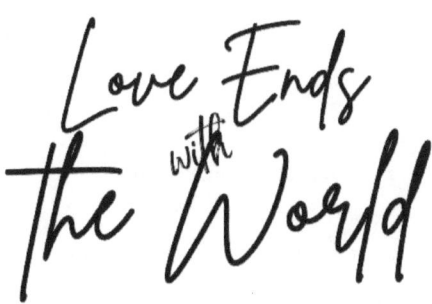

Poignant Tales of Love and Sacrifices

Nitish Mondal

BLUEROSE PUBLISHERS
India | U.K.

Copyright © Nitish Mondal 2024

All rights reserved by author. No part of this publication may be reproduced, stored in a retrieval system or transmitted in any form or by any means, electronic, mechanical, photocopying, recording or otherwise, without the prior permission of the author. Although every precaution has been taken to verify the accuracy of the information contained herein, the publisher assumes no responsibility for any errors or omissions. No liability is assumed for damages that may result from the use of information contained within.

BlueRose Publishers takes no responsibility for any damages, losses, or liabilities that may arise from the use or misuse of the information, products, or services provided in this publication.

For permissions requests or inquiries regarding this publication, please contact:

BLUEROSE PUBLISHERS
www.BlueRoseONE.com
info@bluerosepublishers.com
+91 8882 898 898
+4407342408967

AUTHOR: NITISH MONDAL
nitish.mondal60@gmail.com
+91 9818086262
+91 9810875516
+91 9818898450

ISBN: 978-93-6261-011-9

Cover Design: Sadhna Kumari
Typesetting: Pooja Sharma

First Edition: July 2024

Disclaimer

All the three stories contained in the book are more or less 'non-fiction'. As a writer, the author might have taken some creative liberty to make the storylines captivating and engaging. However, please note that the instances are inspired by happenings of real life, as narrated to the author by his elders. That is the reason why the book has been termed as 'fiction'. I might have skipped petty and common unrighteousness here and there, nevertheless no rosy picture has been painted with a view to attract my benevolent readers. The names of most of the characters have been camouflaged to upkeep their integrity.

Nevertheless the author of this book does not assume and claim any responsibility or liability to anybody for any disruption caused by errors or omissions. The information contained in this site is provided on an "as is" basis with no guarantees of completeness, accuracy, usefulness or timeliness.

 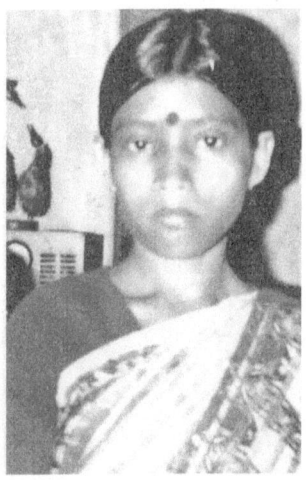

I dedicate this book entitled: 'Love Ends with the World' to my Brother-cum-Friend, 'Smritish Mondal', and the most lovable sister, 'Ms Minu Mullick'.

Your irreparable loss will be mourned until I breathe my last. Though unable to see you, yet feel your presence every moment. Your thoughts, courage, fraternalism and everlasting memories are my source of innovativeness. May Lord Krishna bless your souls with rest, tranquillity and heavenly peace!

Acknowledgement

There are many people who are instrumental in shaping my life. A lot of you have been incorporated in this book, but by no means, all. I am indebted to each and every one of you for your unconditional support, friendship, love, inspiration and guidance.

First and foremost, I wish to express my thankfulness to **my family** for their unflinching support and assistance in my passionate ventures.

My gratitude to **Ms. Nitisha Mondal**, my editor, for language editing and polishing the book. A big thanks to her, without whose support, I would have lost in the copy editing world and perhaps my book would not have seen the light of the day. Thanks to **Blue Rose Publishers** for publication of the book, designs of the front & rear covers and for the flattering photographs which reflected my personality.

I wish my **parents**, my late brother, **Smritish,** and my late sister, **Minu,** had been here to see this book come to life. I am sure they would have been proud of me.

I am always thankful to **Amol Ranjan Das** – my childhood friend – for my evolution from an average into a writer. This transition would not have been possible without his inspiration and encouragement.

Last but not the least, I expect my book would inspire students, workaholics and idles (like my erstwhile self) alike.

Foreword

'L O V E'   'L O V E'   'L O V E'

Perennial Love Of My Mom Ends With The World

- My First Shelter : Mother's Belly
- My First Universe : My Mom
- My First Restaurant : Mother's Breasts
- My first Bed & Toilet : Mother's Lap
- My First Doctor : My Mother
- My First Teacher : My Mom
- My First Thermometer : Mom's Palm
- My First Friend : My Janani
- My First Cycle : Mom's back
- My First Lawyer : My Mom
- My First Love : My Mother
- My First Weapon : Mom's Love and Affection
- My First Kisser : Mom's Fondness & Tenderness
- My First & Last Belie : My Mother
- I Speak : My Mother Tongue
- Giver of Unconditional Love : My Mom
- I share my all my secrets : With My Mom
- Purest form of love : My Mother's Love

- Most Selfless person on the Planet : My Mom who loved me before my birth
- The Angel for me on this Earth : My Mother

***

Don't leave your Mother when she is old.
Your Mother didn't leave you even when you were young.
Don't leave elderly Mom alone far from her loved ones.
Embrace her and tell her how much you love her when she is alive.
Love your Mom and treat her with Loving Care.
For you will **only know her value** when you **see her empty chair.**
Mother's love has no Limits, knows no Boundaries & is Unconditional.
Do whatever you can for her when she is alive.
Mother's love is the purest love you can find on this earth.
Never live with regrets for not having said
how much you loved her in her presence.
Parental love is the only love that is
truly selfless, unconditional & forgiving.
Mother is the most **Selfless** on the **Planet**, beginning to
Love her **Children** even **before they are born.**

***

Synopsis – 'Love Ends with the World'

The book brings out three different stories with 'Love' being the central theme. While one expresses the **love for motherland**, the other two present the **love for one's village & family** as well as **close bonds of the horse with his master**.

1. Sacrifice of Four Malevolent Friends!

There was a huge pond in my Mother's village, named 'Talpukur'. My Mother once told me that a child would go missing mysteriously every alternate day. The villagers were unable to explore any solution in spite of all their efforts. A sorcerer and a priest were invited for a rescue operation, but in vain. However, when the priest was unable to detect, he asked if there were any women in the village bearing unethical characters! That was enough to make the lives of the four friends hell. They were courageous, intellectual and adventurous. They were, in fact, guiltless. All those elderly village women, basically illiterate & orthodox condemned those girls publicly. They lodged a strong protest with the Village Pradhan to take them to task in order to get rid of the tragic occurrences in the village. The village Pradhan fell prey to the uttermost pressure tactics of those elderly women. Four friends were summoned by the Village Pradhan. Prior to deciding the nature of punishment, the Gram Panchayat wanted to know from those girls if they had to say anything to defend themselves. They volunteered to dig up the real culprits behind the disappearance of the children of the villagers in a week's time. The Village Pradhan cautioned them vehemently that if they failed to detect, they would have to leave the village once and for all.

Were they able to dig up? Who was the real culprit? Was he a man, animal or lizard? If so, what was their modus operandi to detect? What happened to them and their families? Did the Pradhan shunt them out of the village? Let us find the answer in the book.

2. **Dusk & Dawn**

"Tale of woes of Twin Sisters ... "We heard from our mother that our Dad was a captain in the Navy. We had a three-storeyed house in the heart of Calcutta. We were studying in the Convent school and led an enjoyable and luxurious life. Our mother, Smt. Protima, was as pretty as a picture. Both of us were quite studious. Our parents wanted us to be the freedom fighters and to fight for the sovereignty of our motherland. It was rightly said: 'Man proposes and God disposes'. Unfortunately our lives were lost in torturous & embarrassing Red Lights at the age of 9 years. We were victims of policemen who promised to help us. We had to compromise with our destiny, had to give in and spend our youth at Prostitution. Among others, even scavengers & cobblers were our customers. When business was slow, we had to parade on the streets in a semi-nude state to attract customers. A customer forcefully made me (Debi) swallow drugs. When I became sick and bed-ridden, my customers were transferred to my sister. What a piteous incident! There are numberless people who hate and abhor girls like us but are never prepared to assist us. My younger one, Rubi, had a secret lover, Ravi, who used to be one of her customers. Ravi promised Rubi to take both of us out of the brothel. One day, when Rubi was engaged with another customer, Ravi was allotted to me.

What happened to them! Were they able to come out of the brothel? Was Ravi successful in his venture? Ultimately, what happened to Ravi? Was Rubi married to Ravi? Did they lead a normal life? Explore all these by going through this book.

3. Singapore - A Country of Delight

All are well aware of the dreadful water crisis worldwide. Scarcity of water has disastrous effects on humans, animals as well as the flora and fauna. It has abundant water resources. The people of Singapore keep their country as glittering as priceless diamonds. It has made tremendous progress and achievement by converting saline into drinkable water. They have abundant indigenous water resources of their own. Since the tap water is as good as mineral water, the houses do not even require water purification devices. It is indeed a country known for greenery and immaculacy. Even a heavy storm is dust free. Since the country is free from filth, leaves of the trees look gorgeously green. It has indeed beautified the country all the more. My son-in-law, working in Singapore, shared with us that he was refunded a few thousands (Singapore Dollars) as the Government received a huge sum in the form of income-tax returns. Integrity and probity of the administration is unparalleled. Mosquitoes, stray animals, wild birds, nomadic people, gipsies & beggars are invisible. As the country is dust-free, the mesmerising beauty of the Sea is impeccable. The contribution of the erstwhile PM, Lee's magic wand and selfless service to the nation to root out corruption is monumental. Public transport is as good as a private vehicle. Women's safety is of utmost importance. All can move freely on the road even in the dead of nights. If I had not been there physically, I would have really felt remorse for my whole life for not being in the glorious country. It is virtually a Ram Rajya in all respects.

***

Characters / Glossary

Sacrifice of Four Malevolent Friends

1. **Anjana** : Ambidextrous, Black Belt in Judo (Leader of the Group)
2. **Amola** : Die-hard love with Ayushi (looked like an androgynous)
3. **Ayushi** : Good looking and a dare devil girl
4. **Ajanta** : Archer
5. **Amol** : Elder brother of Amola
6. **Bidyut Kr** : Anjana's fiancee
7. **Sanjana** : Sister of Anjana

Anjana, Amola, Ayushi and Ajanta are four friends.

Dusk & Dawn

1. **Kedarnath** : GGF ('K')
2. **Aroti** : Wife of Kedarnath/Sister of Binoy('B')
3. **Kananbala** : Sister of Kedarnath
4. **Binoy ('B')** : Brother-in-law of 'K'
5. **Minu** : Binoy's wife:
6. **Abhinandan** : Son of Kedarnath & Aroti:
7. **Krish** : Son of Binoy & Minu
8. **Stormy** : Horse

9. Charlie	:	Chief of the Navy
10. Swatantra Bahini	:	**(Organized by 'K')**
11. **Ansh Guha**	:	Captain of the Navy
12. Protima	:	Wife of Ansh
13. Debi & Rubi	:	Daughters of Ansh/Protima (Twin sisters)
14. **Prostitutes**	:	Sona and Mona (Debi & Rubi)
15. **Jackson**	:	Deals in Girls
16. **Lalu Prasad**	:	Kingpin — dealing in Girls
17. **Ravi**	:	Driver (Friend of Rubi)
18. *Bone*	:	Sister
19. **Bhai**	:	Brother
20. **Dr Chakroborty**	:	Nephrologist
21. **Bhai Phota**	:	Bhaiya Dooj
22. **Boudi**	:	Sister-in-law
23. **Isla**	:	British girl (friend of Krish)

Contents

SACRIFICE OF FOUR MALEVOLENT FRIENDS! 1
   Sacrifice of Four Malevolent Friends!.. 2
      Introduction 2
      Talpukur's Dilemma 2
      Sorcerer and Priest Invited for Rescue Operation 3
      Four Girl Friends Bearing Brunt of Predicament................. 6
      Four Friends Decided to Dig Up Culprits 7
      Spending Whole Day on Mango Tree with BINOCULARS 9
      Celebration on Penultimate Day 10
      Amola's Die-Hard Love with Ayushi 11
      Chits-Chats & Shero-Shayaris 12
      Are All Creatures of Bengal Exceptionally Brilliant! 14
      Unflinching Love for Ayushi 16
      Anjana's Battle with Crocodile 17
      Anjana's diary: Fifth day to Seventh day 19
      Serious Conditions of Anjana & Amola 23
      Anjana Pleaded Her Betrothed to Wed Sanjana 24
      Amola Begged Ayushi to Wed Amol................................... 25
      All Friends were Considered Epitome of Goddess............ 27
   Conclusion 28
      Lord Krishna's Raas Leela with Gopis 29
      Anjana being Incarnation of Gopi 31

DUSK AND DAWN 33

Dusk and Dawn 34
Role of Blood in Charismatic Acts 35

Chapter - I 37
Who Doesn't Know About Rana Pratap's Chetak 37
Miracle Stormy 38
Deep Love for Stormy 40
How Stormy saved Child Abhinandan! 43
A huge statue of 'Stormy' 54

Chapter - II 56
How Does A Mother Carry Baby in Her Tummy 56
Putana was sent to kill Lord Krishna 57
Mother Kananbala Temple with Remembrances 66

Chapter - III 68
Stormy's Death Led to Mental Trauma 68
'K's Appreciation to His Better Half Under The Influence Of 'Tari' 71

Chapter – IV 73
Britishers Officially Created Prostitutions 73
From Warm and Yellow Lights to Torturous Red Lights .. 76
She Fought like a Ferocious Lioness 78
British Law was the Law of Jungle 81
Feminines are Epitome of Love & Compassion 88
Celebration of 'Bhai Phota' 91

Debi Kisko Kahego Tu Maiya 99
Mystic Ordain of Lord Krishna 109
Kidney Transplantation and its Nitty Gritty 111
State of Ecstasy upon Post-Surgery 111
Krish Engrossed in Debi 112
It is not important how long you live, but how you live ... 113
Marriage of Krish was in Doldrums 117
Even Renowned Vishwamitra fell Victim to Beauty 120
Quotation by Swami Chinmayananda 125
Consequence of a Negative Attitude: 125
Bring about a change of our Negativities 126
Law of Chastity should not be restricted to Feminines only 127
Debi Expressed Her Inability to Go Ahead 129
Krish Fell in Love at First Sight 135
What is Dating! 137
Celebration kicked off 139
Reception Day 144
Wedding Night and its Romanticism 147
Why Sexagenarians Opt for Sense Gratification! 150
All Indians are not Mir Zafar and Jaichand 156
Court Scene with Brief Interrogation 158
Conclusion 162
From an Author's Perspective 162

SINGAPORE ~ A COUNTRY OF DELIGHT..................... 165

Singapore - A Country of Delight... 166
Introduction.. 166
Purification of the Sea Water.. 166
Natural Disaster cannot Jeopardise Traffic System 168
Sincerity and Honesty.. 169
No Stray Animals & Beggars are on the Road 169
Culture in Singapore 171
History of Singapore 172
An Independent Republic... 173
Heaven for Tourists 174
Public Transport is as good as a Cab................................. 175
Flirtation and Teasing Are Unknown................................. 176
My Experience - Changi Airport & its Surrounding 177
Mesmerising Beauty ~ Sea of the East-Coast 180
Wild Birds have no Room in Singapore 183
Enjoyed at Sea-Beach to my Heart's content at Night...... 187
Background of Clinking Glasses 191
Education System... 193
Peace of Mind Gives Passions to Life................................. 194
Singapore was in a Topsy-Turvy state................................ 196
PM Yew a Superhero 196
Cooperation in the Socio-economic Fields........................ 197
Cleanliness is the Hallmark of Civilization 199

Yew's Magic Wand to Remove Corruption	202
Deadly against Personality Cult	203
Was Lee a Dictator	203
Establishment of Ram Rajya	204
PM, Yew, Mastermind of Today's Singapore	205
Conclusion	207

SACRIFICE OF FOUR MALEVOLENT FRIENDS!

Sacrifice of Four Malevolent Friends!

Introduction

During those days around 140 years or so, as Sundarbans Reserve Forest (SRF) located to the south-west of present Bangladesh between the river Baleswar in the East and the Harindanga to the West, adjoining to the Bay of Bengal, is the largest contiguous Mangrove forest in the world. During the rainy season, hundreds and thousands of miles of areas were inundated. It was one of the most dangerous natural disasters. West Bengal was highly prone to floods which led to erosion and threats to other aquatic species. It resulted in loss of life, deterioration of health condition, widespread devastation, waterborne diseases and damages to personal property. The cubs of several animals viz. tigers, lions, bears, deers, wild kittens, water buffaloes as well as various kinds of snakes, lizards, etc. used to wash away from one place to another with the current of the flooded water. It was so disastrous, at times even wild reptiles were found having flown into the village by the current of the water.

Talpukur's Dilemma

Our mom once told us that there was a huge pond, as large as a river, in her in-laws' village named 'Talpukur'. Most of the villagers used the pond for washing, bathing and carrying water to their homes. The pond was very deep and large as a result of which its water remained unsoiled. In a series of unfortunate events, a child would mysteriously go missing every alternate day in the village. It went on for more than a month or so. It was a matter of great concern for the villagers as well as for the people of West Bengal.

All the villagers were round the clock alert to detect or dig it up. Unfortunately, they were unable to explore any solution.

Saying so, she abruptly got up. When asked, we were informed that she had to accomplish a lot of domestic chores. We all enthusiastically volunteered ourselves to lend our helping hands to assist her. Our mother further reminded us that she would tell us what actually happened in her in-law's village which she had heard from her mother-in-law. However, to our dissatisfaction, she would tell us in piecemeal otherwise it would take more than a couple of weeks. I could vividly remember that it took almost a month to complete it. A few of us literally cried and shivered in fear. My elders felt a thrill of fear and tremor in their arms but they camouflaged their feelings. The way Mom narrated it, with action, diction, style, intonation, articulation, illustration and expression, it appeared as if it were happening in front of us. I am sure it would surpass Bollywood's way of presentation. During those days, we assisted our Mom most willingly. I am, in fact, sorry to confess my inability to write as potentially as illustrated by my Mom. I also beg apology to my revered mother for not having written it when she was alive. However, I would try hard to write without giving rise to apprehensions as a solid mass of rock is not beaten by the storm, so, a sage is not moved by praise and blame. Our mother, to our jubilation and ecstasy, continued:

Sorcerer and Priest Invited for Rescue Operation

The villagers invited Hari, a sorcerer and well-known wizard. He claimed to have magic powers and solved many similar cases of haunted, horror and evil spirits. He charged a huge sum of money and promised to drive away ghosts, if any, from this village perennially. The villagers did not have any alternative but to fall prey to whatever amount he demanded. Thereafter, he encircled a particular area. In the centre of it, there was a massive banyan tree, perhaps a thousand years old. When several villagers gathered there, many birds living in the tree flew away. Seeing them leaving the tree, Hari told them that there were many ghosts living on the tree. It was a haunted tree. But as soon as they saw him (sorcerer), most of them left the tree in the guise of birds, out of fear and panic. Hari vehemently declared that there were a couple of ghosts - very strong, stout and powerful. They were ultrahazardous and were instrumental in creating nuisance in the village. If they were allowed to remain there in the village, they would surely kill all the villagers within a couple of years. The villagers started shaking like a leaf. All the villagers shouted at the pitch of their voice: "Don't only turn them out but kill all of them instantaneously." Hari got a golden opportunity to demand a huge sum for that. All the villagers agreed to pay the balance amount when all the ghosts would be rooted out from the villages forever. Hari angrily retorted: "You are not convinced about my magic traits to kill the ghosts. I do not challenge your belief. I am prepared to refund what you have already paid and leave the village right now." All the villagers knelt down in front of him and fulfilled his demand by paying the balance sum. Hari asked one of the villagers to come in front of him. Madan, a thin chap of 12 years was sent before him. Thereafter, he ordered someone to give him a '*matka*' i.e. pitcher. He filled the pitcher with 20 litres of water. He chanted *mantras* for a few minutes, threw something on the burning dried grass & leaves and subsequently hit Madan several times with a broom. There was an obnoxiously strong smelling gas. Madan shouted with unbearable pain and pleaded from time to time to condone them. Strong and noxious fumes were unbearable. Madan's parents wanted to come to his rescue. Hari prevented them from doing so by saying that it was not Madan who was shouting but virtually the ghost was crying in acute pain. Hari asked his parents not to worry for their son. On his advice, Madan held the heavy pitcher with his teeth and walked for a couple of yards. Hari again informed the villagers that it was not Madan but the ghost carrying the pitcher. The villagers asked Madan for authentication and verification. His voice became very heavy, uncommon, strange and peculiar. Literally, it appeared to be the voice of a non-human. With this peculiar voice, Madan begged apology to Hari and assured him that they would leave the villages forever and would never return. They also pleaded to Hari not to torture them unnecessarily as they were not instrumental for the disappearance of the children from villages. They had been living in this village for the last around 50 years and were always friendly with the villagers. They saved many villagers, who entered the village at midnight, from wild animals several times. Hari asked them to leave the village instantaneously. They agreed to do so. Hari further asked them to fell a coconut tree which would acknowledge that they had left the village. In the meantime, many villagers shouted to forbid him to knock down their coconut trees. In no time, the sixty feet tall coconut tree routed out. Seeing his magic powers, all the villagers were convinced and mesmerised. They were all enthusiastic and celebrated the occasion till late at night.

Unfortunately, after a couple of days, once again another boy disappeared from the village. All the villagers were at their wit's end to know what to do. They tried hard to get to know who was behind the mishap but in vain. They were all saddened and downhearted. The Pradhan of the village was approached. He called a well-known Priest, Shankar. As usual, Shankar charged some amount for his invocation to deity and to perform various other rituals. Thereafter, he told with conviction that evil spirits had no role in it. It was not even the handiwork of any human being. However, he failed to explore the real culprit behind these mischievous acts. He assured that he would continue his meditation and invocation at home and would come back with the result. It is undoubtedly a serious issue and must be nipped in the bud. While going back, he asked if there were any women in the village bearing immoral and unethical character!

Four Girl Friends Bearing Brunt of Predicament

Alas! That was enough to create a hue and cry amongst villagers to make the lives of a few girls hell. They were, in fact, not bearing immoral characters or so called sinful girls. But they were courageous, plucky, valorous, intellectual and adventurous. All those elderly village women, basically illiterate, conformists and so-called orthodox, who strictly opposed unconventional thinking, behaviour and attitude; vehemently condemned those girls publicly. They along with other such orthodox women lodged a strong protest with the Village Pradhan to take them to task in order to get rid of the tragic occurrences. They alleged that the village got polluted and owing to immoral activities of those girls, village deities were no longer in the villages. Literally, the stroke of bad luck was due to the divine curse. They further alleged that no human being could make good unless those immoral girls were reprimanded. The village Pradhan fell prey to the utmost pressure tactics of those elderly women.

Four girls viz. Ajanta, Amola, Ayushi and Anjana were summoned by the Pradhan. However, nobody could prove their immorality. Nevertheless, the village Pradhan was coerced to take some action against those four girls. Prior to deciding the nature of punishment to be awarded, the Gram Panchayat, consisting of elderly villagers, wanted to know from those girls if they had to say anything to defend themselves. They sought an hour's time to let the Gram Panchayat know about their decision. The Gram Pradhan declared a lunch break for an hour.

Four friends had a closed door meeting and recollected what the sorcerer and the Priest predicted about the ghosts and human beings having no role in the mishap. "We are dead sure that the culprit is well inside the village. We are quite certain and sanguine to be able to detect. There was the consensus of opinions that they were surely and certainly going to be defamed by the Village Panchayat. It would be a stigma and blot which would damage the reputation of their families eternally. It was better to die than live in dishonour. All those four girls were well known sports personalities and never said 'no' to any act of bravery, courage, fearlessness and valour. "Why are we getting scared of doing something great for the villagers where our ancestors were born and hearth and home for our parents and all of us?" All of them got up and proclaimed valiantly: "We are the authors of our lives, we should not be afraid to edit or change the script. We will do a miracle and sort out the mishap even at the cost of our lives once and for all. We will not allow our brethren to die like this!" They invoked Radhey Krishna and prayed for the success of their mission.

Four Friends Decided to Dig Up Culprits

They approached the Gram Panchayat and volunteered to dig up the real culprits behind the disappearance of the children of the villagers. If it was agreed upon, they longed for a week's time to find out. Initially, Gram Panchayat was not in agreement. The reason was crystal clear. If they were successful in their mission, it was an embarrassment for the Gram Panchayat. Nevertheless, the Gram Panchayat had to concede to their pleas in view of the public demand. There is a saying: "A person who is on the verge of death, will go to any extent for survival." Ajanta vigorously and resolutely pleaded to Pradhan for certain prerogatives which would facilitate them to accomplish their mission. They would like to be at liberty to discuss with the members of the family of the victims and they must extend their wholehearted support and cooperation to them. Anjana reiterated that all of them would stay together for a week in the Club Room of the village and there would be no interference and access from any quarters. Amola sought permission to have possession of swords, sticks, iron rods and thick pieces of wood for support as a weapon. Ayushi desired to have a free hand for this task. All the villagers and Gram Panchayat were bewildered at their bravery and temerity. All agreed to concede to their prayers.

They collected very important pieces of information from the victims' families. It came to light that all the boys and girls disappeared during the day time. They came to the conclusion that nobody was murdered as none had seen anybody's dead body. Some lad did not turn up after taking a bath; there was a swimming competition in the village where ten young swimmers took part. One of them did not come back home after the competition. There was a mango tree close to Talpukur. 'Talpukur' denotes a huge and massive pond. The tree was known for delicious, sweet and large mangoes. It bore countless mangoes. Shibu loved mangoes and was prepared to do anything for it. He was an expert climber as well as swimmer. He used to come in the evening to collect the fruit from the tree. All the four youngsters found most of its branches bearing mangoes touching the water of Talpukur. They covered a couple of miles of jungle, adjacent to Talpukur, but were unable to discover any trace of blood, bone, skull and hair of humans. Three days went by.

The whole day they kept vigil on Talpukur and the forest areas. During day time, everything went off well except uproar, clamour, tumult, noise and hustle bustle of the children. All four wished to join them but their duties shackled them. In the dead of night, they kept vigil, observance, and patrolled around Talpukur one by one. When one of them took a round of it, the other three kept themselves ready with bows and arrows, swords, bamboos and iron rods to come to her rescue in case of any exigency. Though they were not able to make any headway in their search yet, as good luck would have it, all the four days, there was no predicament. While Ajanta was expressing her unhappiness for having given an awful life, Anjana reminded them: 'We are not given a good life or a bad life. We are given a life. It's up to us to make it good or bad. No matter how difficult yesterday was, just know that today is our day. So, we must stay positive at every moment of our life'. In the meantime, Ayushi countered Anjana: 'Why do good people always suffer? Where is Krishna in this Universe?' Anjana reacted: 'Lord Krishna is not in the Universe, the whole Universe is in Him! Take a few moments to sit quietly and just be thankful for what all you have bestowed by Him.' Anjana further added: 'All things in life are absolutely temporary in nature. If they are going well, enjoy them; they will not last forever. If they are going wrong, don't worry, they can't last long either.'

Spending Whole Day on Mango Tree with BINOCULARS

The following day, Anjana - six feet tall, stout, plucky and an intellectual youngster - decided to spend the whole day on the mango tree with binoculars. She was maintaining a diary where she used to write down the day's events, record an account of the whole day, with date, place and time of occurrences. All of them met in the evening. Ajanta, Amola and Ayushi talked about the fate of their families in their absence. What would happen to their old parents and siblings? Perhaps, they had not taken a prudent and judicious decision. In the meantime, Anjana joined them. She listened to their discussions. Anjana asked them smilingly if they wished, they might leave the group honourably. She would try hard till her last breath to explore the culprit. Anjana further retorted:

"We all are defamed and tarnished in the village. Most of the villagers look at our parents with contempt and disrespect. If we want them to live with honour and dignity, we should stick to what we have committed and never think of backing out. She further added: *'Our life must be dedicated to upkeep the honour and dignity of our parents, otherwise it is worse than leading a life of gutter worm.'* Anjana further reminded them about the proverb: 'Look before you leap'. We should have pondered over deeply prior to making any decision. However, I assure you that our lost prestige will soon be restored and our families will start living with dignity and utmost respect. But for that we all have to take pains and make honest and sincere endeavours. Undoubtedly the choice is ours". Ajanta, Amola and Ayushi were remorseful. They all begged apologies to Anjana. They reiterated that they became sentimental which was totally uncalled for. They assured that they would never back out and would fight selflessly till their last breath.

Celebration on Penultimate Day

Anjana was enthusiastic and proposed a celebration. All her mates were astonished. On asking, Anjana reminded them only a day was left: "We do not know where we will be on the seventh day onwards. My dictum is: 'Do or Die! Nothing should be in between'. Let us make our 'get together' a memorable one. Once we do our task with sincerity and utmost honesty, there will be no room for repentance. As you know, I have a boyfriend. He has sent some eatables and a packet of cigarettes. We all know cigarette smoking is injurious to health. Nonetheless today is a special day. It is not the time to despair, but to enjoy ourselves. Today is not the time to think about what is injurious and what is heavenly. Everything is fair today which is a source of enjoyment, amusement and entertainment. No shackles and chains can bind and restrict our source of pleasure, recreation and fun for today. No barrier can come in our way. It is a time to sing, dance and enjoy ourselves". All of them lit cigarettes and, having wished, started smoking and throwing rings of smoke to one another. Thereafter, they held the chicken pieces and gnawed them with their hind teeth and enjoyed their delicious flavours. They kept chewing, munching and nibbling. They also embraced one another from time to time.

Amola's Die-Hard Love with Ayushi

Ayushi was good looking with feminine attraction and sex appeal. As regards Amola, she looked like an androgynous. She was neither clearly masculine nor feminine in appearance. She had a body build and other physical characteristics of a blend of both normal male and female features. Androgyny refers to sex-role flexibility and adaptability and therefore may be mistaken for being a member of the opposite gender. The androgynous person is considered more popular, interesting and physically attractive. Many such individuals identify as being mentally or emotionally both masculine and feminine.

Amola: "I am in deep love with Ayushi though I had never expressed my feelings to anyone. I had never romanticised my feelings in any way. It is felt and camouflaged within my heart. I know that nobody would accept my love. They would rather laugh at me. I don't mind if people chuckle at me. I damn care what others would discern for my selfless love. Love is nothing but a set of emotions, behaviours, beliefs with strong attachments and affection. The concept of love is always unimaginable and it may occur to all and sundry irrespective of gender, creed and religion - from the richest men to beggars. It is a natural feeling that comes automatically in one's mind. So, where has the lover erred? Was I at fault when my first experience of love developed with my revered mother? Pure love is always selfless whether it is with one's parents, brothers & sisters, boys and girls or even animals. I always thought to inform everybody shouting from a Park Row Building (once the tallest building in the world) "I love you, Ayushi, more than I love anybody else in the universe. In order to substantiate my 'love', I am prepared to jump from the Park Row Building as I know that will be tantamount to my salvation. There is a saying: 'A person's most valuable asset is not a brain loaded with knowledge, but a heart full of love.' I Love You For All That You Are, All That You Have Been, And All That You Will Be".

Chits-Chats & Shero-Shayaris

They all decided to keep enjoying to their heart's content as it was not known what would be their fate upon completion of a week. Anjana narrated a unique love story between the love of the Moon and the Sun. "Once the Sun and the Moon fell in love and decided to enjoy themselves by travelling the world together. That happened until the Moon betrayed the Sun and slept with the Morning Star. Since then as punishment, the Moon and the Sun could never meet. The moon travels by night and the sun by day". All shouted together: Lovely, fantastic ... Nice one.... Haa ... Haa ... Haa.

Ajanta asked: "Why do couples hold hands during their wedding?" Ayushi replied with a smile: "You don't know, it is nothing but a formality just like two boxers shaking hands before the fight commences." All clapped, whistled, saying Bah bah bah and bah.

Anjana: *Mooje Koi Nashe Se Mohabbat Nahi*   (*I am not fascinated by*
Chah To Oon Palo Se Rahi   *intoxication.*
Jo Nashe Ke Bahane Se   *Intoxication is just an*
Saath Bitate Hai Dosto Ke   *excuse to spend*
   time with my friends.)

It is the 'real beauty' of the programme, everybody retorted. All the friends confirmed with firm belief that nobody will be allowed to keep aloof from one another. All of them shouted and reminded the villagers:

'Friendship is just not a matter of an asset or some kind of a liability. It is a silent promise or a commitment that I was; I am; and I will always be there for you'!

They all started chit chatting, dancing and singing in joy. All of a sudden, Anjana apprised them that it was 7 pm. Let us jump into action. After having relaxed for a couple of hours, they chalked out their schedule. She further reminded that 'Success is never PERMANENT. Failure is never FINAL. So, never stop effort until your victory makes history' (Quotes by: Naaz).

As planned, at 12.30 am, the goat was tied with a rope close to Talpukur. Anjana was incharge of that area, in the Western side. The remaining three would look after the jungle areas in the Eastern, Southern and Northern parts. The standing instructions were that nobody would encroach on the duty of others unless asked for. All will be with their preferred weapons. As expected, the goat started bleating from time to time because of hunger. Otherwise, there was a pin drop silence except croaking or hooting of frogs and hissing of snakes. It was a moon-lit night which was charming, fascinating and a beautiful sight. It dazzled our eyes. It bathed the whole world with her stillness. But four of them were not there to enjoy the scenic and panoramic beauty where one could hear a pin drop of the moonlit night. They were always concerned with the accomplishment of their mission. Anjana contemplated that in case the goat became the victim of crocodile tonight, the mission would stand accomplished. It was 2 O'clock. Anjana stared at Talpukur like a mother looking for her lost child and the lover gazing at the beloved. At 2.30 am, there was a thunderous splashing in the water. Anjana saw through binoculars that a huge, literally massive and monstrous, crocodile was proceeding towards the goat. Seeing the crocodile from a distance, the goat kept bleating and jumping hard to sever the rope. The crocodile crawled surreptitiously, looking in all directions if anybody was there to harm him. I noted it took around 4 minutes to cover such a short distance. The crocodile gripped portions of the goat in its jaws, went back to the pond and rotated rapidly in the water to tear the prey apart.

Are All Creatures of Bengal Exceptionally Brilliant!

Look at this crocodile! During the day, it will all along keep itself under the water. It will not float for a fraction of a second even by mistake which is against its nature. It will not show its face throughout the day. I don't know if it has been greatly influenced by the cultural legacy of West Bengal.

I started pondering over the West Bengal is proverbially the land of rivers. The State is the home of the Royal Bengal tiger, which is the national animal of India. It is also known for its sweets and snacks such as *rasgulla* and *mishti doi (sweet curd)*. It is a land of patriots, legends, intellectuals, artists, freedom fighters as well as abounds with rich cultural heritage. To cite a few names - tips of the iceberg - Viswakabi Rabindranath Tagore, Satyajit Ray, Sri Aurobindo Ghosh, Mother Teresa, Netaji Subhas Chandra Bose, Swami Vivekananda, Raja Ram Mohan Roy, Bankim Chandra Chattopadhyay, Soumitra Chatterjee, Amartya Sen, Khudiram Bose, Bidhan Chandra Roy, Ramakrishna Paramansa, Kazi Nazrul Islam, Sarat Chandra Chatterjee, Jyoti Basu, Leander Paes, Ishwar Chandra Vidyasagar, Shakti Chattopadhyay, Jagdish Chandra Bose, Chittaranjan Das, Dr Rajendra Prasad, Uttam Kumar, Kishore Kumar, Manna Dey and Hemant Kumar Mukherjee, Saurav Ganguly, etc.

"I did not divulge to my friends about the incident that took place at the mid-night of the penultimate day and the fate of the goat. I rather charged them that there was a dereliction of duty. The goat must have run away under the cover of darkness owing to our slackness. All of them were not happy with my charges. Nevertheless they might have thought that it would not be prudent to counter me as I was the oldest among them and they considered me their leader. Sometimes they also call me 'Subhashini' which derives from 'Subhash'. All of them believed that I had extraordinary leadership skills and fighting traits with charismatic oratory. It was a solar powered village. But generally solar energy was not in use from 11 pm to 4 am in that particular village. The reason was unknown. However, on the seventh day, special permission was sought to illuminate the village for the whole night. All the villagers were asked to confine to their homes between 10 pm and 5 am. However, in the evening of the seventh, the last day, we planned our modus operandi. Anjana informed all of them to be alert with their weapons to look after Eastern, Southern and Northern areas. Anjana reiterated not to breach the understanding and trespass her area until and unless they were asked to do so. Soon after their discussions, Anjana proceeded to the prayer room to offer prayers to Lord Krishna and meditate.

Amola had a doubt in Anjana's way of speaking and taking utmost responsibility and offering her friends the least responsibility. She knew that Anjana wrote a diary which she was able to trace. Amola was full of admiration and appreciation while going through the contents of Anjana's diary. She considered herself a very lucky one to have a friend like her. She never shared with her friends what she got to know on going through the diary of Anjana. Knowing all about Anjana and her potential for the well-being of her friends and the villagers, her eyes flooded with tears. While eulogising Anjana, she could remember having read somewhere: "The importance of good people in our LIFE is just like the importance of HEARTBEATS. It's not visible but silently supports our life". She never longs for credit and appreciation for what she has been doing every day for 24 hours X 60 (1440 minutes) X 60 (86,400 seconds). What a friend! It was 10 O'clock. We were on duty, with our weapons, as discussed.

Unflinching Love for Ayushi

Amola: Anjana was with a sword on her left hand and iron rod on her right. She was found taking rounds of Talpukur a couple of times. This was done to tempt the crocodile. Though the Eastern side was my area, I was unable to take my eyes off Anjana's brave acts. It was midnight. All of a sudden, I thought to check what Ayushi was doing. No sooner did I have a cursory glance at her than I became sentimental and started crying. I was crying in speculation of a predicament, crying happily, as I loved her so much. Even I, for one, did not know what prompted me to cry when I was buoyant and cock-a-hoop at her very sight. It was really the most magical feeling in the world. Had I shared my feelings with anybody, who had not tasted the fondness of 'love', I would be construed mentally ill by them. She made me feel unbelievably in good spirits and I could not imagine my life and identity without her. Soon, I chanted a prayer to Radhey Krishna: "If 'death' is destined to one of us in this combat, let You make my death inevitable since I cannot think of, even in my wildest dream, living in the absence of Ayushi. Thereafter, I thought to concentrate on my duty. The clock turned 1.30. It was unbelievable what Anjana was doing. She lay where the goat was tied. I murmured: 'How can you do that'? She could not afford to invite her death! The goat was taken away from there by the crocodile in no time the previous day. How could I allow her to do that? But she was too adamant to listen to anyone. It would rather mess up our whole plan and everyone would hold me instrumental for any failure. She was indeed like a candle which burned brightly all the way down to the end.

Anjana's Battle with Crocodile

It was 3 am. No sooner did I move towards the duty side of Anjana, I heard a tumultuous noise. In Judo, when you fight an opponent or while striking a punching bag, it is not just about intimidation, there is a science behind all those grunts and hissing. Why do fighters make these sounds when striking? There are different types of breaths for various movements, with many ways of incorporating breath modes with the timing of a punch or kick. Making noises will come from maintaining a proper form, your speed, and engaging your body to help keep your endurance up so that you can stay in the fight and hit with more power. I could visualise from a distance that there was a fight, literally war, between Anjana and the crocodile. The crocodile was able to hold her leg and dragged her towards Talpukur. Anjana was like the ambidextrous Arjuna, the third of Pandavas, the son of Pandu, world's renowned archer, husband of Draupadi, was not just the best archer, but was also equally adept at using his right and left hands with equal speed. When the iron rod slipped out of her hand, Anjana punched the humongous reptile. The crocodile was least affected by her punch. It seemed: 'If the dog barks, the mountain is not injured' (Chinese proverb). She somehow could hold the iron rod and hit the humongous reptile with it. He in turn, attacked her with his powerful tail without giving up her leg. They have big muscles that attach to their hips and hind legs that allow them to move their tails side to side with strong thrusts. I was surprised to see its tail. It was longer than a full sized human, maybe 7 ft. I did not want to interrupt without Anjana's signal. Seeing all of us, if the crocodile was able to flee away, all her endeavour would go in vain. In the meantime, I informed all my friends about the combat and asked them to be ready and alert. They all were waiting anxiously for the 'call' from Anjana. The ambidextrous Anjana, Judo, Black Belt, hit his tail with the sword and then in no time, she struck his head with the iron rod. She kept on rolling over to take her leg out of its jaws. As soon as the jaws got loosened, she kicked its eyes with the other leg. The crocodile, in acute pain, surrendered her leg instantaneously. But attacked her body with double strength. Anjana, while shouting in severe and acute pain, counter attacked it by piercing the iron rod into its eyes. Thereafter, we observed that crocodiles are probably the most vocal of all reptiles, since they can produce a wide variety of sounds. When the iron rod was pierced, it chirped as a distress call and thereafter it uttered a loud hissing sound, that is generally used as a threatening call to ward off rivals. Nevertheless, the crocodile might have been ashamed that his ferocious body, and massive size was not good enough to vanquish the dainty looking human. He had no alternative but to beat a retreat. Anjana shouted: "Encompass the Talpukur area; don't let it go". As we all were waiting for her call, in no time, all of us surrounded the crocodile. Amola being an archer, shot an arrow on its half tail as the remaining half was separated by Anjana. The crocodile turned aggressive and attacked Ayushi vigorously. She fell down unconscious. Anjana was unable to lift herself despite her best efforts. The crocodile held Ayushi's leg and dragged towards Talpukur which was just a few feet away. It was about 4.30 am and everything was visible in the daylight. Amola ran towards Ayushi and got her free from the crocodile's grip by striking him hard with the iron rod on its head. It made a countermove and jumped on Amola with its assumed 18 ft height and presumably weighing around 2,000 kg. Amola fell down and was about to roll over the water of Talpukur. In the meantime, Anjana, while still laying down in acute pain, threw an iron ball at the crocodile, which hit his head grievously. The crocodile in no time caught hold of the leg of Amola and dragged her towards Talpukur which was a yard's distance away. Ajanta, an adept archer, shot the arrows from the bow on the crocodile at full draw. When the crocodile became powerless and on the verge of death, it raised its head for a few seconds, perhaps to look and salute Anjana and her mates for their valour and gallantry. He lay down soon after that conceivable brooding over: 'How come the society becomes patriarchal where such audacious and plucky women folk exist! Hey, Govinda, my last wish in my next birth is to be as merciful, charitable, courageous, manly as Anjana'. Anjana's fiancee, Bidyut Kumar, and a few villagers appeared and tied the monstrous crocodile.

Anjana's diary: Fifth day to Seventh day

FIFTH DAY: When I saw a dozen mangoes packed in a bag lying on the bank of Talpukur, I was sure and certain that Shibu was the victim of the water-borne animal. That is the reason why I decided to spend the whole day on the mango tree with binoculars to identify it. I concentrated the entire day, watching the kinds of water animals floating on the water even for a second. As good luck would have it, I saw a massive crocodile for a couple of seconds on its way to catch a large fish. Thereafter, it disappeared and was never seen again despite my endeavouring hard to have a glimpse of it. But it seemed to be very shrewd. It may also be possible that he is aware that he is in the midst of the human habitat. I am sure that it must be waiting for the rainy season to shift to its own habitat with the current of the flooded water. It also happened many a time in the village earlier as well. That is the reason why it never exposed itself during day-breaks. The million dollar question is how to get it exposed. I started brooding over accumulating all my common sense and experiences on the water animals. It is also certain that it was not able to get adequate fodder for all these five or six days. The crocodile is a monstrous amphibian which is in need of enormous food to survive. It surely and certainly cannot survive on fishes alone for a long time. During the day time, owing to tight security and vigil, it is not even able to float on water. I assume, if it spends the whole day in water, it surely comes on land during late evening or at the dead of night. If I tell the Village Pradhan to drain away or discharge the water from Talpukur in order to seize the crocodile, nobody would listen to what this unconscionable girl says. On the other hand, surely, it is a Herculean task which will take at least a month's time and, for sure, nobody will be willing to do that without having any clue or a piece of evidence from reliable sources. Nobody will pay heed to my observation. It may also be possible that during the course of draining out its water, the crocodile slips away to neighbouring ponds. Why should they listen to what I say? For them, I am an immoral girl. Moreover, according to many, we are instrumental for what is happening in the village. They will laugh at all of us if we tell them about the crocodile. Hence, no point in sharing this important piece of information with my friends either. My friends may come on my way and may not allow me to do what I intend to.

SIXTH DAY (Anjana's diary)

Amola, Ayushi and Ajanta were a bit concerned as today is the penultimate day. I assured them to shun any kind of concern. To be afraid and scared must be out of our dictionary. Some solutions will positively emerge. Crocodiles have night vision. They can see at night because of tiny mirrored receptors in the back of their eyes. It is also confirmed that they are highly intelligent animals. So, I need to be smarter. First of all, I will have to tempt and allure it. We arranged a goat and I got it deprived of fodder and water throughout the day. It will bleat throughout the night because of hunger. All the planning must be worked out in the absence of the knowledge of my friends.

Finding my friends gossiping, I have chalked out my plan. It is getting dark. Nothing will be visible within half-an-hour. The darkness is generally associated with danger and fear. The light is contrary to darkness. It is the symbol of purity and illuminated thought. It is wrong and unacceptable to me as our cherished ambition is going to be served in the night's darkness. I am planning its nitty gritty sitting in the darkness. Hence, how can darkness be associated with danger and fear! Darkness never represented danger and fear for the Marathas either! The battle was fought in the dead of night between the Maratha army under Chhatrapati Shivaji Maharaj and General Kartalab Khan of the Mughal Empire. The Maratha defeated the Mughal forces. Shivaji Maharaja's attacks on Shaista Khan were at midnight. The whole city was covered with darkness. Shivaji Maharaj and his forces surreptitiously and expeditiously entered the palace under the cover of darkness. Most of his attacks used to surprise the enemies. So, night's darkness made Shivaji Maharaj in high feathers and won many a battle. The clock went from 1 to 2 .... In this turmoil, I assumed the lion came along roaring, and perhaps said in a loud voice: "Don't you all know that I am the king of the jungle. How dare you awake as of now!" I retaliated: "If you are the king of the jungle, go to your queen and make it a fun night."

SEVENTH DAY (Anjana's diary)

It is the day of doing something charismatic or to perish forever. This day will also either enable my parents and only sister as well as the families of my three friends to raise their hideous heads and live with respect and veneration or to lead a life of gutter worm. My life is undoubtedly priceless and, naturally, I cannot afford to waste it. The lives of four families rest on my shoulder. I am prepared to lay down my life; I am ready to sacrifice myself but not before the accomplishment of my cherished mission. Today, I will fight until my last breath. I have bent upon dying, not prior to fulfilment of the following task:

1. Catch the crocodile, which is very difficult, but certainly not impossible;
2. Prevent it from going back to the pond; or
3. Injure it to the maximum possible extent to enable others to lay hold of it.

<u>I also learnt a few tips to combat crocodiles</u>:

1. Their scaly skin is too tough to penetrate. Sometimes even on land, daggers do not have any effect.
2. Eyes of the crocodiles are their most vulnerable, delicate and vital parts.
3. Another endangered part is its head.
4. It can bite through a human arm or a leg that will pose not much problem if the fighting is on land but do not allow them to drag you in the water.
5. If in combat, you are badly injured but somehow you are able to run away, you should maintain a straight line. It is a misconception moving about in a zig-zag to evade a crocodile.

I know my friends will never allow me to lay where the goat was kept the whole night. They were a little suspicious when I charged them for negligence of duty. I strongly forbade them to trespass my area until they receive a request from me. My utmost endeavour will be not to endanger their lives. It is indeed a massive, huge, gigantic and mammoth crocodile. Even if four of us attacked it, the crocodile may get scot free upon inflicting deadly assault on all of us. Hence, it will be appropriate if I fight with it till my last breath and all of them pounce on the injured, tired and fatigued crocodile. In that event, there is every likelihood of the fulfilment of our cherished aspiration and on top of it, the loss from our side will be minimal.

Serious Conditions of Anjana & Amola

All of them were rushed to the hospital. The condition of Anjana and Amola was serious. As regards Ajanta and Ayushi, though their condition was stable, they would remain in the hospital for necessary treatment and observation for a few weeks. The news of their bravery, audacity, gallantry and fearlessness spread far and wide like wildfire. The renowned doctors were invited from an acclaimed hospital by the village head. All the villagers were full of appreciation for them. The Village Pradhan convened a meeting where all the villagers were invited. In the meeting, he proclaimed:

"At the outset, I feel proud and honoured to garland the parents of all the four young girls. They are, in fact, instrumental in saving all of us from the clutches of the monstrous crocodile which has been unknown to us for more than a couple of months. Had these superhumans not been here in our village, I fail to understand how many more children, men and women would have been the victims of this maneater! Seeing their parents shedding tears, the Village Pradhan asserted: I would have been proud and the happiest man if I were blessed with such brave, valiant, charitable and merciful young girls. Their names will be written in the golden letters in the annals of village history. We would also recommend their names to the higher ups for appropriate acknowledgements and awards for their sacrifice and incredible bravery. I, on behalf of my Panchayat, hereby recommend government jobs to all the four brave girls or their dependants, as the case may be. I also declare a cash award of Rs.500 to each of them. God forbid, in case of any unfortunate demise, Rs.1,000 will be awarded to each. All the expenses towards hospitalisation and convalescent period will be borne by the Village Panchayat. I also request the families of these four youngsters to approach the Heads of the Village Panchayat whenever they have any issues. We all salute them and three cheers to the members of their families".

Anjana Pleaded Her Betrothed to Wed Sanjana

The families of all the four friends along with Bidyut Kumar visited the hospital every day. Anjana and Sanjana were sisters. They were more of friends than sisters. Anjana reminded her sister: "You were always helpful to me. Sanju, do you remember when we were school-going: You were punished by our parents for some mischievous acts committed by me. You always used to come to my rescue whenever I committed blunders whether it was outside or at home. When I joined Judo class, it was you who paid my fee by teaching a few students".

Didi, for God's sake, do not talk about all these.

No, Sanju, please let me tell, otherwise, it will be too late.

"*Bus karo, Didi!*" (Stop it, Didi), Sanjana while weeping.

Sanju, "My soul won't rest at peace, if I am not allowed to express my gratitude to you". She suddenly developed acute chest pain and a breathing problem. She continued: "The time has come to return everything to you". She happily put Bidyut's hand on Sanjana's and pleaded with folded hands as she was not able to talk. Sanjana and Bidyut told her instantaneously: "If it is your last wish, we accept your ordaining willingly and most happily."

Despite the best treatment, doctors confirmed that the days of Anjana and Amola were numbered as the crocodile attacked both of them dangerously which typically caused lacerations, abrasions, punctures, fractures and amputations. The pain from a crocodile bite was unbearable. Hence, the painkiller medicine had to be injected. Though it relieved their pain to a great extent, yet it led to serious cardiovascular issues, heart diseases, bloating, abdominal distention and bowel obstructions. It also caused damage to the kidneys. No sooner did the Village Pradhan get to know her condition than he appeared before Anjana. Anjana with her gesture pleaded to the Village Pradhan to offer the job to Bidyut.

Village Pradhan: Don't worry! We are with the members of your family. He consoled and assured her that her wishes would be fulfilled.

She suddenly felt acute chest pain and shortness of breath, developed fainting or dizziness, coughing persistently while blood oozed out. She fell on Sanjana and kept looking at her with tearful eyes, full of love and affection, and suddenly shouted saying: 'I am leaving, my dear Sanju'. All end……. The doctor checked her nerve and declared her dead. With the instructions of the Village Head, all the doctors, nurses and whosoever was present in the Hospital, stood up and observed two minutes 'silence' in the memory and honour of Anjana and prayed to the Allmighty to endow peace to the departed soul.

Amola Begged Ayushi to Wed Amol

On the same day, the condition of Amola deteriorated. The doctor called her parents and informed them about her worsening condition. Many villagers turned up at the hospital to meet her. Ayushi was next to Amola's bed. Amola's elder brother and parents were with her. Seeing her temerity and bravery while saving Ayushi from the clutches of near death by endangering her own life, Ayushi could understand that it could not be the price for her friendship only. She recollected that once Ajanta apprised her that Amola was in die hard love with her. At that time she made fun of Amola's love as it was next to impossible. It seemed to be a day dream for her. She also cursed Ajanta for speaking hanky panky which did not have any head and tail. Ayushi could remember that she ceased to talk to Amola for a couple of months. Now, everything became crystal clear to her. Amola asked Ayushi to look after her parents in her absence. She informed her that it goes without saying that her father loved her by the core of his heart. She did a lot of mischievous acts in her life, but it was her dad who always came to her rescue. He forbade her (Amola) to take part in the life risk venture. Her dad relentlessly asked her not to worry for their honour and so-called dignity. Once he also questioned her: what he would do with their honour and dignity if he lost her! She didn't hide anything from her dad, including her die-hard love for Ayushi. That is the reason why Thomas Fuller rightly proclaimed: "My son is my son till he is married. But my daughter is my daughter throughout her life". Aeschylus very rightly said: "Call no man happy till he is dead". She was not able to talk on account of her ceaseless breathing problems. She was coughing and confronting breathlessness from time to time. Doctors also advised her not to talk. Ayushi forbade Amola to talk. "No, it cannot be. I know the time is very short, Amola retorted. She informed Ayushi that she had no alternative but to share her last wish with her. Ayushi, "I wish you to remain in my house soon after I bid goodbye to this mundane world. I make a fervent request to you to wed my elder brother, Amol, and take care of my dad. I won't be able to leave this world peacefully unless you promise me to do so." Amola held the hands of Ayushi, and continued oozing blood in her cough. Ayushi assured that her last wish would be honourably fulfilled by her. No sooner did Ayushi agree to marry Amol than

Amola died of a stroke. The doctor declared her dead upon checking her pulse.

All Friends were Considered Epitome of Goddess

All the Villagers and Village Panchayat turned up and garlanded them profusely and covered their bodies with tons of flowers. Many children and even those older than Anjana and Amola touched their feet as a mark of respect and reverence. Children blew cronches. A few women were of the view that they were incarnations of goddesses. The way they fought and saved the lives of all of us was indeed unparalleled. The village head arranged buses to take as many persons as was desirous of going for their cremation. During that period, females were not allowed to attend funerals. But the Head of Gram Panchayat made an exception. All were allowed irrespective of caste, creed, gender and religions. Manual bamboo and wood pyres were used for cremations. The Sarpanch arranged tea and snacks for all those who had attended the cremation. After cremation, the Sarpanch with the members of the families of the bereaved girls collected the ashes which were placed in an urn and consecrated it to the sea. Thereafter, on the 13th day of demise, the Sarpanch with the members of the families of Anjana and Amola held a ceremony, Pind Sammelan or Terahvin (pret-karma), where they performed rituals for the peace and tranquillity of the deceased soul. The Sarpanch with the cooperation of all the villagers celebrated the occasion for two whole days. Puja and havan were held. All the two days, from morning to late evening, food was distributed to all the villagers. Thereafter, not only did the villagers live peacefully but progressed by leaps and bounds.

Conclusion

Stories Reflect Author's Nature, Personality and Psychology

The individual glimpses are generally found in stories. The author, despite his honest endeavour, is unable to write the story that he had originally heard, got to know and thought to write. Sometimes his instincts do not permit him to write in accordance with the original version. Take the case of somebody who got scot free even after having committed a heinous crime. Some authors are deadly against the acquittal of such criminals. They, therefore, exaggerate what had happened with the criminals, and they sum up by putting the criminals under life imprisonment or have them hanged. The author's momentary or partial viewpoints are always present even in the original stories. Hence, the stories positively reflect the author's nature, character and his style of writing.

I would further substantiate my contention with the following examples. The example of Krishna as '*Makhanchor*', one who steals butter. A few interpreters while studying deeply conclude that it is a childlike attitude. Krishna was so innocent and simple that he might have thought that every house in the village to be his own house. Hence, he was at liberty to go to every kitchen of his playmates and run off with food items he liked most and shared the same with his playmates. Since it was a playgame for Him with his playmates, He might not be aware of the difference between taking away food from his own house and His mates' house. He construed it as a playful game in order to have fun with his mates. Whereas other authors, without knowing much about Him, might critically highlight Krishna's stealing butter from one house to another. They further add fuel to the fire by saying that It might encourage other children to do so. But this is not the proper understanding. How can anyone explain the Bhagavad Gita when they do not know much about it? Such an attempt is like asking someone, who is idle, indolent, lazy and inert, to join Azad-Hind Fauj of Netaji Subhash Chandra Bose. It would be nothing but tantamount to inefficaciousness.

Lord Krishna's Raas Leela with Gopis

As written by **Swami Prabhupada in 'Krishna - The Supreme Personality of Godhead'**:

(**Please read between the lines**.) Krishna is the supreme personality of Godhead and has no desire left unfulfilled. Lord Krishna's Raas Dance with Gopis is on the platform of Yogamaya and not of Mahamaya. The dance of young boys and girls in this material world is in the kingdom of Mahamaya. On the material platform, when a servant serves the master, he tries to satisfy not the senses of the master but rather his own senses. The servant would not serve the master if the payment is stopped. That means that the servant engages himself in the service of the master just to satisfy his own senses. But on the spiritual platform, the servitor of the supreme personality of Godhead serves Krishna without payment and he/she continues to serve in all conditions. That is the difference between Krishna consciousness and material consciousness.

To further add to the knowledge of the so-called intellectuals, most of the Gopis in their previous lives were great sages and experts in the study of the Vedas. Lord Rama was described as being superior to the Gandharvas in 'beauty'. (There is no male equivalent of 'pretty' and 'beautiful'. 'Handsome' is a word that is less strong and more casual than pretty and beautiful. Hence, for male, we may use 'good-looking' or 'gorgeous' which can also be used for a feminine gender.) However, when Lord Ramachandra appeared before the Gopis, they were mesmerised, speechless and dumbstruck by Rama's captivating and eye-catching appearance. Gopis evinced their heartfelt desire to have Him as their husband. Lord Rama gave them the benediction that their desires would be fulfilled when He would appear as Krishna. Therefore, the desire of the Gopis to have Krishna as their husband was long cherished.

The loving affairs of Krishna with the Gopis are called 'parakiya-rasa'. The attitude of a married man who desires another wife or vice versa is called '*parakiya-rasa*'. The Gopis wanted Krishna to be their husband, but actually there was no possibility of his marrying all the gopis as the gopis were already married. But because they had that natural tendency to accept Krishna as their supreme husband, the relationship between the gopis and Krishna is called 'parakiya-rasa'. Their attitude towards Krishna was that of paramour love. Therefore, the loving affairs of Krishna with the Gopis are called 'parakiya-rasa'. This 'parakiya-rasa' is ever-existent in Goloka Vrindavana, in the spiritual sky. There are many other circumstances and instances which show that Lord Krishna is not bound by the rules and regulations of the material world. People, in general, must follow the instructions of Lord Krishna as given in the Bhagavad-Gita and should not even imagine imitating Him in the *raas* dance.

Nevertheless 'parakiya-rasa' is pervertedly reflected in this material world with obnoxious lyrics of the songs accompanied by the most vulgar dance to suit the likings of the Producer or Director of films or theatres to meet their vested interests. It is most abominable. There is no possibility of enjoying this transcendental 'parakiya-rasa' within the material world. It is stated in Srimad-Bhagavatam that one should not imitate this parakiya-rasa even in dreams or imagination. Those who do so, drink the most deadly poison. This material world is the perverted reflection of the spiritual world. It is, as for example, just like the reflection of a tree on the bank of a reservoir of water; the topmost part of the tree is seen as the lowest part.

Anjana being Incarnation of Gopi

In the above story, one cannot help but observe qualities of mystery, power, audacity and valour associated with the protagonist Anjana. Upon her brave martyrdom, the villagers owed their safety, prosperity and peace to her. According to my mother, Anjana started to be perceived as the incarnation of one of the Gopis who might have committed a minor offence in her past life. Hence, as a punishment, she was sent to the mundane world with a condition that if she chose a life of comfort and bed of roses, she would have to come back here repeatedly. On the contrary, if she opted to fight for the causes of human beings, she shall go back to the spiritual world soon. This is, of course, the villagers version of her valiance and valour. One may question the authenticity of such a claim and rightfully so. However, isn't the idea of any deity descending to this material world attached to their selfless sacrifice in protecting humanity?

Later the Village Pradhan with the wholehearted support and financial assistance of the villagers erected a large statue of 'Anjana', remembering her for generosity, gallantry and humanity. It is considered a place of great sanctity for all and sundry. One can see worshippers from far-flung areas visiting this monument and kneeling down in prayer.

However, this takes my thoughts away to our soldiers who are laying down their lives at the altar of our motherland. They are perhaps the greatest assets of any country. If we cannot protect the nation from foreign invasions all other growth, progress and development become nullified. Moreover, most of them are a very selfless lot who put the interest of the country above their priceless lives. They serve at places away from their homes and families and have to lead a rough and tough life. Unfortunately, their families are not adequately compensated upon their martyrdom. One might emphatically question that it is a part of their duties. Yes, there is no iota of doubt in that. But how many of us - Ministers, MLAs, MPs, Police Departments, Doctors, Law Courts, business tycoons, Government employees and so on - getting fat salaries, discharging their duties honestly, sincerely and with dedication!

Thus, isn't it fair to conclude that the **selfless love** of the four malevolent friends for the villagers and soldiers for their motherland are 'perennial' and which **ends with the world**. I leave it to my readers to brood over on this.

***

DUSK AND DAWN

Dusk and Dawn

Dad believed:

Keep a Green Tree in Your Heart, Birds Will Surely Come and Sing... (Chinese Proverb) ...

Introduction:

The central message of the story is the illustriousness of our Dad and his predecessors. That remained the greatness on their part. How our dad left his hearth and home of his ancestral village and arrived in the capital of India, empty handed, with massive liabilities of six children for the sake of their upbringing, was a million dollar question! He was simply working as a clerk. His salary was so small that he could hardly make both ends meet. Nevertheless he left no stone unturned to gain his objective. He was indeed unyielding when the question of their career was at stake. I could recollect once I asked Dad: 'What is life?' He beautifully narrated 'A Tale of Two Cities' to define what exactly life denoted. Then we were too young to grasp the crux of it. However, when we grew up, we got to know about it bit by bit and perhaps one life will fall short to understand it in toto.

QUOTE

There is something strange and unique about the **geography of Israel**. There are two seas in Israel — The **Sea of Galilee** and The **Dead Sea**. The Sea of Galilee is **teeming with life** as it contains 27 species of fish. Found nowhere in the world. Its shores are full of birds and lush with vegetation.

WHEREAS

The Dead Sea, on the other hand, **contains no life**. It's toxic and bitter. Yet they are both fed by the same river - **The Jordan**.......... ????
How could two Seas, fed by a single source, be so different?

THE ANSWER IS:

<u>The Sea of Galilee</u> receives water at one end and gives it at the other. <u>The Dead Sea</u> has no outlet. Hence, it receives water and keeps it all within itself.

IT IS ALSO WITH LIFE.

If you only receive but do not give, you do not live.

So, GIVE, LIVE and LOVE.

UNQUOTE

In fact, our Dad was strict and inaccessible to all of us. He was a borderline dictator. He was one with John F. Kennedy, whose dictum was: "Never negotiate out of fear and never fear to negotiate" However, on the top of all these, we may call him a benevolent dictator as he always looked after the interests and bright career prospects of his children. Whatever he used to decide that would have been final and unquestionable. Even my mom had a little to say. I too failed to understand him. He was a hard nut to crack. There was a reason behind that. He belonged to a family where his forefathers led variegated lives - from zamindars to downs and outs. Along with ancestral property, zamindari blood flowed in his veins. While reading this story, my readers will get to know how blood affects the family tradition.

Role of Blood in Charismatic Acts

I would cite a historical fact of the role of blood in our activities. Had it not been so, Panna Nurse (Dhai), would not have saved

Udai Singh, the son of the king of Mewar, by sacrificing her own son in order to save the heir to the throne at Mewar. When Banbir, the wicked man, burst into the room, he roared and asked Panna: where the prince was. She dressed her own son in the Prince's clothes and dressed the prince in her son's to appear Udai Singh the most ordinary. She showed her loyalty and courage to go beyond limits to save the only heir of the kingdom. It goes like: Panna was loyal to the dynasty and her duty was to save Udai Singh's life. Panna realised that Udai Singh must be saved for the future king of Mewar, even if it meant sacrificing her own son. She put the sleeping Udai Singh in a wicker (Bamboo basket) and with the help of a trusted maid, smuggled him out of the palace. Panna Dhai laid her own son on the royal bed and presented him as 'Udai Singh'. He was cut into several pieces in no time in front of Panna Dhai. Her son's blood oozed out and she bathed her in it. Nevertheless, Panna Dhai stood her ground, without shedding a drop of tear, never making the enemy feel that he was her son. I am really at a loss to understand how any mother could do that. A mother's love is the purest form of love. It dares all things and crushes down remorselessly all that stands in its path. The child is the reason for her living. Nothing in the Universe is more precious than her love. The question arises when the king was killed and Rani Karnavati committed Jauhar, Panna Dhai would have got the King's son, Udai Singh, killed and might pose her own son as Udai Singh. She could have tried her own son for the future king. There was no iota of doubt that she was loyal to the dynasty and her duties. Secondly, it might be possible that it was in the back of her mind that her son could never become king as he did not have the royal blood. I would try to substantiate the blood and its utility from my forefathers' point of view.

Chapter - I

My great grand-father, (GGF), Lt. Shri Kedarnath, was a zamindar. Generally, the meaning of zamindar was a collector of the land revenue of a district for the Government during the Mughal rule in India. But he was a zamindar in the sense that he owned miles and miles of ancestral domains treated as jagirs. He was not the zamindar, who was a landlord, collected rent from peasants and paid revenue to the Company. But here, my great grandfather was the owner of vast areas of land. During his time, the system of zamindari was recognized as landlords, who let out their lands to tenant farmers in return for a share of the produce or price of the crops. Zamindars were large landowners with complete proprietary rights. Once my grand-father, Rajnikanto, wanted to know about his estate. They were both on the back of the horse, Stormy. He told his son, Rajnikanto, if Stormy - very strong and stout - galloped very fast for half an hour in each of the four directions, even then it would not be possible for him to cover our entire estate.

Who Doesn't Know About Rana Pratap's Chetak

It is said that horses have been part of human's lives for thousands of years in a mutually beneficial relationship that has only grown stronger over time. Owing to this long-standing alliance, these animals are the best equipped to understand human emotions and have developed a unique sense of loyalty. In fact, these faithful companions sometimes turn into heroes when their masters are in danger and come to his rescue at the cost of their lives. The example of Maharana Pratap is best suited in this respect. He was the last man to flee from the battlefield. Beating a retreat was out of Rana Pratap's dictionary. But when Chetak got to know that his master was badly injured and was on the verge of being captured by the enemy, he saved Rana Pratap's life in the Battle of Haldighati, in the Aravali Mountains of Rajasthan. He ran 5 km with one leg - broken by the opponents - and jumped a 22 feet canal, reaching his master at safe place and left his last breath.

Miracle Stormy

Stormy was loyal and obedient but a little stubborn sometimes. If Stormy had anybody in this universe, he was his master, Kedarnath, and vice versa. He loved his master by the core of his heart. They both were made for each other. It is said: "Some horses will test you, some will teach you and some will bring out the best in you". My GGF used to assert: "Passion for riding cannot be described in terms of words. A ride on a horse gives you a fantastic experience and monumental pleasures and happiness. That is the reason, people address the animal as a 'horse' while Kedarnath babu, lover of horses, used to say: He is my best friend, my love and soulmate. It is a part of me and so am I. I am hale and hearty because he is my care-taker as well as healer. I have an immediate connection the moment I meet and see him. The bond is so strong that I am drawn to him". This nexus developed over a period of time. 'I experienced a love so deep, powerful and vigorous that I begin to doubt if I really have ever truly loved anyone else'. There is a phrase: 'If wishes were horses, beggars would ride on them'. But if my GGF was asked, he would have said: 'If wishes were horses, I'd need a spacious and comfortable stable'. Though it might appear a humorous wish for somebody but for our GGF, it was a factual fact because he saw many a master lived in a mansion but the stable was like a pigeon-hole. He was of the view that a horse was neither a 'pet' nor a 'friend'. He was surely your best friend, a listener, a partner and a team mate. It did not matter for your horse whether you were walking through the jungle, a river or likely to confront ferocious animals on the way. Because it was your horse who would be there for you, to love you, to save you, to talk to you, to listen to you and to sacrifice his life for you or cherish every moment with you.

One day Binoy ('B'), the brother-in-law of my GGF, met Kedarnath. Binoy wanted to borrow Stormy for a couple of hours to visit the neighbouring village in order to discharge an urgent piece of sale and purchase deeds of some property. At first, Stormy showed his lack of interest in giving him a ride. Kedarnath was also not in favour of letting Stormy out since it was like the blistering heat of the desert. He tried to persuade Binoy to go soon after the sunset when the climate would get much better. Nevertheless Binoy stuck to what he said. He further instructed, showing a bit of harshness, "Kedar, don't be compassionate and empathetic towards your horse. The horse is meant for services. It is not a show piece". Kedarnath did not like such harsh words against his dearest Stormy. But since his brother-in-law was elder to his wife, he was unable to counter. He had to agree reluctantly. Stormy could understand each word of how Binoy reacted. Nevertheless Stormy had to abide by his master's instructions.

Binoy sitting on his back ordered him in a harsh voice to gallop fast. When my GGF went out of sight, after covering a mile or so, he felled him into a large pond. He straightway went to Kedar and lodged a strong complaint against Stormy and angrily asked him to give the horse left and right and further added that his reckless gesture must not be tolerated. The horse not only felled him into the pond but also danced in front of onlookers and children. They further added fuel to the fire by singing filmy songs with the dance tune of the horse, making the situation more embarrassing for Binoy. He further retorted: "Had I been the master of this bloody horse, I would not have spared him. I would have taken it to task.

He would have also been deprived of fodder for a good number of days."

My GGF, Kedarnarth, asked him softly: "Dada, please keep cool! I understand what Stormy has done to you is gratuitous. I would forbid him to do that in future and also assure you that he would not repeat it in future." Binoy got extremely aggravated. "It seems that your horse has not committed the mischievous act. It is you who have done it! He shouted at the pitch of his voice, I am sure, you have gone mad! How are you going to teach this stupid donkey not to perpetrate the idiotic act!"

Deep Love for Stormy

Kedarnath could not control himself. He reiterated: "Dada, for God's sake, don't call him a donkey or even a horse. He is 'Stormy', my friend. I never treat him as an animal. He does not have anybody in this universe except me. But I have a large family to enjoy with at all times. He serves me day in and day out. What I give him in return - only fodder! Is his service tantamount to that? No, he deserves much more than what he has been in receipt of. He undoubtedly deserves: love, fondness, tenderness, attachment, intimacy, kindness, sympathy and endearment. On top of it, we must deal with him with forbearance, patience, leniency, mildness and self-restraint. If he sometimes plays pranks on us, we might welcome it. However, Dada, you being an elderly person, I beg apology on behalf of my friend". It denoted K's colossal love for Stormy. Surely, more than anything else in this world.

Binoy was reddened from impassioned, embarrassed, indignant, outraged, and exasperation of emotional upset. He left his sister's home disdainfully, publicly announcing: "I will never be back unless you punish your horse severely". Stormy lent his ears from a distance and could grasp each and every word of their conversation. Seeing the reactions of her eldest brother, my great grandma, Aroti, was aggrieved at the outcome. GGF skipped his dinner that night. Stormy also did not touch any fodder soon after the predicament. The following day when 'K' offered him fodder, he did not touch it and his eyes were flooded with tears. He kept licking his master's feet. When Kedarnath did not have his breakfast, there was an awkward silence. It was a joint family. All the members of the family, approximately 50, assembled together and persuaded 'K' to have his breakfast and pleaded to forbid Stormy to indulge in misconduct in order to restore peace and tranquillity in the family.

In the midst of the uproar, it was aired that somebody saw Stormy galloping somewhere all alone at a great speed. No sooner did my GGF hear that than he started accosting his name: "Stor .. Stor.. Stor.. my.. My friend, my love, my world .. Where are you? Where have you gone, my beta?" He went out of the room and started running hither and thither approaching and addressing aggressively to whosoever he came across on the way, he got them stopped and asked them impatiently the whereabouts of his Stormy. He came back in the evening. Being tired, exhausted and disappointed, he lay on the floor. My Great Grandma tried hard to persuade him for dinner but in vain. He had not taken even a drop of water for more than 24 hours. All the members of his family gently and persistently endeavoured to convince him that Stormy would be brought back soon and he should not feel worried and concerned. Some children started crying, some were mourning and shedding tears. A few elderly women broke down and sobbed like a child. Many women commenced praying to Lord Madhav: "*Om Shri Krishna sharanam namah*". It is an invocation to the beloved Banke Bihari, surrendering oneself to Him with utmost devotion and conviction in order to take you under His shelter. This chant is said to take away all the grief and miseries from one's life and mind, giving eternal peace. Some were of the opinion that if this persisted for a couple of days, GGF would be infected with serious mental trauma.

Our Great Thakuma, Aroti, wife of Kedarnath, was at a loss to understand what to do. The condition of the family was in a state of mess. She was an intellectual lady. She tried hard to patch up the differences between her brother and husband. One day she went to her brother's house. Her brother and family welcomed her and were hospitable to her but he did not mention anything about her husband. She broke the ice before leaving her brother's house. Dada: "Do you have time to listen to me, maybe for 10 or 15 minutes?" He could guess that she wanted to tell something about Kedarnath. He retorted: "Undoubtedly, Aroti, but it should not be anything about Kedar". Listening from her brother against her husband, she was unable to control herself. She immediately surrendered whatever gift items were given to her. She also ignored the escort, arranged by her brother and started moving on her own. Binoy could understand that his sister was extremely unhappy with what he had said directly against her husband. Since her childhood, she had been polite and submissive. But once she went against somebody, she became a hard nut to crack if she was not persuaded immediately. In order to repair the relationship, he held her hand, pleaded with her to come back home and he was prepared to listen to what she would say. Initially, she was adamant to go back. But on his insistence, she thought not to create any scene outside and in front of villagers. Binoy smilingly asked: Aroti, you wanted to say something! Thus Aroti narrated to her brother how Stormy was instrumental in saving child Abhinandan.

QUOTE

How Stormy saved Child Abhinandan!

Aroti: As you know, our child was born after a decade of our marriage. Your Jamai (Kedarnath), you and I visited a number of temples. In some temples, we had to go barefoot for about 5 kms in scorching heat. Had you not joined us, it would have been an upheaval task for me and your Jamai to go to every temple. With Lord Gopala's grace and your blessings, 'Abhinandan' was born. Dada, it was around 12 years ago, when our kid, Abhinandan, was hardly 2 years old. I had to go to attend the birth ceremony of one of my childhood friends. I could not negate her request as she gladly and heartily took part whenever she was asked to do so by me. She never said 'no' to any of our work. Perhaps, you also knew her. She was Shukla. Other members of our family went to some other village to attend a wedding in our relations. Your Jamai was all alone at home. While he was with Abhinandan, a man came in a great hurry and informed your Jamai that a disaster occurred in their house. A couple of Englishmen were creating a nuisance. He tried to contact members of 'Swatantra Bahini' (SB), but none were available. Hence, his involvement will save them from their plight. He, as you know, is a well-known social worker, on hearing this, could not wait any longer. He immediately went out with him, leaving the child under the charge of Stormy. There was a bear in the village. It was very shrewd and opportunist, lifting many a baby from time to time. Finding a golden opportunity, the bear entered the house and approached the sleeping child. Stormy then placed itself between the baby and the bear. A fierce fight occurred between the two. The bear was very strong and powerful. It somehow managed to jump on Stormy's back and caught hold of its neck. Stormy immediately galopped out of the room with the bear on its back and dashed it against the powerful wall of the building which led to its collapse. The bear was seriously injured and fell down. But the arrogant, wild and ferocious bear ran towards the room where the child was lying. Stormy galopped and soon stood like a rock to shield the entry point of the room. This time the bear attacked Stormy aggressively. There was a child who was witnessing all these from a distance. He immediately rushed in and informed a few villagers. The villagers came with lathis. Seeing the villagers, the bear fled instantaneously. Your Jamai also returned by that time. Stormy drenched in the pool of blood. Seeing his master, he just raised his head towards the baby. Perhaps, he wanted to say his brother was safe and sound. GGF saw from a distance that the baby had a sound sleep. He asked his men to call his wife back. He immediately called up a team of veterinary doctors. He sent his men and vehicle for the doctors to come in no time. The blood oozed profusely from his neck and other parts of the body. Initially, he examined if Stormy was breathing. He then instructed his men to apply antiseptic medicine on the injured parts. He put Stormy's head on his lap and massaged his body, crying bitterly like a child. It was a hot day. He asked his men to fan him.

A team of doctors came. After treating him for a while, they informed 'K' that Stormy's condition was very very serious.

'K' shouted at them. What do you mean? How very serious!

Doctor: It required major surgery.

'K' : How dare you say very serious!

Doctor: It needed a huge sum. There was a doctor, Mohan, who was not aware how much love 'K' had for his Stormy. He told him: "Sir, you will get an Arabian horse with that amount".

By this, 'K' lost his temper and asked him if he was married? Finding no response, 'K' kept on shouting at him.

Dr Mohan: Yes, Sir, 'I am married'.

'K' : How much do you love your wife? Tell me, tell me quickly!

Dr Mohan : 'I love her by the core of my heart.'

'K' : Thundered whether he would replace his wife if he explored a better one in her presence.

Dr Mohan : Remained quiet keeping his head down in utter shame.

'K' handed over rupees five hundred in advance. (It was 120 years ago).

Team of Doctors: It was a huge sum. 'We don't require this much of an amount'.

'K' : Don't waste time unnecessarily. Do your duty. I want to see my Stormy not only 'alive' but hale and hearty. Tell me how much more you are in need for Stormy, my son's treatment. In the meantime, I also came back. Hearing about Stormy's heroism to save the child by putting his own life at stake, I could not control my tears. After giving necessary first-aid, Stormy was immediately taken to a veterinary hospital. He came back after a couple of months of treatment.

UNQUOTE

Binoy: It was not fair on your part and Kedar should have informed me. It revealed that I was not a part of your family. I knew Kedar tried to avoid me.

Aroti: No, Dada. It was not that. He wanted to share it immediately with you. But it was I who forbade him to divulge it to you lest you should give me left and right for not taking due care of the child.

Binoy: It was a blunder on your part. Unfortunately, I always treated Stormy as an animal and nothing beyond that. But the amount of love, gallantry and faithfulness he displayed to save Abhi was beyond my imagination. Hurry up! We should move fast.

In the meantime, Binoy sat beside his brother-in-law. He assured him that he would explore the lost Stormy. Seeing him back and calling him by his name, 'K' felt better. He asked: "Dada, are you going to help all of us to find my Stormy?" Binoy reassured him and asked his sister to arrange dinner for both of them. Hundreds of men were sent in all four directions throughout the night to look for Stormy. As ill luck would have it, there was no clue of his whereabouts. 'K' got up early in the morning, had an early bath, put on a holy dress and straightway went to his house temple. Having chanted: 'Shri Krishna Govinda Hare Murari, Hey Nath Narayana Vasudeva' for an hour in front of Lord Krishna idol, he took out a revolver. All the members of his family became silent spectators since he had already closed all the doors of the temple. He said: "My Stormy is my soul. Now, Lord tell me: 'Can anybody live if his soul gets detached from him? I leave it to you! I have not much patience to wait for my dearest Stormy. If I fail to get my answer soon, I have no choice but to renounce this material world'. 'K' was an ardent devotee of Lord Keshav. No sooner had he determined to leave this mundane world than a few people came from a distant village to inform that there was a horse who had been in the water of the huge lake for more than a day. It was raising its muzzle above the water. (The muzzle is the part of the horse's head that includes the area of the mouth, nostrils, chin, lips, and front of the nose). As soon as they heard that 'K', 'B', their sons and a few villagers reached the spot in no time. It was a huge lake close to a deep forest surrounded by half a dozen villages. Despite his being there for more than 24 hours, it was the sheer grace of Lord Krishna that he was spared by wild animals of the nearby jungle. Thankfully we were able to come here before night falls. Everyone noticed something popping out of the water in the middle of the lake. But it was difficult, if not impossible, to identify whether it was Stormy's.

Binoy: Kedar, is there any way to get Stormy back from the lake?

'K' recalled that he could whistle in a unique way. And as soon as Stormy heard the whistle's sound, he would rush to him. He got completely carried away by the sound of my whistle. Binoy impatiently asked him: What was he waiting for? What prevented him from doing that? He must whistle outright. 'K' suggested otherwise. Let us swim as close as possible to Stormy as the sound of the whistle may be inaudible from here. As per the modus operandi, they swam hard and carefully approached the mammal. As soon as their eyes met, tears of joy came gushing from all the three sets of eyes. With a lot of effort, Stormy pulled himself out of the water and limped his way back home. Everyone was ecstatic and overwhelmed to have Stormy back. But, unfortunately, he had a high fever rising around 102 degrees. Both Binoy and 'K' ordered their men to arrange a large room for him adjacent to 'K'. Veterinary doctor was called in. All of them along with the doctor stayed awake the whole night to look after Stormy. Horses seldom lie down. They are big animals, their blood flow is generally restricted if laid down for a long time. This is harmful for their internal organs, that is the reason why they only recline for REM (rapid eye movement) sleep. This results in them dozing while standing up at various points throughout the day.

Perhaps the dawn of rejuvenation, cheerfulness, merriment, jollity and high spirits set about. While both Binoy and Kedar were dozing off before the day-break, Stormy came near them and started licking their legs. Both 'B' and 'K' opened their eyes and were delighted to find Stormy in a much healthier state. As soon as they woke up, Stormy raised his two front legs to apologise for his misdeed. Both of them in turn embraced Stormy, begged pardon and promised never to repeat their mistakes either. Generally, horses show affection to their masters by an act of sharing breath. He thus brought her nose close to her masters and then started breathing heavily. This tendency extends to horses showing love to their masters as well. The scene of enthusiasm in the family was incredibly lively. Some were dancing and a few singing songs of joy. People with zest are happy, but this went beyond happiness or pleasure. This showed how all were closely attached to Stormy and had passionate longings for his prompt recovery. GGF celebrated the occasion with pomp and show. He invited all the villagers for a feast which continued for a couple of days.

Our ancestors lived in Govindopur. It was around 80 kms from Sunderbans. About 120 years ago, the erstwhile Sunderbans were not like the present one. It was a natural site without much interference from the then Government, surrounded by a deep forest. There was barely any human existence in their surroundings. It was a real disaster during monsoon season though. During the rainy season, aquatic animals, arboreal animals (living on trees); while terrestrial animals (living on land); and amphibians (both water and land animals) were available in abundance. It was home to Royal Bengal tigers as well. Since there was not much access to human beings, one could enjoy natural and panoramic beauty.

Floods were one of the most dangerous natural disasters. West Bengal was highly prone to floods. The cubs of various animals washed away from one place to another with the current of the flooded water. Their parents had no alternative but to follow their offspring, throwing themselves into the current of the water. Sometimes they entered the villages and had to settle down in nearby shrubs, mini jungles or where there was inadequate flood water. It was a real danger for both animals and human beings. Those animals found it very difficult to make their both ends meet owing to absence of their prey. So, they would generally enter the villages post-dusk to escape being caught in darkness and attack the women on their way to relieve themselves, early in the morning. Survival was a challenge for both humans and animals alike. Also many priceless colourful birds were flown to far-flung areas as there used to be fodder for them everywhere. They also fell prey to the villagers and hunters.

Once it was a bright and fine morning after a dark, dull and rainy month. But outside it was like mini Sunderbans. The flood water caused bushes, shrubs and also shrub-like trees to grow everywhere. It stagnated at places and made little ponds and lakes here and there. The animals were unable to go back to their natural habitats owing to ceaseless rain and accumulation of flood and rain water in and out. They were waiting for the pre-winter season to set in. While Abhinandan was playing with Stormy, he made a request to his Dad, Kedarnath, to go outside and enjoy the beautiful morning. 'K' was not interested to go as everywhere there was stagnated water, bushes and mini jungles. So, it was not completely safe for a stroll with his son. Nevertheless, Abhinandan was stubborn and kept requesting his Dad. It was decided that they would leave late in the afternoon and return prior to the sunset. Both Abhinandan and Stormy started dancing with joy.

Kedarnath (K) set out with Abhinandan on the back of Stormy at 3 pm. The weather was pleasant with a cool breeze. Stormy was not galloping, he was trotting, as the muddy roads were very bumpy. When they covered a few kms from home, 'K' remembered that he forgot to carry his rifle. Suddenly, it got dark and started drizzling followed by incessant rain. 'K' was not interested to proceed further. But as Abhinandan was enjoying, pressed hard to go a km or so. No sooner had Stormy trotted half a km, than 'K' saw a couple of beautiful tiger cubs just a few yards away from them. He thought of helping them out lest they should be the victim of predators soon. He alighted from the back of Stormy in view of helping the cubs. Abhinandan was about to get off but Stormy jumped with a loud bray. Abhinandan was not happy with Stormy's behaviour.

Abhinandan: What happened, brother? Stormy, without answering his question, went straightway to 'K' and kept braying loudly. 'K' knew that it was a signal of 'danger'. 'K' was unmindful of Mom tigress which was not too far away from her cubs. It was a Royal Bengal tigress, around 9 ft. long and weighed more or less 200 kg. Stormy was tall, stout, brave and courageous. When his master's attention was drawn to the tigress, the latter was about to jump on 'K'. Stormy dropped Abhinandan near the deep bush and stood in between his master and the tigress, on his hind legs with the forelegs off the ground, preventing her jump on his master. The tigress' jump was obstructed by Stormy and as a result of which the tigress fell on Stormy. Both Stormy and tigress fell down. When the tigress came back to attack 'K', Stormy returned ferociously and kicked her violently with his hind legs. Thereafter, Stormy saw her two cubs just a couple of metres away from their Mumma. In order to save his master, he started trotting after the cubs, braying fiercely, jumping every now and then, showing his intention to kill them instantaneously. To save her kids, the tigress leaving 'K' alone, attempted to attack Stormy. Stormy was around 7.5 ft. and strong and quite intelligent. The tigress tried to attack Stormy from the front as it was dangerous or even fatal for the predators to attack any horse from its back. But Stormy negated its attack by quickly reversing his position and resisted by kicking her with his hind legs. As bad luck would have it, Abhinandan, a child of 10, in all his naivety, appeared at this fierce battle spot holding a bamboo stick. In order to save his son, 'K' came running from a distance. Finding Abhinandan nearby, the tigress leaving Stormy, attempted to attack the child. Yet again, it was Stormy's turn to save Abhinandan. Stormy, without thinking of his safety, attacked the tigress with full force. Finally, the tigress got the opportunity to hold its crest (the top line of the neck). Stormy fell down; the tigress was on its head with 200 kg weight. Its favourite way of taking down its prey is to lunge at the animal's neck and hold on tight with its powerful jaws. That was what the tigress did. In that case, either the prey will die from suffocation or it may bleed out first if the tiger's canines sever an artery. It generally hunts and chews on its prey with its four sharp teeth. It also takes a bite at the jugular vein on the neck. 'K' and Abhinandan, finding no way out, went on raining stones after stones at the cubs. Abhinandan was adept in shooting catapults (Gulel). Fortunately, a few stones struck the cubs badly and it started roaring (cry of a lion/cub) in acute pain. No sooner did they roar in pain than 'K' chased the cubs from a few metres away and kept pelting stones in order to scare the tigress. Mother is like an angel, who would protect her child no matter what! For every child, his mother holds a special place in his heart because she is the first person the child sees after taking birth. This is the reason why a child and a mother have a unique and special bond. (The author himself is well aware of it through his own personal experience which he had written and narrated in his maiden venture in the form of his Biography.) In the animal kingdom as well, mothers' roles are more or less the same as humans. Many species rely on their moms for nourishment, comfort and protection. As cubs grow up, mothers teach them survival skills like hunting, grooming and socialising. That's why modern zoos and aquariums rely on mother animals to raise their babies wherever possible. The tigress left its prey immediately and ran away with her cubs. 'K' could somehow contact 'Swatantra Bahini' and explained this through a villager who was passing by on a bike. In the meantime, 'K' and Abhinandan checked Stormy's vein and pulse and could understand that his condition was very serious. The members of the Swatantra Bahini immediately rushed in, in a large number, on heavy bullock carts with a veterinary doctor. When 'K' asked the doctor about the status of Stormy, the doctor knew how much 'K' loved Stormy, he reserved his comments. It would be appropriate if he was taken to Hospital as soon as possible. Stormy negated it by making a 'neigh' which 'K' could well understand. Then 'K' immediately asked: "Are you interested in going home?" He agreed. Knowing his critical condition, K's heart was broken in thousands of pieces and on each piece, he perceived nothing but Stormy, Stormy and Stormy. It was getting dark. 'K' asked the doctor to apply first-aid immediately. Thereafter, Stormy was taken home. A team of doctors turned up in no time. Soon after checking, they informed 'K' to spend some time with Stormy and there was no point in taking him to the Hospital. Stormy was surrounded by hundreds of villagers. While hugging Stormy, 'K' and Abhinandan reiterated that they were instrumental for his condition. 'K' reiterated that nobody on the earth would fight for his master-cum-friend's life the way Stormy did. 'We would have been no more if you had not put your life at stake'. Both of them cried bitterly and 'K' asked his friend, "How can I live without you? We are indeed indebted to you which cannot be repaid by us by any means. You saved my son and this time, both of us. I failed to be both a responsible owner and a caring friend. I am sure, nobody in this mundane world will lay down his life even for his son. But it is you who have done it without considering any value of your own life. We have heard of Chetak. With due respect to him, he was well nourished since he was nurtured in a palace. But I was not able to give you nutritious food and adequate love and affection. Sometimes I took you to task for your innocence. Why have you given your life and left me in the lurch? You communicated with me entirely through your body language. You understood every word of my language quite clearly; unfortunately, sometimes, I failed to. I could recollect one of my experiences, when I bought another horse in your presence. Out of jealousy, you ceased to eat. You lapsed into depression. I was constrained to sell that horse to a new owner at a different location. You might be thinking that when you tried to save both of us, the tigress felled you down and was sitting on your head, taking out the flesh from your neck with her powerful jaws, why did I not do anything to save you? Yes, I had my vested interest. At the same time, I did not have any weapons to fight with. It was pitch dark as well. Nothing was clearly visible. Last but not the least, had I gone there empty handed and laid down my life, your sacrifice would have been futile. Instead, we both were raining stones at the cubs to scare their mother. But it took a few seconds for the tigress to inflict you with fatal injury. I had the temerity to go to your rescue. But it was you, who forbade me to do that with your gestures and actions". In the meantime, Binoy joined. He embraced Stormy, touching his feet, and begged apology for mistreatment with him. There is a saying, when anybody is on the verge of demise, he has a lot of strength in him. It is like a lamp, before getting extinguished, its flame is stronger. When Stormy raised his head, its neck was in a dilapidated state and blood was oozing from all sides of his neck. Seeing his condition, all three of us were devastated. We held his neck with our palms. Stormy licked the tears from our faces and after some time kept his head on my lap, staring at me without shedding even a drop of tears and dropping his eyelids. A little later, he looked at the gathering by rotating his eyes, trying to recognise each one of them and neighed before he closed his eyes forever. 'K' told that through his 'neigh' he happily bade goodbye.

'K' : It is said: In life, we must have two friends. One like Krishna who even without taking part in war, ensures sure and certain win. The other one is like Karan, who despite knowing certain and definite defeat, did not part with his friend.

'K' asked all of us: In which category will the friendship of my Stormy fall? Despite knowing unequivocally that his death was inevitable, he fought till his last breath. Over and above, when a ferocious Royal Bengal Tigress, weighing more than 200 kgs was sitting on his head and neck, drinking his blood and chewing his flesh, Stormy, in order to save his master - never expressed his pain, agony and anguish - did not invite his master by neighing lest his master should be the victim of the tigress.

Like 'K', I too, as an author, am speechless and plead my utter ignorance!

I would solicit my readers to add to my knowledge.

'K' had his own cremation ground. Stormy was taken there and cremated like human beings. The cremation ground was flooded with villagers and all of them attended his funeral as well. All the rituals were performed. Soon after the cremation, 'K', Binoy and Abhinandan collected the ashes and consecrated them to the Ganges. The Brahmin was engaged in performing pujas. Thereafter, all three distributed food and donated cash to the poor.

A huge statue of 'Stormy'

'K' erected a huge statue of Stormy in front of his house, inscribing on it:

'In loving memory of my **FRIEND, Stormy**, who demonstrated incredible testimony to the loyalty, courage, superabundant and unending love saving my child, Abhinandan, and me from a wild

BEAR and a monstrous ROYAL BENGAL TIGRESS by sacrificing your own life. Both of us are alive by virtue of your gracious act. You will eternally live in our hearts and thoughts.

'**IN MEMORIAM**'

"FONDLY MISSED ALONG OUR LIFE's WAY

QUIETLY REMEMBERED DAY IN AND DAY OUT.

NO LONGER IN OUR LIFE TO SHARE WITH YOU

BUT IN OUR HEARTS YOU ARE ALWAYS THERE".

"YOUR LOVE AND TENDERNESS KEEP US GOING.

WE MISS YOU EVERY DAY,

BUT STILL FEEL YOUR PRESENCE

AROUND US ALL THE TIME."

"IF TEARS BUILD A STAIRWAY AND

MEMORIES A LANE,

WE WOULD WALK RIGHT UP TO HEAVEN,

TO BRING YOU BACK TO HOME".

Chapter - II

How Does A Mother Carry Baby in Her Tummy

A few children were chit-chatting with the village Dhaima (midwife). There was a naughty child who was, time and again, pulling her hair and hiding himself behind his friends. His friends were protecting him and encouraging him to do so. She was fed up with the mischievous acts of the children. There was a noblewoman, Mother Kananbala, sister of GGF. She was a spinster, spending time worshipping and singing Krishna bhajan with the members of Swatantra Bahini. She was watching the mischievous acts of these troublesome children. She was quite respectful in the village. The noblewoman asked the children if they were interested in listening to a story of Putana. If so, they might join her under the Krishna tree. There was the Great Peepal tree which is believed to be more than 1000 years old. The villagers called the tree 'Krishna'. Peepal has a huge importance in the culture of India. Peepal trees are sacred in India and are often associated with a God or a Goddess. Peepal offers shade from the sun. This is the favourite tree of the sadhus and the wandering hermits as well. The people who move from village to village would often rest under the cool shade of this humongous tree. The village and community meetings were always held in an open ground and they needed shade. This Krishna tree in this particular village was indispensable to the travellers, villagers, sadhus, hermits and the women. Gautam Buddha after long years of sadhana, at the peak of consciousness and enlightenment was known to have stayed beneath the tree for a number of days in profound awe, joy and gratitude. It is also believed that Krishna died under the Peepal tree, after which the present Kaliyug is said to have commenced. And, it is also conjectured that He will reside in a Peepal leaf after the destruction of this world and until the next world is created.

All the children, the village Dhai along with the noblewoman assembled under the Krishna tree. The children surrounded the noblewoman. At the outset, she asked the children to chant with her:

"Shri Krishna Govinda Hare Murari;

Hey Nath Narayana Vasudeva".

(Murari was born somewhere, grew up elsewhere).

All the children chanted with her. Thereafter, she asked Sonu, who was pulling Dhai's knot: "How many types of mothers exist in the world?" All the children protested vehemently: "We are interested in listening about Putana." The noblewoman retorted: "I shall tell you only when you are quiet and maintain discipline". Sonu responded: "I have one mother". Now listen attentively.

There are seven kinds of mothers according to Vedic directive:

The real mother; the wife of a teacher or spiritual master; the wife of a king; the wife of a Brahmana; the cow; the nurse/Dhai and the mother earth.

The noblewoman informed the children that she would tell the 'synopsis' of what she had gone through from the holy book, Bhagavad Gita'.

Putana was sent to kill Lord Krishna

Kamsa sent a witch, Putana, to kill Krishna. She knew black magic and was adept in the art of killing. Putana was an expert at flying in the sky. She disguised herself as a pretty woman and entered the house of mother Yasoda. She looked like a damsel with elevated hips, attractive and pointed breasts, and honeyed lips, long, curly & bushy hair, slim waist, amorous glance and sheep-like eyes with a sweet smile. A couple of boys appeared ungentle in their behaviour towards her, gesturing one another with some distasteful signs. The ornament she wore made her glitter from head to toes. Her appearance came as a bolt from the blue for the residents of Vrindavan. They assumed that she could be no other than Menaka descended straight from Heaven. All of them were passionate about having glimpses of her by hook or crook. They considered themselves luckiest if Putana responded to their greetings. Owing to her being drop-dead gorgeous, nobody checked her movement. Hence, she could freely move to the house of Nando Maharaj. Baby Krishna was lying on a perambulator. Putana with her black magic could identify that the child was the Supreme Personality of Godhead. She pondered over if she backed out and returned, she would take the displeasure of Kamsa who would kill her instantaneously. If she ventured to kill Lord Krishna, the latter would kill her. Putana was between the devil and the deep sea. However, she was intelligent enough to decide. She thought it would be the best way to attain moksha to be killed by Krishna. As baby Krishna closed His eyes, Putana took Him on her lap and went out of the room in no time. While flying in the sky with baby Krishna, she offered her breast milk to be sucked by Him. Putana smeared the nipples of her breast with fatal poison and pushed them into His mouth. Lord Krishna sucked her nipple and made her breathless. The demon fell down, perspired, got completely wet, and prayed as loud as she could: "Son, leave me; leave me, son; I am unable to breathe". As she died, the real feature of the witch appeared. While falling, her body covered 10 - 15 miles, smashing all the trees to pieces and it is said that there was an earthquake all around. The earthquake was not, in fact, a natural one. It was by virtue of falling a monstrous, huge mountain-like body on the earth. Her nostrils were like mountain caves; her breasts appeared small hills; her hair covered miles of jungle; her two thighs might act as banks of the sea; two hands could touch the sky. All the children started shaking like a leaf and almost scared to death. They prayed: "Please stop narrating. We shuddered to think of her. We are scared." Many of them embraced the noblewoman. It was a bolt from the blue for all those who were present there. Even after having visualised her dead body, on-lookers were not prepared to believe that she was the same Putana whom they had visualised an hour back. Many children were in a state of fit after having seen her dead body. But Lord Gopala was so gracious and magnanimous that He carried out the wishes of the demon by accepting her breast milk. Krishna accepted Putana as one of His mothers since He had her breast milk. It was indeed a blessing in disguise for Putana. Once she was a demon. Prior to having met Krishna, she took Him as her prey. Soon after having met Him, she became the mother of Him. How lucky and honoured Putana was! She soon got liberation. You know, there are many sages, monks and holy souls who have been worshipping and chanting the name of Lord Krishna day in and day out, yet they are not fortunate enough to have His glimpses even. The children humbly asked the noblewoman: Was there any way to have darshan of Lord Krishna? Could we ever see Him? What would we have to do to catch sight of Him? She informed what Bhagwan Ramakrishna Paramhansa had advocated:

- 'You have to have 'love' as the love of 'mothers to their children';
- As the love of 'chaste wives to their husbands';
- And as the 'attachments' of the 'businessmen to their wealth and property'.

- When all these forms of love and attachments are clubbed together and are offered to Lord Krishna, His divine Darshan is inevitable.

So, I would advise you to chant His name day in and day out irrespective of your age. No sooner had she completed than the children were full of appreciation and kept chanting His name. The noblewoman asked the children: "Hereafter, how are you going to address Dhai?" Ma, Ma, Mother! The noblewoman forbade them to crack jokes and tease the woman. She further reminded them that we all feel uneasy with the slightest bite of an ant. How do mothers feel who bear each baby in her abdomen for 9 months or so? All the children embraced *Dhaima* and held their ears as a gesture of apology for their mischievous acts.

It is said that once in the village and its surroundings, there had been no rain for around half a decade. There was an acute drying of water resources, crop failure and withering, scarcity of food items, leaving livestock starving. This caused severe drought. Consequently, levels of water in rivers, ponds and wells dried up dangerously leading to acute water shortage. Trees became nude in the absence of their leaves. They had the appearance of ghosts especially in the nights' darkness. Absence of leaves caused a serious scarcity of oxygen. The significant amounts of water stored up did not last long. The sources of surface water left polluted with dead animals, leaves of the trees, insanitary conditions and absence of cleanliness. Severe famine broke out leading to the death of the inhabitants of the villages. Rates of mortality shot up due to an acute shortage of water and air pollution. The water animals in the ponds were found dead. Villagers had no alternative but to quench their thirst with whatever water was left - muddy, contaminated and polluted. There was an all-round concern, worry, disquietude and perturbation. Gram Panchayats conducted a large-scale yagna for a couple of days to invoke rain god but in vain. There was a hearsay that Mother Kananbala had the potential to invoke Hare Krishno and do away with the predicament. Finding no remedies and solutions, as a last resort, Heads of Village Panchayat along with all the villagers approached Mother Kananbala who was chanting Krishna bhajan under a Krishna Tree. She was quite unmindful of the predicament as her days passed, chanting and singing Krishna *aarti* and *bhajan*. She lived a frugal life and could even survive without consuming food and water for a few days. The village Head explained to her the appalling, dreadful and perilous conditions of both villages and villagers. All of them prayed for her to come to their rescue. They also reiterated that if there was no rain for another year or two, all these villages would not be in the country's map. They pleaded with folded hands to save all of them and the villages from complete annihilation. Upon listening to all these, she pointed a few questions and craved answers from the Heads of Village Panchayats:

- Have I not requested you time and again to erect boundaries around Krishna Tree? Also to construct a few rooms inside the boundary for the monks and sages and others who worship the Tree. My younger brother, Kedarnath, agreed to do that. But it was I who reacted to his doing that. It was the foremost duty and responsibility of the Village Panchayat, first of all, to understand the godliness of this Tree and make the villagers appreciate its sacredness. You should also have hung a 'notice board' by the side of the tree forbidding people to spoil the sanctity of Krishna Tree. Unfortunately, you ignored me every time I approached you.

- Do you know why I told you all these? The village children, even adults, urinated and discharged other bodily wastes at times. Keeping in view of the importance and significance of the holy tree, I had to clean in order to sanctify the entire area. I never divulged all these to anybody. But, honestly speaking,

I knew some day or other, misfortune will certainly befall upon these clusters of villages and its surroundings.

- Do you know who lives on this Tree? Leave it.... You won't believe.... You all will make fun of me. You see, there are four Yugas namely Satya Yuga (the Golden age). In this Yuga, knowledge, meditation and penance held special importance. Treta Yuga (Silver age), Dwapara Yuga (Bronze age) and Kali Yuga (the Iron age). Though it is Kaliyug yet you will appreciate the sun, the moon, the air, the rain, the Sea, the River, water, foodstuff, flora and fauna, etc. all are available which were in existence in all the three aforesaid Yugas. Can you tell me about nature's discrimination on the basis of Yugas? No, nature remains the same. Nature is never biased or partial to any Yuga.

- There are ten prominent avatars known as the Dashavatar. Of these, four appeared in Satya Yuga: Matsya, Kurma, Varaha and Narasimha.

- Vamana, Parashurama and Rama were believed to have lived during the Treta Yuga. Rama is an incarnation of Vishnu. He is the seventh avatar of Vishnu. Vishnu is one of a trinity of the three Godheads of Hinduism. Brahma the creator, Vishnu the protector, and Shiva the destroyer. Vishnu has had nine incarnations on earth as different beings. One of these is Rama.

- Lord Krishna is the eighth avatar of Lord Vishnu. He was born to Devaki and Vasudev in the Dwapara Yuga in the form of a human with divine powers.

- Kalki is a descendant of the divine into the material realm of human existence. Kalki being the tenth incarnation. He has been described as the incarnation who would appear at the end of the Kali Yuga.

There was no point in discussing religious gospels before you. It was tantamount, sorry to say, to cast pearls before swine. Heads of the Village Panchayats, while touching her feet, humbly requested her to condone their blunders. Indeed it was a matter of ignominy and humiliation that they did not give any importance to her counselling. They agreed that they did not have any rights to be the heads of the villages. They prepared to step down immediately if she wished. Alternatively, as per her counselling, boundaries covering 50 kathas (two and a half bighas) of the area, being Krishna Tree in the middle, a few pucca rooms, lavatories, washrooms and an office room would be constructed within a month. The heads of the Village Panchayat volunteered their own saving funds for this purpose. Over and above, a Priest would be appointed to worship Krishna Tree and Bhog and Prasad would be offered to the deity as decided by the Brahmin. As regards hospitalisation of monks, sages and holy men in the temple, it would be at the discretion of Mother Kananbala, using temple funds. She appeared delighted and agreed to dilate on this issue as soon as the construction got over. All assembled inside the newly constructed temple. Krishna Tree was close to the temple. There were two rooms, a kitchen, one spacious hall, an office room, a bathroom and a lavatory duly constructed. A Priest, a scavenger and a manager were appointed for its maintenance. In the meeting, it was proposed to nominate Mother Kananbala as President of the 'Krishna Temple Brotherhood'.

She expressed her happiness over the construction of the temple, rooms, etc. and offered a suitable name for its Association. She outrightly rejected any post. Citing that she may be here today, but elsewhere the day after. However, she promised to do good to others as long as she lived. She would strive hard to restore happiness, prosperity and tranquillity of the villages. She would not leave until and unless there were rains as well as prosperity in the villages. However, she suggested that the charge of the temple must be endowed to a person who believed in worshipping Jagatpati with utmost reverence and his/her dictum should be final and binding. She suggested a spiritual personality. However, she informed all of them that she would continue praying in the temple for a week at a stretch. Not only would anyone be allowed to enter the temple but no one should even be visible around the temple compass especially during the night for a week starting from the day after. All kinds of Pooja *samagris* (ingredients) for a week must be kept inside the room adjacent to the gate by today. Nobody would access the temple unless the main gate of the 'Krishna Temple Brotherhood' was found open. All agreed to her proposal.

It was assumed that the first three days of the Puja were successful. The main gate of the temple was found closed from inside for all the first three days. The Heads of the Village Panchayats ensured that nobody was in and around the Krishna Tree especially during nights. Earlier before the start of the Pooja, there was a stench. The smell and odour was like some waste materials, rotten eggs, food and vegetables, hair and dirt that clogged in the drain pipes for a few months. It felt like some sort of degradation. We used to breathe polluted air, we were also quite doubtful about the food we ate and the water we drank. Day in and day out that made the villagers very uncomfortable, unhealthy and unsightly. From the fourth day onwards, the villagers were wonderstruck to find chirping birds and blooming of flowers, which had almost disappeared for the last many months. On the fifth day, villagers could sense pleasantry - a drastic change in the air while the night seemed comfortable. Nobody knew the source of such a sweet fragrance. Everything appeared to be transforming miraculously.

The surroundings were so pleasant that the villagers preferred to roam outside for the whole night. On the penultimate day, villagers were surprised to see an illuminating Krishna Tree from a distance with pleasant fragrance all around the place. When there were sudden rains, the villagers became enthusiastic and their happiness knew no bounds. It was greeted by the cheers of ecstatic villagers. Initially, there was a drizzle of rain for a while. After some time, it stopped. Thereafter there was a shower of rain. It again ceased to take place after half an hour or so. It was a pleasant surprise, rather strange, for the villagers who had been missing them badly for the last five years or so. The villagers were astonished, finding ponds with water filled to the brims. The village heads and the members of the Panchayat came in different groups and advised all the villagers to get in and forbade them to come out of their houses. This latest development came to the villagers as a bolt from the blue, who were earlier concerned even about their survival. The last day, the seventh day, was full of miracles. People could not believe their own eyes when they saw many peacocks dancing on the road adjacent to Krishna Tree. Villagers winked their eyes in utter surprise at what they were watching. They had beautiful, multi-coloured - dark greenish-brown and blue-feathers. They spread their wings out like a fan or umbrella. Was it a village or Heaven! Many people cried out pointing at the Krishna Tree which was infested with peacocks and peahens. Villagers looked at it from a distance most astonishingly. Trees that were bare for years suddenly bloomed with beautiful green leaves. Surprisingly, though it was not the spring season yet there was greenery all over. Villagers were so captivated in the panoramic and scenic beauty that they forgot to have their meals. Earlier many villagers decided to leave their hearth and homes and would settle down somewhere else, but now, they could not think of leaving their village at any cost. Many villagers were gossiping around their ponds; a few were singing songs eulogising the place, village, where they were born; some were chanting 'Hare Krishna mantra'. It was a fantastic evening. A few villagers could see the shadow of a herd of cows at Krishna Tree. In the meantime, the Heads of the Village Panchayat turned up and drew 'Lakshman Rekha' (a boundary line) and strictly forbade everybody to cross that. At midnight, it started raining cats and dogs and went on till morning. In the early morning, there was a deafening noise. The huge temple gate opened automatically. All the villagers went to the temple in groups. The Heads of the Village Panchayat and its members were found standing, surrounding the temple gate. All seemed unhappy, disappointed and tears trickled down their cheeks. Upon finding that their spiritual mother was no more, all the villagers burst into tears. The Heads of the VP decided that sandalwood must be used to conduct the cremation ceremony (mukh agni). 'Ks' family, the family of his brother-in-law, were around Mother Kananbala. Seeing Stormy, 'K' asked him: "How will you go? Should we arrange a vehicle for you?" Stormy was a few yards away from them. He questioned Stormy: "Why are you standing at a distance?" Stormy's eyes were flooded with tears. Binoy Babu asked him loudly: "Are you not one of the members of our family?" All of a sudden, when he tried to drag him closer, he could realise that Stormy had already left for his heavenly abode. He reiterated: "If it was my hallucination, how he stood close to me, how I could see him, how come we talked to each other!!

Mother Kananbala Temple with Remembrances

Binoy asked the villagers not to collect funds for her cremation ceremony. He would bear all expenses. The Heads of the VP intervened and politely, humbly and with folded palms told him: "Dada, we know, you can well afford to do that. But our men are very keen in doing something for the noble cause of their spiritual mother. They have already collected funds for her cremation". Binoy had no alternative but to give in. The body of Mother, Kananbala, was full of natural aroma. She was covered with tonnes of flowers. Heads of the VP asked whoever was interested to touch her feet, as a mark of respect, might form separate queues. There were long queues. All of them evinced their keen interest to go for their mother's cremation too. Mother Kananbala was taken for cremation accompanied by a large number of villagers and outsiders. After performing all the rituals, praying over the body before cremation, the mourners collected the ashes and consecrated it into the river. Soon after coming back, the name of 'Krishna Temple Brotherhood' was changed to: 'MOTHER KANANBALA TEMPLE'. A large statue of the miracle lady was erected in the Temple with 'REMEMBRANCES':

Your Memories and Love Showered on us;
Will Always remind your presence in our hearts.
May your soul rest in eternal peace!
You will remain in our hearts forever.
We dedicate ourselves to ideals you left behind.

Chapter - III

Stormy's Death Led to Mental Trauma

Aroti: 'K' was unable to lead a normal life. He was always obsessed with the thoughts of Stormy. Aroti was very concerned about her husband. She called up her brother, Binoy, and shared with him all about her husband. She also reiterated that if her husband was haunted with never ending thoughts of Stormy, he would get a bee in his bonnet about it. It might lead him to depression very soon. She also enquired: 'Was there any way to help him to control his feelings?' While saying that, she was teary-eyed and started weeping continually. Her brother retorted: Everything cannot be achieved in life. 'For some people 'ifs' and for others 'buts' remain to be brought off'. However, I assured you that necessary changes would be brought about in 'K' soon.

'K' was all alone in the stable. When he saw his brother-in-law, he escorted him to his room. He told 'K' that he asked his men to prepare 'drinking *Tari*'. (For the information of the readers: It is made of dates or palms. In the early morning, before the sun-rise, if it is consumed, it is like nectar, the most delicious fruit juice. But after 10 am onwards with the sun rays, some sort of fog develops in it. Thereafter, it is boiled and as soon as it gets cooled, it's consumed. Then it becomes a kind of liquor, though not having any contents of alcohol, spirits or wine, etc. It's like calling a 'cauliflower' a flower. It is not a flower in any way, yet its suffix is 'flower'. In the same way, 'Tari' does not have any alcoholic contents yet it does intoxicate consumers). We both would enjoy a bit and, thereafter, we would decide what to do for the welfare of our village and also to ensure that no Stormy would have to die a similar kind of death in future. In the offing, 'K' mildly turned down to join in any such party.

Binoy: Listen 'K': It is said that:

"Worrying is a total waste of time and energy.

It does not change anything.

It messes with your mind and steals your happiness".

And

"There is always another chance for everything in life.

But the fact is that there is no chance of another life.

So, Dream it, Mean it, Live it, and Love it".

'K':   But....Dada......

Binoy: Don't cut in when I speak...............

Stormy sacrificed his life .... Why? To see you depressed! To see you broken-hearted, down in the mouth and low-spirited! To see Abhinandan confined to a room day in and day out, sitting idle at this prime age and spoiling his career. Further, had Stormy watched you from heaven, he would have surely repented for having been brutally and savagely killed by the ferocious tigress for your and your child's sake'.

I endorsed what you say, Dada. Nevertheless, it is said that: "Time, friend and relation are such components which are though received free of cost or cheaply yet their values are realised only when they are lost. However, some of the biggest culprits are stress, heartache, guilt, pain, woe, remorse, depression and grief. I have been the victim of all these soon after the demise of my Stormy. Sometimes I am unmindful of these emotions, but they still affect my behaviour, attitude and day-to-day life. Occasionally, I feel like talking to someone about my nostalgic feelings and writing in a journal which are great ways to sort out what I am feeling and why! But I have been so obsessed with Stormy, I fail to understand why

I am not able to forget everything and start my life afresh. Every time my mind keeps taking me back to the dreadful scene of stormy being brutally massacred by the fierce tigress, while I feel merely standing there and as if I were watching waves of the sea".

All Tactics of *Sam, Dam, Dand* & *Bhed* could not Avoid Devastating War

Binoy: Answer a couple of my questions: "You being an ardent devotee of Bishnu, how come you were not able to control your mind; how come you were unable to get rid of the predicament? He continued countering his brother-in-law by reminding him: Lord Krishna, eighth incarnation or Avatar of the Hindu God 'Vishnu' and also as supreme, who is considered the highest Avatar in the Universe, who endeavoured hard to avoid the war with the offer of settlement of just five villages to Pandavas. Lord Krishna adopted all tactics of *Sam, Dam, Dand* and *Bhed* to avoid the war which He could not. Narayan asserted that everybody gets his/her fruits of individual Karma. 'B' reiterated that even Murari has nothing much to do. He cannot interfere in the 'Karma' of a person. In view of all these, if you were not able to save Stormy, it was nothing but predestined.

The gospel of Binoy babu brought about a moment of epiphany in 'K'. Aroti was delighted to watch her brother and husband involved in a philosophical discussion accompanied by laughing and talking freely. While looking at Aroti, 'K' jokingly asked: 'Dada, you are, in a real sense, muscular, tough, and energised. But how come Aroti is feeble, incapacitated, weakened and chicken-hearted! She is not able to withstand hardship and strain! Aroti with a reddened face rushed in like a hurricane, hitting all the chairs and tables on the way, retorting violently: "Do not talk of me, better talk of yourself! You are most sentimental and emotional. You become the cause of worry and concern for all of us. Whenever any mishap occurred in the family, it was you who stopped talking and started living like Robinson Crusoe".

'K's Appreciation to His Better Half Under The Influence Of 'Tari'

Both 'B' and 'K' had a big laugh for a couple of minutes. 'B' kept appreciating her sister saying Robinson Crusoe ... fantastic! Thereafter, 'K' humbly requested her to cool down. He questioned her: "How do you know about Robinson Crusoe?" She typically answered in a sharp but witty manner. "You know, I am a Graduate. I can afford to help and assist you in every way you crave for". "I know, I know. You are both jack and master of all", responding 'K'. Saying this, he held her hand as a gesture of love and made her sit beside him. She settled down after a lot of hesitation. 'K' started eulogising her beauty. "You are really an enchantress. I am not aware what magic you put me under a spell? Whenever you are in front of me, I become spellbound. No sooner do I see you than I forget this mundane world and I am in the periphery of divinity. Not only are you a paragon of beauty but also a high-quality woman who loves her partner deeply and cares for him with empathy, kindness and loyalty". He asked her brother how come she was an epitome of beauty with confidence and emotional intelligence! 'B' could well understand that 'K' was talking about all these things under the influence of 'Tari'. Nevertheless he was enjoying. 'B' had never observed 'K' in such a romantic and jovial mood. He was pleased to see his sister happy and gay. Though Aroti could well understand that 'K' was exaggerating, nevertheless, she was happy that he was gleeful, beaming and buoyant after a long time of his being in a state of exasperation which she did not want to mar. 'K' was also delighted to explore for the first time how graceful, charming and dashing her better half had appeared at the time when she not only loved but also fought with him. However, who does not like compliments! Women do love compliments like: 'You have a great smile.' 'You are a paragon of beauty.' 'You have deer eyes.' You are a 'Mrignayani' — epitome of beauty. 'My friends always speak high of your charming face.' Soon after that 'K' started humming a few stanzas from a Bollywood song:

"Mere Neendon Mein Tum,	(You are there in my sleep
Mere Khwaabon Mein Tum,	and in my dreams.
Ho Chuke Hum Tumhari	I am totally lost
Mohabbat Mein Ghum"	in your love).

She felt a bit of shame mixed with deep love. Aroti covered her face with both her palms like a college-going girl. She looked at her brother to watch his reaction. When she detected that her brother was enjoying it, she asked if she would arrange some more dry fruit to enjoy with the drink. 'B' told her smilingly that he was already enjoying himself to a great extent by watching them too closely. It was for the first time 'B' was enjoying the banter between Aroti and 'K'. Aroti reminded her brother that she would not allow him to leave without having dinner. They all had dinner together in a very very cordial atmosphere after a long time.

Chapter – IV

I do not care for liberation, I would rather go to a hundred thousand hells, 'doing good to others (silently) like the spring', this is my religion.

— Swami Vivekananda

Britishers Officially Created Prostitutions

After oppressing India, draining its wealth and filling their coffers for 100 years, the Britishers openly abused rights of Indian women and officially created prostitution and called them Chaklas, which means brothel, in the pretext of giving economic independence to the poor Indian women. The status of women, at the dawn of British rule in India, reached the lowest level in the society. The rate of literacy was so low that hardly one woman in a hundred was able to read or write. Raped Indian women were forcefully turned into prostitutes by Britishers. That was the reason why the Britishers were eye sore to our GGF. Kedarnath organised a Force named: *'Swatantra Bahini'*. Initially, there were around 25 members in this Force. They were stout, heroic, courageous and brave warriors. They welcomed death but never learnt to give in. No sooner did they get command from GGF than they jumped into action without caring for their life. They did not mind going through fire, deep forest or the ocean to attack Britishers or their protagonists. Kedarnath put them in a school where they were taught 'The Ramayana', 'The Mahabharata' and 'The Bhagavad Gita'. They were taught that mother and motherland were truly greater than heaven - *Janani Janma-bhoomi-scha swargadapi gariyasi*. The members of the *'Swatantra Bahini'* were instilled with patriotism. They were taught what Lokmanya Tilak, great freedom fighter, once said, on receiving news of his wife's death while at prison, 'Presently, I have no time for personal sorrow. My country's sorrow is my sorrow'. They were also motivated by the speech of Bipin Chandra Pal, an Indian nationalist, writer, orator, social reformer and Indian Independence movement and freedom fighter.

QUOTE

i) Mother and motherland are greater than Heaven. A mother's love for her child is eternal. No matter how many children she has, her love for them will be unconditional. Moreover, only a mother can give her children undivided attention irrespective of their qualities and looks.

ii) As for the motherland, it is the land where we belong. We will always be more welcome in our own motherland than in any other country. Our motherland has a rich heritage that we should always be proud of.

iii) If any single person starts to walk towards the responsibility, after some time, he realises that he is not alone while many people have started following him and the crowd also increases with time and he feels the situation is going from better to best. So, don't complain, only give solutions and do not take part if you know it is not good for our country.

UNQUOTE

They were also taught and enlightened about great patriots of India and their sacrifices for their motherland. Personalities with distinguished courage and ability, admired for their brave deeds and noble qualities with the principal aim of liberty. Patriots are those who love, support, defend and sacrifice their lives smilingly at the altar of their motherland. The dictum of patriots is: Give us your blood, your sacrifices and patriotism to achieve freedom. A patriot will be ready to help his fellow countrymen whenever they are in danger. They were injected with the value of discipline and morality. They were imparted various training of warfare too. Their duty was to explore and assassinate the British people who were brutal, violent, savage and wild against the Indians. In the event of the death of anybody especially in the hands of the British people, their children were taken care of and all the expenses of litigation, if any, were borne by GGF.

All of a sudden, one of the members of *Swatantra Bahini* met 'K' and informed surreptitiously that girls were bought and sold by a Britisher named Jackson while Lalu Prasad was the kingpin of the deal. He along with other persons of his den met in secret, typically to engage in an illicit activity, by convincing our illiterate and poor girls to earn huge amounts of money in exchange of engaging themselves in sexual activities. 'K' discussed this issue with 'B'. The latter advised the former not to take any action in haste until and unless they had some documentary evidence. Or else, we would nab those anti-social elements, involved in these activities, and finish them secretly and surreptitiously under the darkness of night. After a couple of months, 'K' found Lalu chasing a couple of girls with malicious intentions. 'K' followed him with a rifle which made the miscreants beat a retreat immediately. Both the girls held K's feet in reverence and cried their eyes out to beseech them from all those pimps. 'K' escorted them to the place where *Swatantra Bahini* was sheltered. They were twins of 14 years. Their garment was shabby and torn. They were scared and frightened. A sudden sound in the doorway startled them. 'K' asked them to be stress free. In order to instil confidence and a little credence in them, 'K' emphatically told them that not even the ray of the Sun or sunlight dared enter in the periphery of that area without his consent. Nevertheless the twins were not much convinced. 'K' called a few members of *Swatantra Bahini*. A few stout and robust men appeared before them. They obeyed 'K' and stood in front of him, bowing their heads as a mark of respect. 'K' asked them: "If somebody comes to pick them up or tries to cause any harm to them; what are you going to do?" They took out sharp daggers in no time and told 'K' that they would stab them instantaneously. 'K' asked Ashim, one of the members of 'SB', to help them freshen themselves and arrange new garments for them. As they did not have female garments, both the girls had to satisfy themselves with males' garments for the time being. 'K' had lunch with the twins. He assured them that he would remain there for a couple of days. They could relax now and he would catch up with them again in the evening. 'K' asked Ashim to escort them to their room.

From Warm and Yellow Lights to Torturous Red Lights

This was the story of Debi and Rubi, twin sisters. Debi was not aware where she should start from. She retorted that there is a proverb: 'Morning shows the day'; 'All's well that ends well'; 'Every cloud has a silver lining'. We did not know the authenticity of these phrases so far as we two sisters were concerned; if all these phrases were really applicable to them.

QUOTE

As narrated by Debi and Rubi:

"We heard from our revered mother that our respected father, Mr Ansh Guha, was once a captain in the Navy. We had a three-storeyed house in the heart of Calcutta. We both were studying in the Convent school and led an enjoyable and luxurious life. Our mother, Smt. Protima, was as pretty as a picture. Both of us were intellectual and studious. Our parents wanted us to be freedom fighters and fight for the sovereignty of our motherland. It was rightly said: 'Man proposes and God disposes.'

Once all the naval staff members and their families had a pleasant trip for a couple of days and were sailing on a Viking ship. The Chief of the naval staff, a Britisher, Charlie, was quite impressed with the beauty of our mother. He planned to make friendly and cordial terms with our father. He straightway barged into our room where all of us were talking, chatting and enjoying ourselves. My father could not believe his eyes. He was completely taken aback. However, he stood up to salute him. Charlie was in no mood to be formal. He straightway hugged my dad jubilantly and told him that they were on a pleasant trip, hence, there was no room for official formality. They were all friends. He extended his hand, Ansh and children shook hands with him. But Protima folded her two palms to wish him, against her wish, in the Indian style. Charlie was not at all comfortable with her gesture.

Later there was a 'drinks party' where wives of all the naval staff members took active part. On knowing Ansh had been serving in the Navy for the last five years, Charlie assured him that soon he would be promoted to the next higher rank. All the other staff members were looking at one another with surprise and were at a loss to understand what made Charlie curry favour to Ansh all of a sudden. Charlie started looking crazy. It appeared that he had kept an eagle eye on somebody. A while later, he enquired about: "What happened to Protimoo? Why has she not turned up at the Dinner Party? Was she all right? Have you forbidden her to join? On the contrary, I'm happy that all are here to celebrate the occasion. This occasion comes once in a blue moon. I expected her to be here to enjoy herself with all of us". Dad angrily retorted that she was a teetotaller. Now, a few staff members could understand the reason for Dad being his 'blue-eyed boy'. Mandeep, a staff member, taunted Dad that 'his ten fingers were in the ghee'. The other members saw eye to eye with Mandeep. Dad found it very difficult, if not impossible, to pocket the insult and embarrassment. He had no alternative but to be quiet. He knew: 'Where ignorance is bliss, it is folly to be wise there'. He became sentimental. He knew that all of them mistook his silence for an admission of guilt. Charlie raised a glass of Whisky and shouted 'Cheers'. All of them followed suit. Dad consumed many pegs of drinks in order to forget his humiliation and ignominy. Charlie arranged a sumptuous dinner. Alcohol switches the brain into starvation mode, increasing hunger and appetite. It prompted them to have food without looking hither and thither.

She Fought like a Ferocious Lioness

Charlie sneaked out of the party to avoid being heard or seen by anybody. He straightway went to Mom's room when we were playing outside. She was all alone in the room. Seeing Mom so attractive, pretty and irresistible, Charlie could not control himself. He went straight to her, hugged her and tasted her lips like peaches and honey. She tried hard to get herself freed, but in vain. As he was under the influence of alcohol, addicted to his highest position and he being the master of slave India, all these were petty issues for him. But perhaps he no longer knew what he was indulging in. He was not aware that he provoked an Indian cobra which is a venomous snake in self-defence when it is cornered. He was 6'4" tall and stout. He threw her up and caught her on his shoulder. While he was removing her saree, Mom was able to get herself free from his captive. "Oh! You look like a paragon of beauty with this mini clad! Maybe, you will be '*Apsara*' if the rest is removed. She was about to open the door to go out. In the meantime, Dad appeared. She embraced him while wailing and crying. She looked violent, aggressive, deadly and frenzied. Her vermilion smeared all over her cheeks, nose, lips, ears and heads; long dilapidated hair covered her face, neck, shoulder and back; her *Shakha*, white bangle – made of 'Conch shell' and *Pola* is a red coral bangle – worn by married Bengali ladies, all were used by her as weapons which took active part in her fight with Charlie. As customs have it, one has to wear a pair of each in both hands. Shakha and pola form an integral part of the wedding trousseau. It is worn by the bride in the wee hours of the marriage day amidst rituals and customs and continued wearing until the death of her spouse. Also, the white bangle signifies purity, and the coral signifies fertility and happiness – were broken while they were used, attacking Charlie's head many a time, raiding his face with her long nails and assaulting his hands and lips violently with her sharp teeth. Charlie was badly wounded and smeared in blood.

But, as usual, on seeing beautiful girls, men's thought process gets drastically changed as they lose their sense of rationality. As per Bhagavad Gita: 'Lust cannot be satisfied by any amount of sense enjoyment, just as fire is never extinguished by a constant supply of fuel. This material world is shackled by sex life. In the ordinary prison house, criminals are kept within bars; similarly, the criminals who are disobedient to the laws of the Lord are shackled by sex life. While one enjoys sense gratification, it may be that momentarily there is some feeling of happiness, but actually that so-called feeling of happiness is the ultimate enemy of the sense enjoyer'.

Fuelled by the condition of his wife, Dad erupted in anger and charged Charlie fiercely: 'Have you thought that India is under you and you have all the bloody rights to act as per your whims and fancies over the Indians?' "Don't worry, I will ensure that you get the next higher post in a month's time. I can give you in black and white right now", retorted Charlie'. Dad blasted: "You bloody, shitty, sodding Charlie, damn you and your fecking and damnable post. I am going to tender resignation". "I have decided to send you to hell, saying so, Charlie took out his revolver. If I set eyes on some woman, she is mine. Protimoo is lucky enough that she will be my wife. If she wants, I am prepared to divorce my present wife and make Protimoo my queen. I will shift to London soon after marrying her. I feel that she has not been used potentially! She will find the difference when I take her to London soon after our wedding. I have abundant money, a prestigious job, a sovereign motherland i.e. London - the capital of the United Kingdom, a city of dreams, stands on the River Thames, the atmosphere is unique and unparalleled. We both will enjoy to our heart's content. I will take her away from India and its dirt and pollution. Saying so, he was slowly and steadily coming close to Mom.

Dad retorted: What do you know about India and her geography'? Do you know what Max Muller once said: 'If I were to look over the whole world to find out the country most richly endowed with all the wealth, power and beauty that nature can bestow - in some parts a very paradise on earth – I should point to India.

Charlie said sarcastically: 'You have interpreted wrongly. Max Muller meant in his affirmation that India is most richly endowed with beauty of women'. Saying so, he ran towards Mom. I do not know if it was good or bad luck, the electricity suddenly went off. Dad, in no time, seized his revolver and gave him a hard kick. Power was back within a couple of minutes. Charlie was lying on the floor, Dad kept his right leg on his head. He smashed his face with his leg as a punishment for dishonouring Mom and kept kicking Charley's head as retribution for degrading the image of our motherland. In the meantime, the police and other staff members appeared.

Charlie shouted at the pitch of his voice: "Arrest this bloody bastard; don't let him leave!" Dad pumped all the six bullets on Charlie. The room was flooded with blood.

British Law was the Law of Jungle

In short, my dad was arrested. Mom disposed of the wealth and property she was in possession of for litigation. But, alas! It was their court, their Lord Justice, their laws and hence utter injustice for our brethren was the justice for Britishers. The law was worse than the law of the jungle. The police could arrest anyone without a warrant and detain anyone without a trial. Our Dad was asked about his last wish. He reiterated what Mahatma Gandhi once said: 'There is a higher court than courts of justice and that is the Court of Conscience. It supersedes all other courts'. Our Dad was hanged till death. We were reduced to penury. All our relations were at loggerheads with us and we were kept at arm's length. Their accusation and condemnation added fuel to the fire. We started living in a slum and could not even afford to go to the government school. One evening, it was raining cats and dogs. We did not have any food for the whole day. When there was no alternative, we had juice extracted from the grass and leaves of the tree, and it tasted like the best food in the world. Hunger is the best sauce. Jackson and Lalu came to abduct us. Our mother held their legs praying and begging to spare us and in exchange they could use her. They raped Mom wildly and beastly and while Mom was crying in keen and sharp pain, they took both of us away. What a destiny!

We were hardly nine years old - became so-called prostitutes, call girls, girls of the streets, a whore in a brothel. We were renamed Sona and Mona at the brothel. We had no alternative but to accept it as our home. The lady pimp was our 'Maa'. She looked after us and sometimes gave us money to buy dresses and have outside food for her own vested interests. She meant business and we had to work. We were not aware what type of work we would have to do. Initially, we just worked domestic chores viz. washing clothes, cooking, massaging *Maa's* legs as well as our face and body with some body lotion. We were given a few tablets to consume on a daily basis. Both of us found ourselves much more mature physically than our actual age. One day, a man came to our room and promised that he and his brother would take both of us outside the brothel and would marry us. But he brought us to the dirtiest brothel, promising to return but never turned up. Later on, we came to know that our so-called Maa charged a heavy fee from him. That brothel was owned by a stout woman and we called her *Mausi* (aunty). She looked after us well, as usual, in the beginning. We were given a bed and clean bed sheets. We felt very happy to be among the kind people. Then on the third day, she put make-up on Sona's face and made her stand along with 10 other girls, for the men to book as per their choice. First, I did not understand what was happening. One night *Mausi* was drunk and fast asleep while her brother was in another brothel. Both of us ran away as fast as we could. We saw a policeman on the road and innocently told him about our tragic story without comprehending Alpha and Omega of the intention of the policeman. He promised to help us. He and his friend raped both of us. We cried and shouted with a tremendous amount of pain. We got scared upon finding our private parts were profusely bleeding. Seeing the police van, the policeman & his friend left, leaving us all alone.

We returned to *Mausi* and told her everything innocently. First of all, the doctor gave us medicine after a few stitches. We were locked in a dark room for a week and beaten mercilessly. At the same time, they made sure not to hit our face, breast, thigh and stomach. Thereafter, I (Debi) had to compromise with my fate and destiny and conceded what *Mausi* wanted me to do. But Rubi was not prepared to indulge in that. She was severely beaten several times and deprived of food & even water for a couple of days. But she was determined. *Mausi* was not in favour of punishing her every now and then as it would have an adverse effect on her mentally and physically which might adversely affect her business. Nevertheless she was shrewd enough in her trade. When there was a customer for Sona and they were locked in a room, Mona was made to watch from a distance how her sister was cooperating in the act. In that brothel, there were 20-24 girls and 10 rooms. During peak hours, we would get around 15 customers a day. Both of us would get three or four customers a day each. Our rates were Rs.20 each for an hour which was much higher than other girls. 50 per cent of the money earned went to *Mausi*. The customer had to separately pay 25 per cent extra to her as service charge. Mainly college boys, married men, many goras (foreigners), restaurant owners, drivers, divorcees and even sometimes scavengers, cobblers & stray beggars were our customers. 'That cannot be cured must be endured'. At the time of the police raid, *Mausi* offered them some money and her best girls as a gift with a room. The business resumed again. When business was slow, we had to parade on the streets semi-nude to showcase our beauty, attracting men with our sex-appeals. We were surprised to see even seven year old girls were not spared; they were forced in this trafficking business.

When I was all alone, I pondered over why millions and trillions of people in this Universe are handicapped, orphans, underfed, dying and undergoing acute trials and tribulations and why millions and millions of animals are suffering in multifarious ways in this world. It is all because of their '*Karmas*'. None can get rid of *Karmas*. There were many NGOs who regularly organised shows, gatherings and events on HIV and AIDS & sex workers rights. We insisted on the clients to wear condoms which was important to be safe from the killer diseases for both of us. But customers paid an extra 25% as a bribe to *Mausi* to avoid using it. There were quite a few drug users. They were usually addicted to nicotine and heroin. They forced us to try drugs with them as well. One customer forcefully made me swallow while he was kissing and had sex, rather raped me. I suffered unbearable pain. To my utter shock, he was enjoying my pain. My pain was accompanied by his laughter and acute physical force. Such sadist people are, in fact, worse than wild and ferocious beasts. If I ever have the great fortune to have a glimpse of Lord Gopal, I would have a volley of questions to throw at Him for His kind answer: "Why feminine genders are made weaker than males? Why is it painful for females? Why are males made much more powerful than females which enable them to overpower the latter and play with their honour and dignity as per their whims and fancies!" Soon after swallowing drugs, I was sick but for *Mausi* I was instrumental in losing a lot of business. She ruthlessly, mercilessly and brutally transferred my customers to my sister who had to do overtime for my sake. Even when I decided to resume to save my sister from being overloaded, my sister asked me to take rest for a few more days. What a piteous incident! Seeing all these, I decided to shell out the loss by engaging myself with the job while I was badly ailing and even during my period days. Nevertheless, we had no alternative but to be there and considered it our home. Even if I had left that place where I would have gone? Society will always label us as prostitutes, with least consideration of the circumstances that pushed a girl to make such appalling choices.

Being a prostitute, I got to learn that no girls and women were prostitutes willingly and voluntarily. They are either forced by so-called unavoidable circumstances in the family or people like Charlie, Jackson or Laloo Prasad who dragged them into this, I would not say profession but *Dhanda*. It is said: 'Only the wearer knows where the shoe pinches'. There are a number of people who are available everywhere to hate, condemn, abhor, castigate, abominate and execrate girls or women like us but are never prepared to assist or help those who are forced into this. Even if we get an opportunity to change ourselves, we won't be able to steer clear of the 'stigma' which we have been carrying with this *Dhanda*. But in case of other professions like peon, chaprasi, scavengers and other minion classes - a servile or unimportant ones - if they rise in their careers, nobody will remember or point out that once they were cobblers, scavengers and so on and so forth. Rather they will be eulogised for endeavouring hard to change their profession. But in our case, it is not so. Nobody would give us any opportunity to grow. People will keep thinking that we are prostitutes until and unless death takes us away from this mundane world. I cannot change their mind set-up.

Rubi had a secret lover, Ravi, and he used to be one of her regular customers. They were planning to marry. One day, Rubi was engaged with another customer, Ravi was allotted to me. He was tall, smart and gentle. But I had to perform my duty. While I was undressing, he approached me humbly asking: "Didi, please put on your clothes." "What .. what .. what..? What did you say? "Are you joking, jesting and clowning? Are you mad? Lo, it is the first time that a mad person has become my client! I started laughing which soon turned into deep lamenting. I spoke to myself: I must have listened wrongly about what he had said". He kept saying: "Didi, didi, didi. I reiterated: "You get the worth of your money and get lost from here. If I know anybody in this world, she is my sister, only sister and nobody else. Even my belief in Gopala is becoming weak, puny and powerless. Today, you will call me 'Didi', tomorrow, you will rape me, the day after you will kidnap me and the following day, you will hand me over to some pimp". "Stop it, enough is enough. Since I called you 'Didi', I cannot even slap you. All persons are not alike". When I got to know about his relationship with Rubi, I was overwhelmed with joy, gave him a sisterly hug. I was teary-eyed. I begged for his apology. He wiped off my tears and told me "Didi, both of you have lost everything. You have nothing more to lose. You know: There are more goals to be achieved; more stories waiting to be created. There are a lot of reasons to be happy in this world. For God's sake, don't cry over spilt milk. Didi, I lost my own sister. I shall tell you that story some other day if I remain alive. My cherished dream is to see both of you out of the brothel. If I am successful in achieving that, it will assuage my guilt for not having saved my only sister. I am prepared to pay any price for it, maybe, at the cost of my life". I came close to him and gave him a gentle 'slap', more out of love and affection than a punishment and forbade him to repeat it any more. No power on earth could separate me from my brother. Saying so, my cheeks were flooded with tears. But that time, I was not shedding tears for expressing my air of despondency, depression, low spirits, grief and a dolorous and repetitive tale of atrocity; it was the tear of joy, ecstasy.

- "Tears of joy are like the summer rain drops pierced by sunbeams". ...**By: Hosea Ballou**
- "Laughing is not the first expression of joy .... A person laughs in idleness, for fun, not for joy. Joy has nothing, but the old way of tears"........ .... **By: Margaret Oliphant**
- "When a baby takes birth, it cries and sheds tears, undoubtedly, it is not the tear of sorrow; doubtlessly, it is the tear of joy, ecstasy and a merriment by assuming that it has taken birth as a human being in this beautiful universe, out of millions and trillions of different types of living creatures" ...... **By: Nitish Mondal**

Baba, we are here only because of Ravi, perhaps he is no more in this mundane world. The sun for all of us is a huge star present in the solar system which gives heat and light for the environment and the growth of organisms. But 'Ravi', friend of Rubi, is, in fact, much more philanthropic and altruistic for both of us than that of the sun. Both of us worship Ravi daily as it was he who got us rid of so-called human beings who were literally much more ferocious and inhuman than wild beasts. He took us out of the brothel at the cost of his own life. We could recollect once we were crying while hugging him. He assured us: 'Unexpected results and problems are part of life. Never lose hope in any condition and situation because darkness of night always ends with the light of the day.' When we told Ravi: 'We lost all hopes and there is no ray of hope to lead a good life'. He vehemently counselled: 'Hope is such an energy by which any dark part of life can be illumined.' In this Kaliyuga and in this mundane world, most of us hanker after unnecessary material things that entangle us by feelings of possessiveness. Who will cease sense activities as everyone is attracted by sense objects? Even great sages are not exceptional. They are also not able to control the forces of their senses and sometimes they engage in such activities for the satisfaction of their sense gratification. Ravi's being in this Kaliyuga is surely a misnomer or misfit. We are sure and sanguine that Narayana will take care of him sooner rather than later."

UNQUOTE

After narrating their tale of woes, both of them kept holding the feet of 'K' with their four arms, tears trickling down from their eyes on 'K's feet. Both of them addressed 'K': "You are our father, you are our mother, we are your friends and you are our Universe. We have lost our father who gave us birth, our hearth and home and our identity. We have become trollop, vamp and prostitute at a tender age. We do not know the status of our mother. We asked you, 'Baba', are we at fault for what has occurred to us?" 'K' burst into tears and could not control the flurry of tears. Somehow he camouflaged a part of it and asked them if they were interested in staying with their father (Kedarnath) and mother, Aroti. They had a son but bereft of daughters. They would consider themselves the luckiest if they agreed to live with them. Both Debi and Rubi retorted, "Baba, we understand very well that we won't get a father like you and a mother like Aroti Debi. Nevertheless, with your due concurrence and permission, we wish to stay here with Swatantra Bahini, learn how to use different weapons — dagger, sword, bow & arrow, rifle and also learn Judo and Karate. We would like to be fearless, strong, powerful and patriot fighters like Rani Lakshmi Bai. We learned about her when we were in IV standard. Her strength was in her courage and refusal to succumb and bow to the cruel British Empire. She fought the British with strength and became a martyr in battle at 29 years of age. Now, we do not have any longings other than punishing black sheep and heartless people like Charlie, Jackson and Laloo Prasad. Baba, we don't want to make our life a bed of roses henceforth. If we stay with you, mother and brother, our life will become simple, pleasant and easy because of your and mother's indulgence and care. We shall be as soft as petals of the rose. But we wish to make us as strong as iron, if not steel. Our mission will be to assist the needy and finish the barbarous, merciless bestial and predatory."

Kedarnath asked the teacher, P.C. Roy, to teach both of them the holy books: The Ramayana, The Mahabharata, and the Bhagavad Gita. They will be taught the value and significance of patriotism, to love their country as the motherland is truly greater than heaven. Shiv Shankar, Dodol, Ashim and Smritish to give them preliminary training on wrestling alongside the spiritual training. Thereafter, they would be taught the use of different weapons followed by Judo and Karate.

Feminines are Epitome of Love & Compassion

'K' discussed the nature of 'motherhood' with Debi and Rubi to prevent them from being hard, heartless and ruthless. In that event, they might succeed in their venture, but they would not achieve success in their life. He told them:

'A tree that wants to touch the sky must extend its roots into the earth. The more it wants to rise upwards; the more it has to grow downwards. So, to rise in life we must be 'down to earth', humble and grateful'. – Classic Quotes

Mother, the ultimate human creation of God, is the most selfless person in this world who starts loving her children even before they come into this world. In other words, feminine nature is composed of a sense of caring, calmness, tender & soft-heartedness. Hence, though you have gone through a tremendous amount of stresses and strains, yet you must not do away with your feminine 'Dharma'. A strong feeling, deriving from the circumstances, mood or relationships with others you confronted, must not be your 'Dharma'. Females are a perfect example of a superlative quality. You must bear in mind that flowers bloom while clouds start raining and not by its thunder. So, "Be like flowers, survive the torrential rain, but keep growing for others to use them to glorify various auspicious occasions and decoration of deities." Adding a positive outlook to those negative moments will help you extract more out of them and become even more resilient to your power. There is an Arabic saying: 'Trust in God but tie your camel'.

Please read meticulously:

A Tamil poem composed 1000 years ago by Awaiyar which in translation reads thus:

- "It is **rare** to be born as a **human being**.
- It is still **rarer** to be born **without any deformity**.
- Even if you are born without any deformity, it is a few and far between to acquire **knowledge and education**.
- Even if one could acquire knowledge and education, it is as scarce as hen's teeth to do **offerings and tapas**. And for one

who does offerings and tapas: The **doors of heaven remain open to greet him.**"

Kedarnath: *Beti* (daughters), my home is also your home. You may shift your stay with us for a change at least once a week as the classes will be for six days a week. Over and above, it is your home, you may come as per your convenience.

Debi and Rubi completed their whole course yet there was not a day when they were not polishing whatever they had learned. Early in the morning, they tendered devotional services by chanting Sri Krishna bhajan:

Krishno Krishno Sudhu Sri Krishno	Krishno Krishno only Sri Krishno.
Krishno Bina Kichu nahi	There is nothing but Krishno.
Krishno namo sudha Niye	Taking nectar with His name
Krishnar-E- Gaan Gai	Chant His name only, only His name.

While offering Radhey Shyam, Radhey Govindo prayers: One day, Rubi asked 'Didi, how can we realise God?' Debi quoted what Sri Ramakrishna Paramhansa once advocated:

- 'One should weep for God. When the impurities of the mind are washed away, one realises God.
- The mind is like a needle covered with mud, and God is like a magnet.
- The needle cannot be united with the magnet unless it is free from mud.
- Tears wash away the mud, which is nothing but lust, anger, greed, and other evil tendencies, and the inclination to worldly pleasures as well.

- As soon as the mud is washed away, the magnet attracts the needle, that is to say, man realises God.'

Rubi clapped, uttering, 'Didi, you made my day.'

Rubi further asked why people were infected with disease. Debi exclaimed: 'Disease is the tax which the soul pays for the use of the body, as the tenant pays house rent for the use of the house'. Soon after that Debi forbade Rubi to appreciate her as it was said by Sree Ramakrishna Paramhansa. Rubi retorted: 'But how many of us knew this'? They kept praying to the Supreme Lord for well-being, bliss and remaining at the top of the world for their father, Kedarnath, and mother, Aroti. Kedarnath, for them, was like an incarnation of God. Though they were staying with Swatantra Bahini yet on every alternate day, 'K' used to be there and have a long chat with them. Aroti endeavoured hard to persuade them to stay with them.

Celebration of 'Bhai Phota'

Debi and Rubi used to come to meet Abhinandan, on the auspicious occasion of 'Bhai Phota' (Bhai Dhooj) and stayed there for a week. They celebrated the occasion with great pomp. The festival of Bhai Dooj celebrates the special bond between brothers and sisters and signifies that the same bond continues life long. A paste of vermillion, curd and paddy is applied as a 'religious tika' on the forehead of the brother. Thereafter, the sister puts flowers, betel leaves, betel nuts and coins over the brother's head and chants:

Bhaier Kopale Dilam Phota	Applied 'tika' on the
Jomer Duare Porlo Kata	forehead of my brother,
Jamuna dai Jomke Phota	The thorn fell in the door of
Ami di amar bhai ke phota	Yama;
Jom jemon hoy chiranjeevi	Yamuna applied tika on the

Aamar bhai jeno hoye chironjeevi	forehead of Yama I applied tika on the forehead of my brother Yama is immortal; My brother should also be immortal like Yama.

On applying phota (Tika), Abhi asked Rubi: 'Sister, what do you want from your Bhai on this auspicious occasion?' 'I wish you to remain my immortal brother'. Mom remarked, 'Rubi, you are a rare genius. Since you are mostly quiet, I thought otherwise.' Debi retorted: 'Mom, she used to stand first in the class and was always in the good books of teachers.' They both had teary eyes. Abhinandan wanted to deviate their attention. He kept his one arm on the shoulder of Rubi and turned towards Debi to know about her demand from her Bhai on this happy occasion. But Bhai, I don't want to disappoint you on this joyous day. I promise, I shall remain buoyant. But I will naturally feel discontented, if you do not ask anything on this red-letter day, How can you expect that I will not ask for a gift from my Bhai on this gala occasion? I will positively ask for a gift but at an opportune moment. And I am hopeful that you will not say 'no'. *Bone* (Sister) as: '*Zamindari* Reet Sada Chali Aayi, Pran Jaye Par Vachan Na Jaye!' (This one is a very famous proverb derived from the epic 'The Ramayana', which means that for making any promise true, we can risk our life or also can die but will not make any promise fail ..... Abhi twisted it to '*Zamindari*' in place of '*Raghukul*') . Haa, haa, haa. 'Bhai, if you talk like this, I am not going to talk to you. Why, what happened! Can you ever imagine that your sister will ask for your life? By holding his ear as a gesture of apology, he confessed his blunder. Ok, agreed, Sister. Think over it and ask for it as you may deem fit.

In order to change the topic, Debi asked: "Do you know, brother, about the origin of Bhai Dooj?" Abhinandan was looking at his mother. Mother asked him to answer. He had to cut a sorry figure on account of his ignorance. Debi requested her mother not to humiliate my lovely brother on this auspicious occasion. Upon giving a brotherly hug, Debi narrated what her mother told her:

QUOTE

It is said that after defeating the evil demon Narakasura, Murari visited his sister, Subhadra. His sister, upon giving him a tumultuous welcome, greeted him with sweets and flowers. She then applied the ceremonial tilak on Govinda's forehead. It is believed that this is the origin of the festival 'Bhai Dooj'.

UNQUOTE

Debi and Rubi announced together: "We are lucky enough to have got a smart and kind-hearted brother who loves his sisters from the bottom of his heart. It is all by the virtue of Govinda's gracious act. They wished their brother a long, happy and tranquil life. Debi then prayed for her brother to get her years of longevity". Abhinandan strictly forbade her to ask for such a wish. Debi reminded him of the futility of such an impious body being lavishly used. Being unable to control his emotion, he slapped her while wailing and weeping. He further countered her: 'Was it in your hands? Have you done the act voluntarily? If it is not in your hands, why will you bear the brunt of it? I will accuse the people of the entire Universe for such a state of affairs. For me, my sisters are my pride, they are as pure as the driven snow; impeccable, serving as a desirable model; having exemplary behaviour. Hereafter, I will keep chanting and praying to Govinda to send Debi and Rubi as my sisters in all my following births'. Saying so, he became sentimental and started weeping like a child. Both Debi and Rubi hugged him and assured that they would never hurt him. They wiped off his tears and asked him to play chess.

Mom: Beta, Debi and Rubi, 'Go and have a bath. It is time for lunch. Abhi, beta, you also go and have a quick bath if you are interested in having lunch together and especially with your sisters'. Oh, sure, today, I will have a quick bath in order to have lunch with my charming sisters. While having lunch, Abhinandan dropped a piece of tail of *Rahu* fish on Debi's 'plate', seizing a head piece of *Rahu* from Debi's, saying, 'I love eating the head of the fish'. 'No, Bhai, I love it too.' Saying so, she snatched the headpiece of the fish from Bhai. Rubi offered the head portion of the fish to Bhai and took the tail portion of the fish from him. Abhinandan kept appreciating Rubi and advised Debi not to be quarrelsome. Debi shouted: "Maa, Bhai is calling me quarrelsome, I am not going to have lunch with him".

Abhinandan: For God's sake, please don't say so, *Sister*. I don't know what Karma I did in my previous births which enabled me to get two sisters of your trait in this birth. I don't want to lose either of you. You take my whole Thali, *Sister*, but for Gopala's sake, don't ever say that you are not going to have lunch with me. I won't mind if you accuse me harshly. What about your devotional chanting? Bhaier Kopale Dilam Phota;

Jomer Duare Porlo Kata...

Their parents quietly observed their love filled banters from the kitchen.

Thereafter, Abhi became adamant while imploring Debi and Rubi to stay with them. He had earmarked two special rooms for them - one was the Physical Fitness Room and the other one was their bedroom. But Debi was not interested in being there. Abhi decided to remain on fast until his demand was met. Debi humbly requested his father for intervention. But 'K' nullified her request with a view to it being between the brother and the sister. Debi had no alternative but to accede to his entreaty. Abhi jumped out of enthusiasm when they agreed to reside with them. He became mad out of joy and ecstasy. He started dancing, singing and taking rounds after rounds, holding his sisters' hands. Suddenly, he fell down. He lay unconscious. While Rubi called their mother, Debi massaged his body to maintain the blood flow. Their parents appeared soon. Debi kept massaging his body. They grew extremely anxious about finding him in that state. Some time later, Abhi gained consciousness. He wanted to know what happened to him. 'Nothing, Bhai, you just fell down while dancing and taking rounds', Debi retorted. While Abhi was talking to Rubi, Debi told her parents secretly that Bhai needed hospitalisation. They expressed their utmost concern and asked the reason. She told them that once it happened with one of her mates when she was (she went silent for a while). Maa asked her to carry on. She was my good friend. It was more or less a similar symptom. As there was a cardiac arrest for a few seconds, I was massaging Bhai's body. I also found a bit of swelling in his hands and ankles. Asked Bhai if his urinary output decreased. Sometimes initially, symptoms may be subtle or may not appear at all. She asked Mom if he had nausea, fatigue or vomiting. 'I did not observe meticulously but I felt he was losing weight day by day', Mom answered. Debi asked Baba not to call a general physician. She suggested a nephrologist as it seemed to be a kidney problem. A nephrologist was called from a well-known hospital. Upon learning the case history and having preliminary check-up, the doctor informed that Abhi did have a mild attack. He appreciated Debi for her first-aid treatment; else Abhi's life could have been in jeopardy. He advised 'K' for immediate admission to the hospital for thorough check-up and treatment. 'K' informed his brother-in-law and 'B' (Binoy) came in no time. All of them conveyed their gratitude to Debi.

Debi retorted: 'Does that mean that we are not your daughters? Certainly not! How can we be your daughters?' We are ...

Mom: "Will you shut up? Don't aggravate me by repeating what you are not! I scarcely take my children to task. But if you exceed the limit, I can be a dangerous mother. I will be harsh on you. Only Madhav knows what you mean to both of us. Soon after the birth of Abhi, we longed for daughters. We prayed to Lord Govinda day in and day out. But how could He, the Omniscient, bless us with the boon of daughters since you were in our destiny! The day you stepped in, we offered prayers to Narayana and distributed money, food and clothes to the poor." Saying so, she was teary-eyed and her cheeks were inundated with tears. She covered her face with her palms and was about to leave the place.

Debi: (Holding her feet while weeping), "Maa, Janani, you are the incarnation of Goddess for both of us. To get parents like you tantamount to achieving god. Mom, do you know that the bee is more honoured than other animals not because she labours, but because she labours for others (St. Chrysostom). But Maa, with your due permission, I wish to discuss: You are my mother and he is my father. My brother is my lifeline. I can put my life at stake for my brother. When the people looked at us disdainfully and treated us like commodities to be chewed, tasted & eaten, it was you and Baba, who had considered us their daughters. We have no words to applaud your generosity and magnanimous act. If we do something for our brother, you must not express any indebtedness or gratitude to us. Honestly speaking, for some reason or another if I get injured, it won't affect me much but I will never condone if anybody hurts you, Baba and Bhai".

Mom: Ok, Ok, agreed. Sorry for doing that.

Debi: I wish to tell you that both of us are here to take care of our brother. One of us would go to Hospital.

Mom: "You are very stubborn and if I disagree with what you say, that will lead to a confrontation. At the same time, you are highly responsible and I know what you do will ultimately be the best for your Bhai".

Abhi was taken to Hospital. Debi, her parents and 'B' accompanied. On having thorough check-up and various tests, the doctor shared the following with the members of the patient:

It was diagnosed that there was a renal failure. It prevented sufficient urine production and urinary retention. There was a lot of acid in the blood and tissues. There was a failure of the right kidney, fortunately, the left kidney is intact. Urine output is a key indicator of kidney health. Too little or no urine output is a sign of kidney injury or kidney damage. The patient may develop diabetes, high blood pressure, fatigue, nausea and vomiting, swelling, etc. from time to time in the absence of the treatment and medication. A kidney transplant is often the treatment of choice for kidney failure, compared to a life-time on dialysis. The former can even treat chronic kidney diseases or end-stage renal disease (ESRD).

In order to be eligible to receive a kidney transplant, the patient must have chronic irreversible kidney disease that has not responded to other critical or surgical treatments. He/She may either be on dialysis or kidney transplant. But it is always 'the sooner the better'. You must qualify for and be able to tolerate major surgery. Compared with dialysis, kidney transplant is associated with better quality of life.

One must be at least 18 years old. Some Centres require a donor to be 21 or a little older. There are some medical conditions that could prevent the interested donor from being a living donor.

Debi made a fervent request to her father that she and her sister would like to go for blood and other miscellaneous tests. In the offing, 'K' did not agree as there was no necessity for the unnecessary tests. When Debi reminded him of the ugly conditions they spent most of their youth in, their Dad was convinced. After the tests, they were joyous to know that they had no infections.

The doctor advised 'K' for Kidney transplant which was much better than dialysis as the patient was young. The doctor reminded all of us that kidneys are vital in the human body as they filter the blood and remove enough wastes and fluid from the blood to keep a person healthy. It would be best if there was a living donor as the life expectancy of the patient would be increased. It would also be common for the transplant recipient to resume a normal lifestyle, including sexual activity, as he/she recovers. Many altruistic donors came forward to donate kidneys out of goodwill gesture. Others were tempted by the huge amount of money they would receive by virtue of donation of a Kidney. Unfortunately, all were rejected in view of their ineligibility. 'K' further increased the amount but in vain. When they were not able to receive a donor after about a couple of months, they decided to let Abhi initially be on dialysis and the transplant would take place on the availability of an appropriate kidney from a live donor. But both Debi and Rubi vehemently reacted to their decision. They were deadly against Bhai going on dialysis. Debi informed that while she was in the Hospital with Bhai, she discussed with the doctor and learned that sometimes Dialysis deteriorates kidney function. It could be a burdensome treatment as Bhai would have to visit the

Hospital every now and then. On the other hand, it was a painful treatment. The quality of life would drastically drop.

No, Mom & Dad, we are the last ones to agree with Bhai being put on Dialysis. Both Dad and Mom shouted at them more, out of exasperation and depression, than any sort of annoyance, "We tried our hardest to arrange it but, you know, there is no success in our endeavour. Can you suggest any means to procure it?"

Debi: "Yes, Baba, I told you Bhai is our lifeline. There is a way out. I discussed everything with the concerned doctor. That was the reason why Rubi and I went for blood tests. Maa and Baba, please, do not interrupt me before I complete. After one kidney is removed, that too, the right one, for donation, the other one undergoes a process known as 'Compensatory Hypertrophy', that is, it increases in size and takes over the function of the other kidney as well. The donor, especially, if young, leads a normal life after donation. Most donors who work in an office, return to office within two to six weeks post surgery. Donors with more physical exertion in their profession, generally need four to six weeks of recovery before resuming work. And I am just 19 years old, sturdy, robust and strong. How can I say 'no' to Bhai! God forbid, if anything goes wrong with Bhai, we won't be able to survive. Our condition will be worse than ...

Debi Kisko Kahego Tu Maiya

Debi: "Dad, please do not find fault with Maa. I know she is concerned about my well-being. She is caring, protective and kind. I will be at a loss to reply if you ask me: Who is better - my biological or sworn mother? In order to save me and Rubi from the bastards, my biological mother allowed herself to be raped. About my so-called sworn mother who for the purpose of my good health and well-being, is prepared to put her only son's life at stake when he is in immediate need of hospitalisation, medication, treatment and utmost care". My condition was like Lord Govinda:

Hi Re Kanhaiya Kisko Kahego Tu Maiya	Hi Re Kanhaiya, whom do you call Maiya?
Jisane Tujhako Janam Diya Kee Jisne Tujhko Paala	Who has given U birth or who has nurtured U?
Kanhaiya Kisako Kahega tu Maiya.	He Re Kanhaiya ……………..??

Though it was also very difficult for Kanhaiya too but He could manage as He is the guide to the whole of mankind. His guidance is godly and it is in the form of Gita. Debi took his father into confidence. She reiterated that if she wished, he could discuss with the doctor taking her medical report. If I am ineligible, we would explore other sources. When her Mom intervened, Debi told her surreptitiously not to make it an issue because if Bhai knew about it, he might turn down the arrangements outright. Mom turned up to father and asked if he was not able to get a donor from the outside world. But despite our best efforts, when we were not able to convince Maa, we decided to leave the house once and for all.

Maa: "What .. What .. What!" As she was tremendously shocked, she fell down and lay unconscious. When she regained consciousness after sprinkling water on her face and fanning her for a few minutes, both 'B' and 'K' convinced her that everything would be done as per doctor's advice. If she was interested in doing something for her ailing brother, let her go for it. In case she was not eligible to donate a kidney, the doctor would never allow her to do so. Aroti whispered: "If ever Didi (Debi's mother) happens to meet us, I will not only have to cut a sorry figure before her but would also not be able to show my face to her. She will definitely charge us for exploiting their innocence and immaturity." Debi told her that her mother would rather be happy that I was able to do something for my brother. Aroti told all of them strictly that she herself would talk to the doctor. Both Debi and Rubi gladly agreed and felt elated for getting an opportunity to do something for their Bhai.

The next day, all of them met the Nephrologist, Dr Chakroborty, in the Hospital. When Aroti briefed him, on going through the various reports and medical history of Abhinandan and Debi, the doctor was fully satisfied with the case history and test reports of the donor and its recipient. Further, the doctor reiterated that there were certain conditions, such as HIV, actively spreading cancer or severe infection that would have excluded or obviated the donor to donate and recipient to receive. The donor was also not diabetic and anaemic. She did not have any kidney or heart diseases. The patient's blood group was 'A' and the donor being 'O' is a perfect match too. Aroti kept on questioning the doctor if there was any room for concern. The doctor reassured her time and again. 'K' asked the doctor if he did not take it seriously, he would like to make a fervent request. The doctor asked him not to be formal, Zamidar babu, you may go ahead.

'K' : How much would be the total cost?

Aroti and 'B' almost shouted at 'K'. What is your problem? Why are you unnecessarily worrying?

'K' : Yes, doctor, please let me know!

Doctor: The transplant cost included pre-transplant tests and investigations, surgery, post-operative care and hospital stay, medicines, and other associated costs. The cost differs from hospital to hospital, but it typically starts from Rs.75 thousand to Rs.1.5 lakhs.

'K' : Kept quiet for a while.

Aroti : Tomar ki hoyeche? Tomar ki matha kharab haye gechey? (What happened to You? Have you lost your mind?)

'B' : Kedarnath, I never expected such a middle-class attitude from you!

'K' : (Looking at his wife, he put a finger on his lips, gesturing to her to be quiet). "Actually doctor Debi is not my real daughter, you know! There was a tumultuous uproar, loud or confused noise made by Aroti and her Brother, Binoy. Debi and Rubi took aback for a while at what their father had said to the doctor. However, Debi had a monumental patience and complete trust in her father. She urged Mom and uncle to have self-restraint and let her father complete his discussions with the doctor. 'K' continued: Doctor, see her greatness and the magnanimous acti! Though Abhinandan is not her real brother, she is prepared for a mammoth sacrifice for him. In spite of the fact that I am his real father, am I making any such sacrifice for my own and only son? I reiterate, doctor, she is not my real daughter, she is my mother-like". Saying so, 'K' became sentimental. He bent down and held her feet with his two palms. Sentimental tears fell on Debi's feet from his cheeks. Initially, Debi was at a loss to understand what to do.

She somehow got his hands unfastened from her feet. Thereafter, both Debi and Rubi knelt down and held their Dad's feet with their four arms and implored him not to make them sinners. While weeping, they informed their Dad that they were not aware of the very reason for losing their parents and well-to-do family. They belonged to an affluent background, and became prostitutes. They further humbly pleaded: "Dad, you are like a Temple for both of us. You know, the Temple is a hospital for sinners and not a museum for saints". 'K' welled up upon hearing this. After some time, both Debi and Rubi wiped off his tears and gave him a big hug saying: "We do not know what our own father would have felt seeing us when we came out of the business of Prostitution. But it was you, who not only saved us from the influential, powerful, authoritative and savage touts, but also got us educated, trained us in various warfares and treated us more than your own children. For us, you are like Lord Krishna though we are nowhere near Arjuna".

'K': "Doctor, would you advise any other specialist from abroad? As you know, we are prepared to pay any amount for the well-being of our daughter and son". "Had there been any other patient, the Hospital might have been tempted by your broad-mindedness! But since you were known for 'charity' and saved our Hospital from being bankrupt earlier, I would say with full confidence that there is no necessity for any Specialist from a foreign country. By doing so, you would be wasting your heaps of money unnecessarily", the doctor retorted. You were requested to report on 10th, Friday, i.e. after two days, with Abhinandan and Debi. Ms Aroti .... 'Sir, please wait for a while.' The doctor waited for a moment and reacted: 'Madam, please do not worry. I would appreciate it if you are brave and intrepid! However, please rest assured, with the grace of Lord Krishna, Abhinandan and Debi will go back home happily on 17th'. Saying so, the doctor bunked off.

On reaching home, Aroti bombarded her husband with a spate of questions: 'Who is going to marry a girl with one kidney? I am telling you Lord Nandagopala will not spare us for treating the innocent baby unethically and making use of a situation to gain unfair advantage to meet our vested interest. Who would convey to Abhi that his kidney would be donated by Debi?' Debi requested her parents to leave it on her. She would convey her Bhai about it. While all were having lunch together, Debi requested everyone to assemble in the evening, where they would chit chat and enjoy themselves with sumptuous snacks, to be prepared by Maa. She began by sharing a memory when she was just around four years old, whenever there used to be rain, even drizzling, her father had an excuse to ask her Mom to cook Pakora. He was fond of having

Pakora with tea during monsoon. He used to say: "Pakora, tea and rain had a sensational combination. Saying so, she welled up and fell on her brother's shoulder. Abhi held her head aloft, rubbed off her tears with his left hand and placed her face on his chest. He kept pleading with her: 'Sister, nobody is able to compensate for the irreparable loss of your parent. But are you not happy that your brother has got sisters like you & Rubi and my parents, who had been craving for a daughter, got beautiful, intellectual, genius and lovable, (not one but two) daughters?' Debi: 'Again you are kidding with me by giving incomplete affirmation. On top of what you said, Rubi and I have godly parents and a brother, which we can proudly boast of.' Abhinandan was happy to have deviated the attention of Debi. Thereafter, they started feeding each other.

The next evening, Binoy, Minu (wife of Binoy), Kedarnath, Abhinandan, Aroti, Debi & Rubi assembled and cracked jokes. In the meantime, a variety of fritters (Pakodas), made of potato, brinjal, cauliflower, spinach, paneer, fish & egg, with tea and coffee were served. At the sight of these mouth watering snacks, both Debi and Rubi were taken aback. However, all of them enjoyed the delicious *snacks* while enjoying cloudy weather combined with chit chats and stories. In the intervening time, Abhi asked his father a volley of questions: 'Who is the donor of my kidney? How much are we supposed to pay? Why is the donor not visible?' Kedarnath asked them to continue their merry-making, he would be back in a few minutes. Debi straightway told Abhi that she would be donating her kidney. Abhi forbade her to crack a silly joke when they were talking about serious issues. All others vouched for Debi. Kedarnath rejoined the group. Abhi shouted, pointing out to his Maa, Mama and Mami (mother, Binoy and Minu), 'Did you not find any other whipping boy, you have made my dear sister a scapegoat. It is not acceptable to me. Mind it, I am not going for a transplantation.' Saying so, he was about to leave the gathering with resentment. Both Debi and Rubi held his one hand each and requested him to be seated. He had to sit reluctantly. He was told by Debi that Baba and Maa tried hard to arrange it from an outside donor but in vain. Ultimately, it was I who rather compelled parents to go for my kidney. Fortunately, upon multifarious tests, I was found to be a suitable donor. Nevertheless Abhi was adamant and reiterated: 'We could have waited. What is the need for immediate transplantation? Dialysis would have served the purpose before a suitable donor was explored.' While both Debi and Rubi tried hard to convince their Bhai, the latter reacted saying, 'I am not going for transplantation at the cost of my dearest Sister, it is my final decision.'

Rubi : 'Ok, Bhai, agreed. Some day or other, if I am in need of any organ of my body and there is no outside donor, are you not going to save my life by offering yours? Can you say that you should not be made a scapegoat?' These are all assumptions and irrelevant hypothetical examples and situations. All these have got nothing to do with my transplantation. All of you should take for granted that there will be no transplantation.' Saying so, Abhi began to leave again.

Debi   : Ok bhai, ok. 'But I don't think you will mind, if we all sit together and gossip.' 'No, not at all', Abhi said. All the other members were not happy with the outcome of the discussions and were ultimately disappointed that nobody could convince Abhi for a transplant. Debi asked: 'Bhai, do you remember that once on the auspicious occasion of 'Bhai Phota', you were curious to give me a gift. I told you that I would ask for it at an opportune moment. I am sure that you still remember it.' Everybody started whispering that something positive was going to emerge. Debi further reminded him that he would not say 'no' to her gift whenever she asked for it in future. You emphatically reminded me: 'My beloved sister, *Zamindari* Reet Sada Chali Aayi, Pran Jaye Par Vachan Na

Jaye!' Without thinking about the pros and cons of it, Abhi asked: 'Yes, my lovely Sister, what is the problem, it still stands.'

Rubi : Bhai, you will not say 'NO' whatever Didi asks from you. As discussed earlier, Debi signalled her Baba, Mama and Mami to support Bhai in order to confuse him. Kedarnath, Binoy and Minu altogether retorted, Yes, of course, yes, how many times Abhi would say that! Should he give it in black and white? Abhi also repeatedly said; 'Yes, *dear Sister*, I will undoubtedly and happily accept whatever you ask from me.' Debi loudly said: 'I demand you to accept my kidney.'

Abhi kept quiet for a while. After sometime, he retorted furiously: 'I do not know whether you are an incarnation of Kaikeyi.' (Queen Kaikeyi saved her husband, King Dasharatha, in the Dandaka forest while he was at war. (As per mythology, her left hand was as strong as a diamond which was a boon from a Saint). Hence, the king accompanied her during wars. She not only saved the king from certain defeat but was also instrumental to win the war. Hence, the king gave her three boons. The one 'wish' of Kaikeyi was not to make Rama the king of Ayodhya. As a consequence, Kaikeyi, reborn as Devaki, had to bear the separation from her son for a long time since she manipulated her 'wishes' for her own vested interests. In the meantime, Yashoda, herself Kaushalya reborn, enjoyed mothering a blue, baby god, Krishna. But, *Sister*, you have utilised the 'wish' in the interests of your Bhai and that too tactfully putting pressure on me for its acceptance. Great! I am speechless.' Everyone breathed a sigh of relief hearing him finally giving in.

'K' announced that there would be a party at night and delicious birds would be cooked. He decided to go shooting. It was not yet dark and the perfect time for shooting. He asked Debi and Rubi to accompany. He further asked them if they had ever tasted the flesh of any wild birds like.... He hardly completed it, both Debi and Rubi interrupted their father and persuaded him not to shoot any wild birds. They substantiated: 'all these birds are unique species. There are many considered endangered or threatened because human activity is the greatest cause of their extinction viz., population, global warming, climate change, destruction of habitat, pollution, egg collection, pesticides and herbicides directly impacting them. Whatever is inevitable, can't be helped; but shooting can be done away with. If these birds become extinct, our posterity will be deprived of all these unique creatures. Both 'K' and 'B' were convinced and promised that they would not only put an end to shooting hereafter but would also cajole others to shun shooting.

It was a wonderful family get-together. Families are priceless, and we always have a soft spot in our heart for our loved ones. So, we must make the most of our time with them during a reunion. The benefits of family bonding are multifarious like: to better adapt to the changes that come with life; it builds confidence, trust, teaches children about interacting with others, and creates wonderful memories that last a lifetime. There is an old saying that goes: 'Families that play together, stay together.' Quality time with our family is paramount in building closer, stronger and cordial relationships. Sharing stories, chit chatting and cracking jokes with one another is a sign of a healthy home. One best way to celebrate this is over dinner. Baba asked, 'Debi and Rubi beta, none is trying to make the gala event an interesting one, I know, you can break the ice.'

Rubi: Your attention please, 'We call our language the 'mother tongue.' All of them asked, 'Why'? 'Because the father seldom gets to speak. Sorry, Baba.' 'K' and 'B' shouted: 'Very nice and very thoughtful as well.' Minu and Aroti: 'If it is thoughtful, I will see that everywhere you hold your tongue.' 'No quarrel, please', Debi requested. I would say something on politicians: "In Mexico an air conditioner is called a 'politician' because it makes a lot of noise but doesn't work much." All clapped.

The starter was served along with a variety of juices. Initially, everyone had his/her preferred items. Abhi had his preferred grape juice as he disliked carrots. On taking a sip, he kept the glass aside. Rubi had a glass of carrot juice and exchanged her glass with that of her brother's. Abhi was singing a melancholic song, sitting all alone. Rubi: 'Bhai, what happened! It appears that you don't seem to be happy!' Abhi: 'How can it be so, *Sister*? As long as my sisters are with me, how on earth, I can be sad!' 'Bhai, where is your glass of juice?' It is there. 'Let's go to the centre, where all are assembled, and we will surprise them by sipping the entire glass of juice in one go.' When Abhi and Rubi entered together smilingly, everyone's attention stuck towards them. They sipped the whole lot in one go. Soon after that Abhi started shouting: 'Oh, no, how come it's carrot juice; who has played silly tricks with me? It's cheating!' Everyone started laughing and enjoying themselves. Debi accused Rubi of the mischievous act. Rubi, on giving a loving hug, said emphatically, 'Yes, I did it, I can take liberty in kidding with my only Bhai at this gala event. She giggled like a child. He is the 'Universe' for me.' 'Yes, *Sister*, you are cent per cent correct, Abhi acknowledged.' Everyone was relishing the moment of joy and laughed in exultation. Abhinandan reminded all of them: 'The importance of sisters in our life is just like the importance of heartbeats. It's not visible but silently supports our life.'

Binoy: 'Aru (Aroti), I acknowledge your son has the 'gift of the gab'. Though I know, the credit goes to your daughters as well. Sister, your family is, in fact, complete in all respects with the emergence of your lovely daughters.'

Aroti: 'Dada, Krish, your son, is likely to come back soon from abroad upon completion of higher studies. Why don't you look for a suitable bride for him who will act as your daughter as well? That way, you can kill two birds with one stone!'

Binoy: That is ok. But truly speaking the ball is in his court. Many a time, I talked about this. But I am at a loss to understand why he ignored it. About a couple of months back, I bluntly asked him if he has already selected any one from there, he may inform me without the least hesitation. He asked me not to distract him as he has gone there for higher studies. I kept quiet as I knew: That cannot be cured, must be endured.'

Minu : 'Observing the nature and attitude of the people of 'Kaliyug', I have almost lost faith in God. All those depicted and written in The Ramayana, The Mahabharata and The Bhagavad Gita seem to me 'gall and wormwood'. I might be turning into an atheist.'

Debi: 'Aunty, please do not say anything anti-Krishna! He is God of protection, compassion, tenderness and love.'

Minu: 'Can you substantiate what you said?'

Mystic Ordain of Lord Krishna

Debi: 'Yes, aunty, I can try, if you are all interested to lend your patient ears. I have gone through various holy books during my training while I was in 'Swatantra Bahini'. One of the holy books was: 'KRSNA - The Supreme Personality of Godhead.' I had the opportunity to go through the book between the lines. I am sure and sanguine, having read the book, if I could forget my suffering, torture, pain, misery, agony, affliction, woe and torment, others can surely and certainly lay aside theirs. In the midst of clapping and cheering, Debi resumed chanting Hare Krishna mantra and quoted the following:

QUOTE

We can see Lord Krishna's control on the universal level. For example, there are so many huge planets; this earth is only a small one. Still on this planet, there are big oceans like the Atlantic and Pacific as well as big mountains and sky scraping buildings. Yet despite all this load, the earth is floating in the air just like a swab of cotton. Who is floating it? Can any one float even a grain of sand in the air? You may talk about the law of gravity and so many other things, but you cannot control it. Your aeroplane is flying in the air, but as soon as the fuel is finished, it will immediately fall. So, if it takes so many scientists to build an aeroplane that floats only temporarily in the air, 'Is it possible that this huge earth is floating on its own?' No, Lord Krishna declares in the Bhagavad-Gita: 'I enter into the material planets and keep them aloft'. Just as to keep an aeroplane aloft, a pilot has to enter it, so to keep this earth aloft, Krishna has entered it. This is the simple truth.

Here is a chance for you to become Krishna Conscious and solve all problems. But if you don't – if you continue acting like animals – you will again have to enter the cycle of birth and death and transmigrate through 84 lakh species of life. It will take many many millions of years to come back to the human form of life".

UNQUOTE

Minu: Fantastic! Beti (daughter), I am indebted to you. Honestly speaking, there has been a conflict in my mind ever since I have met you and Rubi. Now, everything is crystal clear. In other words, even the leaf of the tree will not move without the ordain of Lord Krishna.'

Binoy: Now, let us enjoy the grand and sumptuous main course. Both Debi and Rubi eulogised preparations of different delicacies. All of them shouted in appreciation: 'Three cheers for Minu and Binoy.

Kidney Transplantation and its Nitty Gritty

It was the day of 'Kidney Transplantation'. Fortunately, the transplantation was smooth. There was no complication at all. Only problem arose when both Abhinandan and Debi became anaemic. It warranted blood transfusion. Many outsiders and well-wishers were prepared to donate. 'B' was not in favour of blood being donated by outsiders in the offing. Rubi was prepared to donate blood to Abhinandan. In the meantime, Krish, son of 'B', straightway came to the Hospital from the Airport to the surprise of everyone. He did not divulge the details of his week-long India visit to anyone. His blood was tested and he donated it to Debi. Dr Chakroborty was himself at his wit's end to know how such a complicated transplantation became foolproof. He told Aroti enthusiastically, 'Madam, there is no room for concern. Both of them are ok, and will be much better within a few days. But they will have to be under observation for a couple of days.' There is nothing to worry about. While handing over copies of the tips on post-surgery care.

State of Ecstasy upon Post-Surgery

When Abhinandan and Debi returned home from Hospital, there was a hue and cry all over the village. Most of the villagers greeted them with flowers. A few garlanded them. There had been Krishna bhajan organised by Kedarnath and family since morning. Abhinandan and Debi prayed by chanting His name with utmost devotion.

Thereafter, they showered flowers on Lord Krishna's idol. Their mother escorted them to an open area and made them seated. Everybody asked them if they had any complications. They smilingly answered that there were none. They were served 'sherbet', a rejuvenating, invigorating drink while various kinds of juices were served to others. They were surrounded by all the members of two families. Thereafter, many of them questioned Krish for not having informed prior to arrival. He smilingly informed he wanted to amaze, surprise and astound everybody. Krish asked where his father was as he was not in the gathering. His Mom shared with him that he had gone to buy a buffalo. When she was asked that they already had a buffalo, she informed them that additional milk was perhaps required for Abhi and Debi. It was observed that Krish kept staring at Debi without blinking his eyes. Krish, though smart and highly qualified, was, in fact, introverted in nature. Hence, he was not able to go close and talk to her freely.

Krish Engrossed in Debi

Rubi watched it intensely and purposefully. While others were busy talking to Abhi and Debi, she quietly sat beside Krish and, upon exchanging pleasantries, she threw a volley of questions at him without giving him any chance to react intermittently. "How can I help you, my dear friend? You know, she is my sister, 'Debi. I know you will agree with me that her name resembles her beauty. She looks like an 'idol'!" When he looked at her with surprise, she reacted in no time: Please do not mistake me, I am telling what others tell about my Didi. Isn't it? However, I asked you: 'Is she not an epitome of beauty?' Nevertheless, you know, she is not that smart. Had I been in her place, I would have commenced talking to that smart and handsome guy who was gazing at her. However, do you want me to introduce you to her?" Accumulating courage and guts, Krish thanked her profusely and confessed that he could help himself. 'Nonetheless, I must praise your trait in speech, it was like a Bollywood movie where the Heroine's sister talks to the Hero', reacted Krish. Rubi was intelligent enough to proceed without allowing Krish to complete what he wanted to say: 'Thank God, you can not only stare but also talk wisely and prudently.' Both of them laughed at the same time. It started drizzling. Before leaving the place, Krish thanked Rubi for giving company. She asked him politely not to mince matters. He should rather say plainly that he got some information about Didi and that was what he was exploring. It was about three days prior to Krish's return to London. Kedarnath invited all the members of the family for dinner. Krish got the perfect opportunity to talk to Debi face to face. He could identify through conversation that she was not only the quintessence of beauty but also in possession of great knowledge. While talking, Krish quietly noticed her from top to bottom. He found her exceedingly beautiful and sensuous. She had undoubtedly a captivating charm. She had an average height and a slim body; her skin was chalk white; bushy, long, curly & coal like black hair; big wide eyes like baby deer with its cuteness and innocence as well; full cheeks; narrow nose; fuller lips; narrow forehead and jawline with cheekbones at the widest point of the face; liable to grab people's attention and compliments; physical beauty was heavily associated with her sweet and unimpeachable smile.

It is not important how long you live, but how you live

Krish wanted to introduce himself to Debi but the latter interrupted Krish …… 'You are the only son of your parents, you are pursuing your higher studies in London, you have come here on leave to see and help your cousin but instead of helping him, you helped me by default.' Saying so, she perhaps gave a bit of a smile which she hid with her palm. Krish started pondering over whether both the sisters were chips of the old block. He was mystified whether he should admire her beauty, her trait of being an orator or what not! Earlier, he believed that 'Beauty and modesty cannot go together.' He had no alternative but to make an exception to this proverb when he got to know more and more about the attitude, nature and behaviour of 'Debi'. He murmured: 'Good behaviour does not have any monetary value. But it has the power to purchase a million hearts.' He also recollected the Mother Teresa's quote:

'If your eyes are positive, you will love the world.
But if your tongue is positive, the world will love you'.
Here, he is confused: 'If both eyes and tongue are positive......!!'

In the meantime, Abhi appeared. Debi left saying perhaps Mamma was in need of her help. Abhi asked Krish how he found out about his sister. Abhi could guess that Krish must have some romantic inclination towards Debi. His parents complained that he was always absent minded and did not even talk to them properly. But last time when he visited, he was not like that.

Krish: 'Bhai, what do you feel about 'love'? Are you ever in love?' Abhi looked at Krish astonishingly as they did not have ever conversed with a topic similar to that. However, he told him that he did not know much about it as he was least interested in it. You are a number 1......? Abhi retorted: 'intelligent'? Giving a sarcastic laugh for quite some time, I meant: stupid, fatuous, thickheaded and dumbass. Abhi was bit annoyed with his cousin. But, at the same time, he could understand that Krish was obsessed with the idea of love. Krish later realised that it was not right to embarrass his brother. He sought an apology. Abhi later reminded him that there was no need for that. He countered Krish in order to know more about his feelings and he precisely wanted to know details of his love.

Krish: At the very outset, love cannot be explained in any way. "However, since you are my brother, I would venture my best to let you know what little I know about it. Love is a willingness to prioritise another's well-being or happiness above your own. In other words, it is an extreme feeling of attachment and affection where one experiences extreme joy even in shedding tears". He is so obsessed with love, once he revealed while brooding over his beloved: "You know, given a choice between heaven and love, I would positively opt for the latter. As my beloved, I believe, will escort me to heaven; but if I go to heaven without my love, heaven will become worse than hell for me. Hence, what hell will I do going to heaven! Love is a set of emotions and behaviours characterised by intimacy, passion, and mutual commitment. It involves care, closeness, protectiveness, attraction, affection and trust. Last but not the least, since you do not know 'Alpha and Omega' about love, maybe, this example will enable you to understand a bit of it. But I reiterate it is not an exam, it's a feeling which is not prompted by any vested interest. A pure love is always unconditional: it means to love someone with a pure heart. There are no strings attached. It's beyond any boundaries. I may cover miles and miles all alone at a stretch by thinking about her, chanting her name, picturising her actions, nature, behaviour, attitude, smile and image in my mind and keep reversing time and again without a tinge of lethargy."

On flattering Krish for his reservoir of knowledge on love, Abhi would like to be doubly sure about his beloved, sweetheart. He enquired: 'How and in what way are you going to chant your beloved's name?' Without thinking of any ambidextrous intention in his query, Krish plainly said: 'Why, it is very simple: close your eyes half, forget about the surroundings and keep singing: My love is Debi; Debi is in my sleep; Debi is in my dreams and the universe will perhaps be motionless for me without her.' Now, Abhi could know from horse's mouth his infatuation with Debi. In order to tease Krish, he asked: 'What is love? What will be his feelings in case he fails to achieve his 'love'?' Now, Krish got to know slowly that his brother, Abhi, was attempting to tease him. Nevertheless, his love for Debi was monumental and, hence, there was nothing to camouflage his love. He confessed that 'Love' is a powerful emotion that builds bonds and encourages positivity. This warm feeling extends beyond the romantic type of love. He responded at the top of his voice that he would honour death rather than living without her. He also cautioned Abhi not to instil negativity in his feelings. Abhi was enjoying annoying him. He further enquired of Krish sarcastically: '*Accha Bhai (ok brother)*, you are there in London for pursuing which course!' Krish could not believe his ears. However, since he was brooding over his love, he took his question very lightly. After some time when he came out of his love process, he could understand that his *Bhai* took him as a source of amusement. He was a bit annoyed. Krish could not believe that Abhi knew nothing about love. Had he known a bit of it, he would not have made fun of it! He told him vehemently that he was 'sorry' and, at the same time, 'surprised': 'You know nothing about the birds and the bees; nothing about the world of man and woman. Though you are in the stage of adolescence, your knowledge of love is bleak. If you know these, these will work as oxygen and lift you out of the boredom'. Abhi could understand that Krish *bhai* would continue giving him left and right as long as he would be with him. Hence, he planned to quit at an opportune time. Fortunately, sister Debi was seen coming. He pranked him saying: 'Your Heaven, I mean my sister Debi, is coming and I am leaving'. It was time for dinner.

Marriage of Krish was in Doldrums

It was Saturday. Krish would leave for London on Monday morning. Krish's marriage issue was on the carpet most of the time. When he and his parents were assembled together, Minu asked her son if he had thought or selected anybody as his life partner. Later Binoy joined their discussions. When Krish kept quiet, his father informed him that if he agreed, they would explore a suitable *Bahu*. There was a Zamindar, Ajit Choudhury, known to him, who was blessed with twelve daughters. His first six daughters were married to doctors and the other two to engineers and the next one was settled in London. His other three daughters were at marriageable ages. He showed their photos to his wife, Minu. She wanted it to be shared with Krish. His Dad also told him that Zamindar, Ajit Choudhury, was in favour of early marriage as he was the victim of Bronchitis. He wanted his son-in-law ..... Krish cut in and told his Mom that he liked none of his daughters. His Mom also showed a few photographs which were outrightly rejected. Minu proposed to her husband to call his sister, Aroti *didi* and Kedarnath *dada*. Both of them came and joined. Aroti also shared some photographs and discussed their brief profiles. All of them assumed that his (Krish's) priority was her 'look' and 'appearance' and for him the profile was secondary. He told them point blank not to worry for his marriage. Both Binoy and Minu's fear was that their son might marry a foreigner and settle down there and perhaps that was the only reason he kept rejecting every one. They knew that English women are fashionable. They have long legs, big hips, large breasts, pale skin with Blonde hair and blue eyes. Minu asked Aroti: 'Didi, why don't you call Abhi here? He may be in the knowledge of what is in the mind of my son because once I observed that they had long discussions.' 'That's a good idea', Aroti exclaimed.

Krish was Head Over Heels in Love for Debi

No sooner did he get the message than Abhinandan appeared. Over a cup of hot tea and *Pakora*, while it *was* mildly drizzling, they commenced their second round of discussions. Abhi, upon short interaction with Krish, informed all of them that Bhai was infatuated in love with Debi, *sister*. The latest development came to all of them as a bolt from the blue. All started looking at one another. There were differences of opinions amongst them. They started whispering: 'How can it be! Some say that she is like his sister. The other one disagrees. Hence, in the offing, they are at loggerheads.' Krish tried to reason out by saying that Debi is Abhi's sworn sister and not related to him biologically or by blood. Hence, by no means, she could be considered his (Krish's) sister. Abhi reacted: 'Sorry Bhai, Debi and Rubi are my sisters. It is not my look-out how the people of the world perceive or look at it. Every relation cannot be established by substantiating proof. Had it been so, every child would have sought a DNA test to spot the identity of his father.' Krish requested her brother not to be offended. He never meant to question Abhi's sincere brotherly feelings towards Debi and Rubi.

Initially, Binoy was not in favour of Debi's being his daughter-in-law. Since he was a Zamindar, had a name and fame. They were proud of their only son. Hence, initially, they tried to persuade Krish that his parents were not interested in his marrying Debi.

Krish retorted: 'I will never leave the one I love. Even if you find a hundred reasons to give up, I will find one reason to hold on. There is a Yiddish Proverb: 'If a man is destined to drown, he will drown even in a bucket of water and so to say if I am destined to marry Debi, I will marry her even if all of you are against it.' His parents had no way but to give in.

However, his parents were of the view that Debi's consent must be sought. It was decided to flash the information upon receipt of a green signal from Debi. A dinner was arranged. In the dinner, both light alcoholic (Tari) and non-alcoholic beverages were arranged. There were also arrangements for warm beverages like hot chocolate, pumpkin and apple cider. The room was partially illumined to confuse anybody judging the others choice of drink. While Rubi was enjoying drinks. Abhi asked Debi: 'Would you mind if your soft drink transforms into a cocktail?' 'Sorry, Bhai, it is not my 'cup of tea'. Pointing out, Rubi, she will relish your company. Abhinandan joined Rubi while Krish approached Debi. Debi enquired to Krish: 'Don't you like alcohol?' 'Yes, I do, but if you look down upon my taking it, I promise, I will keep away from it', Debi retorted'. 'Why so'? 'I don't know the reason. But I assume whatever you dislike, there is a reason for that', Krish twitted. 'Oh, great, you may continue with it. You have delighted me with your sugar-coated tongue, Debi smilingly said. Taking another peg, Krish was inwardly thrilled to see her enraptured smile. 'My endeavour will be to see you blissful. It will perhaps be my last day if I ever become the instrument of your dismay', Krish said while staring at Debi." Excuse me .. what did you say? In the meantime, Binoy announced that the drinks party would be over in another ten minutes. Thereafter, there would be discussions at length on Krish's marriage. Both the discussions and dinner would continue throughout the night or until a consensus of opinion was arrived at, whichever was earlier. There was a loud shout in merriment, uttering bravo .. bravo, followed by clapping. Debi was so enthusiastic that she took a leading role in the 'clapping' and was completely ignorant that she was going to be made a woman of the hour.

Soon after the drinks party, all of them shifted to another room. All, except Debi and Rubi, knew about the development. In the meantime, Binoy appeared and informed the gathering that he was going to enlighten about the gist of the discussions that had already taken place. "As parents, we were interested in the marriage of our son, Krish. We wanted to know whether he has already selected his life partner. When we failed to receive any positive response from him, we showed a few photographs which he turned down. Thereafter, we got to know from Abhinandan what Krish once shared with him:

"She keeps coming in my reverie & dreams;
I got myself completely lost in her thoughts.
While engrossing in my thoughts on her,
Virtually forgetting the mundane world.
Praying for her eternal happiness,
That was perhaps my only fault.
Craving to know if there is any other fault on my part".

She is none other than Debi. Hence, we got to know that he is deeply in love with Debi and keen to marry her. We, being parents, were interested to know straight from the horse's mouth".

Even Renowned Vishwamitra fell Victim to Beauty

Debi was stunned. She kept mum for a couple of minutes. Thereafter, she put forth her following points of view: "My sister and I are indeed grateful to *Baba*, Kedarnath, *Maa*, Aroti and, of course, Bhai, Abhinandan. When we were in an utterly hard, hellish and mystifying state, it was our Baba and Maa, who not only came to our rescue, but also gave monumental love and affection which is beyond expectation. Brotherly love and fondness from Abhinandan Bhai is unparalleled and perhaps inexplicable. Baba and Maa are 'living gods' for both of us. It is an exhaustive 'tale of woe' which I have already narrated in detail to Baba. I would give an account of the crux of the trauma, which Rubi and I racked with pain, to facilitate all of you to decide if I am worthy of being a wife of the son of a well-known Zamindar, who has name and fame. Let me start by apprising you of all of our past as prostitutes." There was a lot of hue and cry, especially on the part of Kedarnath and Abhinandan. Kedarnabath asked her: "Don't give all of us half truth. What prompted you and under what circumstances you were trod on that path must be told beforehand! Undoubtedly, you were forced, compelled and coerced to be in that profession. In this context, I would like to remind all of you about the epic sage Vishwamitra and Menaka".

Quote:

Vishvamitra was a prominent Hindu sage, who even frightened the Devas and ultimately tried to establish another Heaven. Lord Indra, King of Gods, is worried about the intensity of Vishwamitra's ascetic practice as it would give the sage enormous powers. Indra, frightened by his dynamism, sent Menaka to seduce him and nullify his penance. Menaka was one of the most mesmerising Apsaras - celestial Nymphs in the three worlds from heaven to earth. She entered the forest, where Vishwamitra was absorbed in his penance, and transformed it into a beautiful garden. Menaka successfully lured and incited Vishwamitra's lust, intruding and eventually broke his meditation. Vishwamitra upon opening his eyes, saw an exquisitely beautiful woman, almost naked, standing before him in a lush and lovely garden. He forgot his meditation and fell in love with Menaka.

Unquote

Kedarnath further retorted that even an acclaimed sage, who intimidated Indra and the Devas and was so powerful to think of creating another Heaven, fell prey to the beauty of a woman. We could well understand the mentality and morality of the majority of men who see women as commodities to be owned and used as per their whims and fancies. I see this as a serious indication of the true weakness of the male mind. The abuse, rape, and murder of women symbolise that the men are obsessed with women. Hence, the majority of them are immoral, unethical and unprincipled especially at the sight of a woman. That being the case, these so-called men in no way can accuse any women of immorality. While Debi was in the weeping mode, recalling her past days, Kedarnath announced a break for dinner. In the meantime, he shared about Debi's past life with those who were unaware of it.

Post-Dinner Discussions - Debi continued: "Baba has shared about my past life with all of you. I never expect to have a better match than this. On the contrary, I do not want to be instrumental in bringing about blemish, disgrace, slur, ignominy and stigma on the Zamindar lineage by attaching my ill-repute with them. No, Bhai, no .. Don't weep. Rubbing tears off Abhi's cheeks .. I will also not shed tears. I will have to be strong enough to nip in the bud the utopian idea which should not be fructified and should never see the light of the day like Platonic models of Ideal State. I can never tarnish the image which Baba and his forefathers have taken almost a century to build. If it is fruitful, the image of your nuclear families and their posterities will have to bear the brunt of recognising me as the wife of your son, Baba. I believe that since I received resentful experiences in life, I am unable to rise again. Every time it appears that I have a sword of Damocles hanging over my head and something bad seems very likely to happen to me. The reason being the memory of barbaric, savage and heathen treatment and tortures by the most crude and uncivilized individuals will always be at the back of my mind. It will never enable me to achieve anything in my life. Secondly, when the mind is seized with the past activities of agitation, distress, owing to inhuman treatment, all my faculties dry up and are unable to set out for any fruitful ventures. However, I understand that my mind must shun all the previous pursuits and undertake a daring journey or course of action that are considered audacious and impracticable for me in view of the nature of infliction of pain, suffering, torment, maltreatment and persecution I have undergone. How can I be his better half? Can a dwarf touch the Moon".

Abhinandan: "My sister, Debi, is as pure as her name denotes - Debi which means goddess and idol. As far as I know, she is as pure as 'milk washed basil leaves'. For me, she is goddess-like - perfect, blameless and spotless. Though no one is perfect, all have human frailty or fallibility, yet my sisters are paragons of virtues and devoid of any evil thoughts like a child, as innocent as a lamb and a newborn.

I would like to quote an occurrence from the Mahabharata war. Dushasana dragged Draupadi by the hair to the court, into the gambling hall, and decided to humiliate the proud Pandava queen by disrobing her in public. Draupadi was on the verge of being unclothed or literally 'nude'. We know that she prayed to Lord Krishna and was able to salvage the last fragments of her dignity. With the grace of Lord Krishna, her garments became endless - yards and yards of fabric appeared miraculously - and she could not be disrobed in public, fundamentally male space. She was undoubtedly embarrassed, humiliated, ashamed, abashed and mortified publically. Yes, the memory of barbaric tortures by the most so-called **civilized** persons could never completely leave her mind. But it always helped her to achieve the goal of her life. When the mind was seized with the past activities of inhuman treatment, all her faculties neither dried up nor obviated her to set out for any fruitful ventures. Rather the fire was set as an act of vengeance round-the-clock. It is also said that Draupadi's inspiration was instrumental for the Mahabharata war and total annihilation of Kauravas. I would solicit your answer: Had Draupadi's faculties dried up as her mind seized with the past activities of inhuman, cruel, harsh, brutal and savage treatment? Was she impious, unholy, ungodly, unrighteous, immoral, blasphemous and irreverent? Was she not better half of her five husbands after the occurrence? Did she not continue remaining an honourable wife of the Pandavas?

The episode of the Ramayana is also known to all: After abducting Sita, and reaching Lanka, Ravana did keep her in his palace, showed his entire palace and offered so many luxuries to her, for enticing her. Ravana could not touch her forcibly as he was cursed by Brahma since Ravana seduced celestial nymph Punjikasthala that if he revelled with any other woman by force, his heads then undoubtedly would break into a hundred pieces. He forcibly kept Sita in Ashok Vatika anticipating that in future she might change her mind and would accept him as her husband eventually. I will give you an instance from 'Sundara Kanda'. Sita got to know that Hanuman's tail was set on fire. She took an oath that if she had never ever thought of anyone other than Rama as her Man, may the fire on Hanuman's tail not hurt him a bit. Can you imagine catching the fire and not feeling the heat? That was the chastity of her '*Pativrata Dharma*' even after being kidnapped, even fire had to change its basic Dharma. Mata Sita was there in Lanka under Ravana's custody for about 10 to 11 months. Could Ravana make Mata Sita immoral, unchaste and impure? If Mata Sita and Draupadi are pious and chaste, how come my sisters are impious and unchaste!! Immoral, sinful, vice and bloody bastards are those who drag naive innocent girls into this business; others who act as silent spectators and last but not the least it is the administration which never cares to bother whether the inmates of the brothels are there voluntarily or forcibly". The police, who are the custodians, can easily be bought and sold by means of greasing their palms.

Krish : I feel embarrassed to even talk about chastity. Even the horrific, dreadful, horrendous and horrifying experiences may become an inspiration for some people to make progress towards a goal. All these dreadful experiences cannot deter them from setting higher goals. Ultimately, it is our attitude which determines how we look at a setback. But to an optimist, it can be a stepping stone to success. To a negative thinker, it can be a stumbling block. On the contrary, I agree, nothing can be achieved if the goals are contradictory. For instance, the desire to be an accomplished writer of holy books as well as being an alcoholic cannot go hand in hand as both are altogether contradictory to each other.

Quotation by Swami Chinmayananda

"Moment to moment you have a choice: to create a thought or destroy a thought in you. Thoughts are creative, they can make or unmake you."

"Even though you conquered battles of the world, you will become the world conqueror only when you have conquered your mind."

"Mind can make a hell of heaven or heaven of hell."

I tell you: 'When people don't know how to recognise opportunity, they even complain of noise when it knocks. But they should bear in mind that the same opportunity never knocks twice'.

Consequence of a Negative Attitude:

We become our biggest obstacles in our life by having a negative attitude. People with a negative attitude have a hard time in every step of their life as it leads to resentment, purposelessness, ill-health, stressful life and frustration for themselves and for those they are associated with. They create a negative environment at home and workplace and become a liability to society. They also pass on their negative mindset to others around them and to their posterity.

Bring about a change of our Negativities

Human nature generally resists change. Change is by and large uncomfortable. Regardless of its positive or negative effect, change can be stressful. Sometimes we get so comfortable with our negativity that even when the change is for the positive, we don't want to accept it. We stay with the negative. In this context, I would like to quote what Charles Dickens once wrote: "A prisoner stayed for many years in an underground dark prison cell. After serving his sentence, he got his freedom. He was brought out from his cell into the bright daylight of the open world. This man looked all around and after a few moments, he was so uncomfortable with his newly acquired freedom that he asked to be brought back to his cell into confinement. To him, the underground cell, the chains and the darkness were more secure and comfortable than accepting the change of freedom and the open world."

During childhood, we form attitudes that last a lifetime. Undoubtedly, it would be a lot easier and better to have acquired a positive attitude during our formative years. Does that mean if we acquire a negative attitude, whether by design or by default, we should stick with it? Of course, not. Can we change? Yes..... Is it easy? Absolutely not. It is by the desire to be positive; to cultivate discipline and dedication and to practise those principles. As adults regardless of our environment, education and experience, who is responsible for our attitude? We ourselves. We have to accept responsibility sometime in our lives. We blame everyone and everything but ourselves.

Law of Chastity should not be restricted to Feminines only

I would like to remind all of you that the law of chastity should apply to both men and women. It denotes complete fidelity and loyalty towards your partners. However, I am sure, people of the present generation may not agree! Those who are chaste, should be morally clean, even in their thoughts and words. I would like to question the chastity of menfolk including me. Giving a man an option: to opt for a purse full of currency notes or an attractive girl — undoubtedly, he will opt for the latter. While calling a spade a spade, given a golden opportunity, how many menfolk are chaste! I am sorry to say that a very few menfolk are chaste morally, in their thoughts and words not to talk of their actions. Let me take my own case. When we were school/college goers, most of our discussion points with our friends were based on girls - their looks, their appearances, their smiles, even their way of talking, walking and what not! We hardly discussed anything other than these. I for one was not able to perceive how come we forgot that we had our own sisters, sisters-in-law, cousins, etc. at home. To be frank, candid and honest, we all knew what used to come in our minds during the course of our discussions on them. Regarding actions, getting an opportunity, perhaps nobody will care for morality, laws, even punishment, and one's name, fame and integrity. Before putting one's finger on the chastity of women, have menfolk ever thought of theirs?"

Binoy & Minu: In view of their discussions, we don't have any objection, rather it would be our pleasure to accept Debi as our daughter-in-law subject to her consent and agreement of her father, Kedarnath.

Minu asked Krish: It was just for our knowledge's sake. Is it safe to have a baby after donating a kidney? I knew this query would emerge. In order to satisfy my parents, I had already studied it thoroughly. According to the nephrologist, 'if the kidney donor is a female and is having regular menstrual cycles and good general health, getting pregnant and having a child is no issue at all. But it will be better if she is not pregnant for at least one year after the donation of her kidney. Even the nephrologist is of the view that the marriage of transplant recipients to non-transplant recipients is not uncommon. You will also be surprised to know that even two recipients tying the knot is not unique. They can lead a normal life. You may like to confirm the authenticity of this from family nephrologist, Dr Chakroborty'.

Binoy & Minu: "We are pleased to accept Debi as our daughter-in-law. Now, the ball is in your (Kedarnath) court. We are begging your daughter for our son, Krish'. 'We feel delighted and elated to marry off our daughter, Debi, to your son, Krish', Kedarnath retorted.

It was 11.30 pm. All were congratulating and embracing one another. Rubi engaged in friendly banter with Krish. 'So, very soon, you are going to become my *Jija ji*. I must get my passport ready'. Krish informed her jokingly, 'You are perhaps mistaken. I am not marrying both of you, your Didi will be my better half and that is the reason my honeymoon will be with your Didi in London'. All started making the spontaneous sounds that were the instinctive expressions of lively amusement, merriment, laughter and cheerfulness and sometimes also of derision, taunting and jeering. It was indeed a lovely and lively moment. Rubi humorously responded: 'I know that, I know that very well and perhaps you are not aware that *'Saali Adhi Gharwali!'* (*sister-in-law is a half wife*). It is a common joke in India between a woman and her brother-in-law and vice-versa. There was tumultuous laughter. All started appreciating Rubi for her wit. The two families were enthusiastic and jubilant.

Debi Expressed Her Inability to Go Ahead

Debi : I am very sorry to inform all of you that upon pondering over at length and keeping in view the name and fame of Zamindar Gharana, I express my inability to proceed further. (The atmosphere was so still and quiet that one could hear the sound of a pin falling. After some time, whispering commenced. When Rubi tried to persuade Didi, the latter forbade Rubi to interfere in her personal affairs. Though Rubi felt offended, she could understand why Debi was stubborn. Krish felt as if he were deprived of every joy in life. He was not at all interested to remain there any more. He asked his parents to book his air tickets for the UK the day after. Krish rightly retorted: 'Man proposes and Debi disposes.'

While Krish wanted to talk to Abhinandan, it was discovered that the latter was missing. There was a frantic search but in vain. It was gloomy all over the village. When nobody was able to find him anywhere, Aroti started running from pillar to post in search of him. She was more concerned about his state of health, being a new recipient of a kidney, if he failed to take medicine and diet on time, he might collapse. Kedarnath was at a loss to understand whether to take care of his wife or to find out the place where his son was. Debi did all she could to detect his whereabouts. But unfortunately he was found nowhere. She decided to ponder over with a cool mind. She was afraid that his brother, Abhi, might have captivated himself in a room, made of iron. The Zamindar families took refuge there upon knowing about some impending dacoity or robbery. The room was full of arsenals to combat dacoits. They soon got to know that Abhi was indeed there. In the meantime, Abhi announced that he would not come out of the room unless she agreed to marry Krish. Debi asked Binoy and Minu to lie to Abhi about the sudden disappearance of both the sisters. They countered that saying so might not be safe. Debi convinced them that once he came out, she would convince him. In case he was not convinced, she had no alternative but to marry in order to save her Bhai. They retorted not to take any decision and action in haste. It was a question about her life and career. They advised her to look before leaping. Debi reiterated: "There is no iota of doubt that your son is a jewel. My concern is about my 'black mark'. I don't want that to adversely affect your taming name and the life and career of your son".

Binoy: You know, my son is stubborn and fussy too. Let me tell you frankly I'm given to understand that he is deeply in love with you. I don't know what he is going to do in case he is unable to have you as his wife. I am apprehensive that he might stay back in London and marry an English lady. There is also a possibility that I might lose my son's presence forever. Nevertheless I shall never advise you to marry against your wish. You take your own decision and that will be my decision too. Kedarnath has accepted you as your daughter and so will you be for me as well. Debi assured them that nothing wrong would happen and their Krish would continue living with them. In the meantime, her parents approached Debi with medicine and food and asked her to have them immediately. Debi was wonderstruck that in the midst of trials and tribulations, her parents were hyperconscious of her well-being. She assailed them with a volley of questions: Baba and Maa, 'How come, you remember about my welfare in this juncture when all of us have been looking for Abhi! You always show great compassion for our problems and difficulties. Are you not made of flesh and blood?'

Aroti: Yes *Beta*, every second appears like a minute, every minute an hour; an hour a day and a day a year. But at the same time, I cannot explain in terms of words how lucky we are to get both of you as our daughters! Having daughters like you is a matter of good fortune. We know what you are! When a priceless diamond is recovered from a gutter, its price remains the same. How can we ignore your well-being? You are our posterity. You will have to take care of our Zamindari in our absence.

(Debi while weeping, holding her Mom's feet with two hands, seeking apology).

Aroti: What happened! What for? You have committed nothing wrong.

Debi: When all of you agreed to my marriage, I committed not only a blunder but a sin. Mom, I am sorry to say that, at the same time, it was also your fault: Why didn't you take me to task? Why didn't you teach me a lesson by giving me a hard slap. I am given to understand that zamindars are very strict, severe, harsh, authoritarian and firm. But you and Baba are kind-hearted, compassionate, understanding, tolerant, merciful, benevolent and generous. It is I who have taken undue advantage of your generosity'. While embracing her with open arms, Aroti blessed Debi profusely: 'May Lord Krishna grace you with good health, tranquillity, long and meaningful life'.

Binoy and Kedarnath were closeby. Debi, while joining her two palms together, bowing the head down in respect, with softly closed eyes, prayed before Binoy to pardon for her misdemeanour and accept her as his daughter-in-law, if considered competent. Binoy Babu started rejoicing in jubilation. He ran hither and thither telling villagers that ultimately he was successful in getting Debi as his daughter-in-law. He kept blessing her joyfully, uttering: 'You have contributed to a great extent to save my family and to enable me to retrieve my son. I am indebted to you, Debi'. Debi said in response: 'Baba, for Krishna's sake, don't be remorseful for nothing. If you do that, it will feed sin on me. I am your daughter, it is always the duty of the children to work in the interests of their parents. Parents should never be obligated to their children'.

Kedarnath: Smilingly, Dada, you need to take my consent before addressing my daughter as yours.

Binoy: Oh, yes, why not! You recovered her and imparted necessary training and education which contributed to her ideal demeanour. I express my gratitude to you from the bottom of my heart'.

Kedarnath: Dada, I am sorry to disagree with you. My teacher used to say: 'I cannot make any student perfect unless he has an inborn or inbuilt trait. I can only remove the dust or junk clouding their minds. But if she does not have God gifted essential qualities in him/her, who am I to explore that?'

Binoy: Today, I am on cloud nine and feeling extremely proud of being the potential father-in-law to such a benevolent girl.

On hearing Debi's confession and consent to marry, Abhinandan came out of the hall and stood face to face with her. While he was about to touch Debi's feet, she forbade him to do that and surprisingly asked the reason for doing the silly act. Krish is elder to me. So, you would be my *'Boudi' (sister-in-law)*. No Boudi, No sister-in-law! 'I also caution you not to be oversmart. I am your sister and you will remain my Bhai. Every year, there will be a 'Bhai-Phota' celebration and I shall take a beautiful gift from my Bhai on that occasion. Do not try to deprive me of the gift.' 'What gift I can give you sister, you have already shared with me the biggest gift which I can never repay! I cannot even say: 'May my life be added to you!' Bhai, if you talk like this, I can take you to task. Earlier I could not punish you as a sister but mind it, from now onwards, whenever I wish to teach you a lesson, I can act as your sister-in-law.

It was 4 am. Binoy asked all of them to sleep at his place for a few hours and return to their respective houses late in the morning, post breakfast. Rubi ironically asked her brother-in-law: 'How are you feeling! You must be as fresh as a daisy and as happy as a pig in mud. Rubi amusingly forbade him to throw her like a fly from a glass of milk. She playfully reminded him not to go very close to her Didi as he has not yet received the licence for the same'. Debi asked her not to be silly and it would be better if she held her tongue. Rubi tauntingly reminded that she didn't know that she (Debi) would already be taking the side of Krish, her proposed husband. Debi ran after Rubi to pull her hair. In the meantime, Krish countered Debi and permitted Rubi to carry on with the chit chats provided she would not object to his reaction at the opportune moment. Abhinandan reacted sharply: 'Nobody is caring for me. Everyone is giving me a step-motherly treatment. 'Krish da, never forget that 'Debi' is my sister and you should not keep her aloof from her Bhai for a long time'. Krish retorted: 'How can I forget your contribution in uniting us! I promise you, whenever you long to meet your sister, she will be with you'.

Everyone had a delayed breakfast. Both Krish and Debi appeared extremely happy. Rubi observed from a yard's distance that they were hardly eating. They were talking and smiling throughout. Rubi felt pleased to see the smiling face of her Didi. After some time, Krish, out of love, raised the spoon full of food to feed his would-be wife. Though Debi felt embarrassed, looking hither and thither, she somehow took a mouthful from the spoon but forbade him to do it again in front of others. Minu saw everything from a distance. After some time, she came back with medicine and milk. She asked the maid to arrange their left-over breakfast and medicine in the nearby room. Thereafter, she asked both of them to have their remaining breakfast in the privacy of the room, so that they may spend some time alone talking and getting to know each other before Krish leaves for London. Soon after breakfast, they sat facing each other. After an awkward period of silence, Krish asked Debi to satisfy herself if she had any query.

Debi: Do you smoke or drink? As you know, I don't have any objection to that. But I am just asking since you want me to ask something about you. At the same time, as you know, cigarette smokers have a significantly increased risk of a shortened life span, interpersonal problems, respiratory problems and may develop cancer too. I would appreciate it if you take it once in a blue moon or in order to celebrate some special occasion.

Krish: Presently, it may not be possible. However, honestly speaking, I never overdrink and rarely smoke, maybe one or two cigarettes, soon after drinks. I will quit both as soon as I become a father unless you want me to continue! Both of them laughed at their heart's content. This is the first question that came to your mind? I know why? Since you were not deadly against them. It was also because you wanted my well-being! That was the reason why I admired you so much. However, I have a query. What do you mean by special occasions? Does a honeymoon come under its ambit? May I request you to join me in drinking on this very very special event which comes once in two persons' life-time?

Debi: "I will never say 'no' to anything which pleases you. Debi embraced Krish out of ecstasy. Krish was not prepared for that. He got disbalanced and fell on the feather bed. In order to prevent him from getting hurt, Debi held him tightly and as a result of which she also fell on him. Debi immediately tried to get out. Krish reminded her that she was not following what she asserted a few minutes back. He reminded her that she would never say 'no' to anything which pleased him. Debi retorted that it would be applicable post-marriage. Thereafter, she informed him that if permitted, she wished to know if he had any affairs in his life. She further assured that it was just a part of chit chats in order to enable her to live with him life-long.

Krish: 'Good one'. As usual, almost all women desire to know them prior to their marriage. However, the latter part of it, to be with you life-long, is beyond comprehension.

Debi: It is very simple. If you want to marry the other woman, that means she is not compatible with you or you are incompatible with her. I want to explore what prompted you or her for separation. If she had any vices, I shall try hard to get rid of those'.

Krish Fell in Love at First Sight

It was love at first sight. We both were pursuing MBBS. She was a British girl. With all conventional features, she was tall with dark brown hair, pale skin, hazel eyes, and a slim body. I did not realise how I fell for her at the very first sight in the classroom! I was bewitched by her smile, captivated by her charming face and infatuated with her mannerism. In the beginning, I kept staring at her without paying much attention to the lecture. She could well understand that. One day, when the class was off, she asked me candidly without any iota of hesitation: 'Are you from India?' When I answered affirmatively, she quickly asked me: 'Would you mind going for a coffee?' Honestly speaking, for some time, I was unable to decide. Without waiting for my response, she held my hand and virtually dragged me towards the Cafeteria. How on earth a man can say 'no' to her invitation! On the top of it, inwardly, I was indeed enthusiastic to get an opportunity to spend some time with the charming and graceful lady. I was in the Cafeteria with her. As it was my maiden appearance, I didn't know why all of a sudden, I became an introvert. It was perhaps for the first time in my life I was sitting face-to-face with a girl. She was Isla. She complimented my short name, my clothes and my English accent. She found everything, I said, hilarious, even though I knew I was not that funny. We had conversations on different issues. She asked for my contact number before I asked for hers. She held her gaze when I was having casual conversations. When I felt shy talking freely to her, she pointed out many couples who were kissing and hugging each other spontaneously. She came close to me. I didn't know why! Perhaps to hug or kiss me. I held one corner of the table tightly lest I should fall. When we were having coffee, she again came very close to me, eulogising my personality, nature & Indianism. I was deeply impressed with her candidness. She held my hand tightly giving me very little opportunity to move myself away from hers. I was so shy and diffident that in order to get rid of the situation, I reluctantly tilted my cup a bit and the hot coffee fell on my trousers. She immediately rubbed it off with her handkerchief. Observing my discomfort, Isla moved her chair a foot away from me. When I looked at her, she smiled a bit. She changed the topic and sought my opinion on her personality & on her apparel. I complimented her saying: it was a real joy to behold her being gorgeous in classic British style outfits, being down to earth and very minimal make-up since there was no dearth of natural beauty in her. She loudly complimented me asking if I was from Tagore's State. I nodded. She again drew her chair close to me in enthusiasm and pecked me on my cheek. I was, in fact, not at all prepared for that. While I was on the verge of falling, Isla tried hard to save me. But unfortunately she slipped and fell on me. Her heavy body and high-heeled shoes wounded my legs. I was not much worried about my injuries. I was rather more concerned about the onlookers who looked at one another and made fun of us. There were a few who considered me lucky and whispered why she had not fallen on them instead. I attempted to get up by avoiding touching her heavy bosoms. But I was initially obviated by her high-heeled shoes as well. She was also unable to get right up as all the furniture fell on us. Hence, there was a little space for her to roll out. After a while, a few of her friends moved the furniture aside and lifted her up. I was mortified. However, that was not the end of the dilemma. Soon after that she bursted into laughter. As I was unable to understand what prompted her to laugh, she took a little mirror out of her purse and showed it to me. My cheek was all red with her lipstick. Seeing me all the more embarrassed, Isla rubbed my cheek with her headscarf. While rubbing my cheek, she started humming a song in broken Hindi: 'Dil Kya Kare Jab Kisi Se Kisi Ko Pyar Ho Jaye'. Thereafter, she asked me if I was interested in 'dating' her. I was wondering if I found myself all alone with her, I would surely feel very uneasy and uncomfortable. But without waiting for my response, she shared with me the date, place and time.

What is Dating!

It refers to two persons in an intimate relationship. The relationship, for most of us, may be sexual, but it does not necessarily have to be so. Many people have happy, fulfilling, healthy romantic relationships without having sex in the back of their minds. I was unmarried and wanted to abstain from it before marriage. However, this doesn't mean that the relationship would lack depth. Sex, for me, was not the only way to establish intimacy with my partner. In short, incompatibility of our ideas and ideologies caused the winding up of our relationship though we were friends.

Now, I have decided to show off my better half, proudly, post-marriage, to Isla. I would boast of an ideal woman - beauty with modesty! Combination scarcely available! Krish asked Debi if she had anything to share with him. 'Bhai, Abhinandan, and sister, Rubi, are my two eyes and Baba & Maa are my Right and Left hands', Debi retorted. I may not be vociferous if you ever bother me for some reason or other. But they should not be given any room for complaint. 'OK, agreed. But how come you are so pretty! It goes without saying that the beauty of the Taj beggars description, and so yours. Saying so, Krish was coming closer to her and when he was on the verge of clasping her in his arms, Debi shouted, 'Yes, Maa!' Thereafter, she got up in no time. Krish became a bit annoyed at being cheated. Debi came close to him, raised his chin and told him smilingly, you might remove one full night from my life's longevity. Krish failed to understand what she meant by that. She reiterated that she promised that the entire (*Fulsajya Ratri*) 'Wedding Night' would belong to him. She would be at his disposal not partially but wholly. She would not say 'no' to anything he would ask for. She would appreciate his patience and perseverance until that time. Krish became extremely pleased with her but, at the same time, asked her to follow what she had said in letter and spirit.

Krish was informed that the University of London remained closed for a month on account of the students' strike which brought about a mini civil war. It was a blessing in disguise for Krish and his parents. The engagement and marriage were fixed within ten days. Debi made multiple requests for keeping the marriage a little late. Krish's parents convinced her that since it was the final year, it would be very difficult, if not impossible, for him to take off from the University for marriage. Hence, ultimately she had to concede to the request of her Bhai, parents and Krish for an early wedding.

Celebration kicked off

Debi humbly requested her parents not to spend lavishly and unnecessarily on the wedding. She suggested that all of them viz. Debi, Rubi, Abhinandan and Krish would extend their helping hands under the overall guidance of their parents from time to time. It was also decided that since they had many ponds, they could make use of them. They had their own granaries as well. She shared with her parents that 'Only the wearer knows where the shoe pinches'. Debi apprised them of the pangs of hunger. When their Dad was no more, they were reduced to penury, pining for a handful of grains. They survived by eating boiled leaves and roots from trees. Hence, they were fully aware of the significance of: 'Hunger is the best sauce'. However, Debi humbly requested her parents to be charitable and magnanimous while arranging langars, offering cash and gifts to the poor and underprivileged. As Swami Vivekanando proclaimed: *'Jibey Prem Kore Jei Jon Sei Jon Sebiche Ishwar'*. It may be loosely translated as: 'Those who love and serve all on this earth are truly serving the Almighty'. Both Kedarnath and Binoy were in favour of her ideal concepts. She suggested making separate arrangements to feed and offer gifts in the forms of cash, blankets, dhotis and sarees to the poor, needy and underprivileged. There would be langars, where people will be fed free, a week before the marriage ceremony.

The langars commenced and a good deal of the underprivileged were fed and distributed cash and kinds separately. It continued for about five days prior to marriage. Countless villagers joined the celebration from the neighbouring villages. There was a lot of hustle and bustle from morning to evening. Happiness, delight, pleasure, mirth, joy and rejoice scattered all over the villages. All eulogised the arrangements made. The cash and the items in kind were distributed by both Krish and Debi. The receivers were ecstatic to accept them from the hands of the bride and the groom. The entire village was illuminated. Various games were available for children. There was a photo session as well. A musician, related to Zamindar, played at the wedding ceremony. They really added a special element to the ceremony. A well-known singer was invited who sang very popular songs and enthused the guests. Debi in her wedding attire was glittering like 24 carat gold from head to toe. Her sweet smile had further glorified and beautified the pride of 'Wedding Mandap'. In other words, in the Hindi proverb: *'Chaar Chand Lagana'* (to add to the grace or grandeur). Many neighbouring villagers were whispering about her extraordinary beauty.

After the Bengali wedding ceremony, the bride and the groom had dinner with the members of the family, relatives and close friends. They entered a room called the *'Bashor Ghor'*. Soon after completing the marriage ritual, Debi, Krish, Rubi, Abhinandan, their relatives and close friends assembled in this room. This was a fun affair wherein all the youngsters gathered together soon after the wedding ceremony. They shared jokes, chit chats, Shero-O-Shairi, dance, etc. Binoy, Kedarnath, Aroti and Minu also joined them infrequently to be hospitable to them. Binoy asked her *Bauma* (daughter-in-law) to take rest for a few hours as she seemed to be tired and fatigued. As usual, Rubi continued cracking jokes. *Jijja ji* was her target. Krish was desirous of complimenting Debi. But when Debi looked at him, he kept quiet.

Rubi asked: If anybody knew how Aryabatta invented 'Zero'. All showed their ignorance. She started: "One day, Aryabhata sat at home and started counting the friends who are not afraid of their wives. That's how he invented Zero (0)." All started laughing to mock Krish.

Krish reciprocated: It takes roughly two years to learn to speak. But it takes a life-time to learn what not to speak. Rubi complimented Krish for being vociferous. All of them pleaded with Krish to throw a '*Sher*', of his college days in front of his beautiful & glittering better half, on this auspicious night. Krish threw:

'Sher'	'Translation'
Mai Tod Leta Agar Tu GULAB hoti;	I would have plucked you if U were a rose;
Mai Jawab Banta Agar Tu Sawal Hoti.	I would have been an answer if U were a question.
Sab Jante Hain Mai Nasha Nahi Karta,	Everybody knows that I'm a Teetotaler;
Magar Pi Leta Agar Tu Sharab Hoti.	Nevertheless I would have drunk if U were Liquor.
(Quote by: Pankaj Kaushal)	(Translated by author)

Debi covered her face with her palms in shame. Everyone roared and hooted with laughter. On approaching Debi:

'Nights change but not dreams;
Paths change but not destiny.
Always keep your hopes alive;
Because luck may or may not change,
But time definitely changes!!'
(Elmore Leonard Quote)

Very true! All of them kept enjoying to their heart's content. Krish asked Nitin to join as he was known for Shero-O-Shairi (It means a small poetry that consists of big meaning. It could also be used as a double meaning talk in India, it's a type of fun activity).

Talaash Meri Thi Aur Bhatak Raha Tha Wo	I was looking for her and she was wandering.
Talaash Meri Thi Aur Bhatak Raha Tha Wo	
Dil Mera Tha Aur Dhadak Raha Tha Wo	The heart was mine but hers was beating.
Dil Mera Tha Aur Dhadak Raha Tha Wo	
Pyaar Ka Taluq Bhi Ajeeb Hota Hai	The nature of love is also strange but unique.
Aansu Mere The Aur Sisak Raha Tha Wo	The tears were mine but she was sobbing.

By: Rutha Aashiq

All appreciated Nitin and craved to know whether he was a *'Phatey Dil Aashiqui'* (frustrated lover)? Everyone bursted into laughter. Madhusudan fell down off a couch on account of his screams of laughter out of ecstasy.

All approached Adhir ..... He being an accountant, highlighted an Accountancy Fact:

"What is the difference between Liability and Asset?"

One of his friends, Subendu narrated:

"In short, assets put money in your pocket, and liabilities take money out!"

Adhir dismissed his answer in no time. He asked Subendu: "Are we here to learn accountancy?" Let me tell you what it actually is: A drunken friend is a liability. But a drunken girlfriend is an asset".

Everybody shouted How? Why? Absurd!!

He responded smilingly: A drunken friend is a liability because you need to arrange his drinks; confront problems when he is hospitalised; and *musibat ka pahad tootana* (breaking a mountain of trouble) when he is in the police station. On the contrary, a drunken girlfriend is an asset as you are able to stare at her from top to bottom to your heart's content; talk rubbish to her and use her as long as she is in a drunken state.

Many shouted: Excellent .. Unparalleled .. Nothing can be better than this. A few whispered jovially: *Aap Ka Charan Kidhar Hai* (Where are your feet)?

Debi retorted: 'Dada, what is going on?'

In the midst of laughter, Minu came with a variety of soft drinks, and Debi got up to assist her mother-in-law. Minu shared with them that she asked all the workers to go home and relax as the coming two days will be very hectic. Debi escorted her mother-in-law to the next room. When both of them sat on the bed, Debi started massaging her mother's legs. Minu got wonderstruck. When asked, Debi informed her that when she came inside the *Bashor Ghor*, she was limping a little. Minu remarked: "I really can't believe my destiny in having you as my daughter-in-law! I am sure, it would not be by virtue of my 'Karma' in this life". While saying so, her cheeks were inundated with tears. She hugged Debi murmuring: 'I must have done a lot of good deeds in my previous births'. Debi retorted with reverence: "Mom, how can you be doubtful of your Karma in this life too. I reiterate, Rubi and I, were literally lying in the gutter as *laawaris* (abandoned) covered with feces. It was my Baba and Maa, wholeheartedly supported by you guys (my present in-laws), who cleaned us up with their love and affection, and made us sacred, consecrated and holy. It was indeed by virtue of our (Rubi and I) Karmas in many past lives that we had been blessed with such unbelievable Maa and Baba, Bhai and in-laws.

Reception Day

It was Reception Day. Arrangements were made to serve free food and gifts to the poorest, underprivileged and downtrodden. When cash, blankets and sarees were distributed, Debi observed that one lady, whose head to toe was covered with a dilapidated saree, went out of the queue without taking the gifts. Debi asked her men to request the lady to kindly accept the gifts while blessing the newlyweds. Finding a couple of men following her, the lady started moving faster to leave the Pandal. Debi whispered to Krish to escort the lady quietly to a room with the help of their men. It was also in the back of her mind that perhaps the lady was getting ashamed to accept gifts for some reason. After much difficulty, Krish with his men could escort the lady to a room. Debi handed over the responsibility of distribution to her parents-in-law, and accompanied Krish to the room in order to meet the lady in person and help her in some way. As soon as the lady saw Debi, she drew her veil to cover her face. But Debi already saw her from a distance. While asking Krish not to let her go, Debi held her feet crying Maa - aa - aa and fainted. While the lady tried to leave and bunk off, Rubi came and hugged her mother. Krish asked Rubi to take care of her while he would take care of Debi. In the meantime, Debi's parents and in-laws appeared, handing over the cash and gift distribution charge to Abhinandan. As soon as Krish sprinkled water on Debi's face, she felt better and gained back her consciousness. Debi, Rubi, Binoy, Kedarnath, Aroti and Minu surrounded Protima, the biological mother of Debi & Rubi. All others were asked to assist Abhinandan in taking care of langars and distribution of gifts. When Protima came to know that it was her daughter's house, she was embarrassed of her state and did not want to spoil her daughter's married life. She was not at all interested in exposing herself and bringing shame to her daughter.

Minu took Debi in a separate room and asked to assist her Mom to put on a new saree despite Protima's reluctance. She knew it was the wedding night for her daughter. When Protima was about to leave, Minu appeared: "Didi, if you are adamant to go away from here, you may go. Who am I to stop you from going? But before departing, you may please note that I'm an ardent follower of Lord Krishna. I am telling you by His name that once you leave this house, I shall keep starving until you come back. I know from Debi *Bouma* (daughter-in-law) about your greatest amount of sacrifices for your family which perhaps nobody with flesh and blood can do. Do you know what Bouma has done for our family?" Debi requested her not to talk about all that. Minu charged Debi, 'Why not, your mother has every right to know about that. She has donated her kidney to her brother, Abhinandan, cousin of Krish.' Protima retorted: "Has she done a great job? It is the most endearing relationship in which there is a lot of love, care and companionship. When one sibling has a disability, the relationship becomes more complex and complicated for both brother and sister. Hence, it becomes the duty of the other sibling to come to the rescue. There lies no point in mentioning it." Minu retorted: 'Both the daughters and their Mom are indeed great. Didi, today is your daughter's *'fulsajya* night', (Wedding Night) I would request you to lend your helping hands in arranging it'. Krish appeared to inform them to postpone it as his mother-in-law must be tired and needed rest. When there was no response from Protima, both mother and son started looking for her. As there was a congregation of huge numbers of relatives, friends and members of the families, finding an opportunity, she was able to sneak out. Debi was downhearted and sat in the corner of a room putting her two palms on her head, crying her eyes out; Rubi was about to leave the room in search of her mother. All the members of the families were saddened and downhearted. Krish and Abhi forbade Rubi to leave home as they would leave no stone unturned to bring her mother back. In the meantime, Kedarnath and Binoy appeared. Krish was asked not to move out of the house as it was his Wedding Night. Kedarnath, Binoy and Abhi moved out in search of Protima. After an hour, when all of them were coming back downcast, Abhi could see a 'shadow' adjacent to a huge pond. In the offing, he ignored it, assuming it was a shadow of flora & fauna. He asked his Dad and Maternal Uncle (Binoy) to go home and he would follow soon. They forbade him to go close to the pond. When Kedarnath and Binoy reached home without Protima, all were quite upset. However, Kedarnath asked all of them not to worry as 'That cannot be cured must be endured'. He further added that it was late at night, they would try hard to discover her during the daybreak. Nevertheless, Debi & Rubi were saddened and weeping incessantly. Seeing them despondent, all enthusiasm and zeal were dampened. However, Abhi was quite suspicious of the shadow. As he went nearer, he heard the sound of soft mewls. In the offing, he was scared as there were a few murders and the appearance of ghosts a couple of years back. Recollecting the contribution of sister Debi, he remained undeterred, kept his calm and continued his march towards the pond to identify the sound. When he went quite close to it, he was jubilant to find Debi's Mom. He could take her back home despite her resistance. Seeing Protima with Abhi, all sounded ebullient and enthusiastic. Hell transformed into heaven soon. It appears that nothing in this world is so beautiful which gives us happiness and joy. It was indeed a wonderful sight. Krish was so enthusiastic he thought the moment was as enjoyable as the pretty face of the most beautiful woman of the world, the innocent smile of a child, the childhood days, the plays of Shakespeare, the verses of Kalidas, the epics of Homer and Milton, the poetry of Keats, the novels and

Bangla songs of Tagore. It is so because all these are so beautiful as to give perennial joy.

Minu and Aroti embraced Protima and expressed their happiness for her being by the side of her daughter and son-in-law on this auspicious occasion. Finding no way to escape, Protima decided to compromise with her destiny. Krish reiterated that the 'Wedding Night' may be postponed for the next day as his mother-in-law was tired and fatigued. Protima intervened and said: "Krish is the chip of the old block. He resembles his parents in character, attitude, nature and magnanimity. *Beta*, (son), no issue, I am all right. As suggested by your Mom, your '*Fulsajya* bed' will be decorated by didi and me". All of them were enthusiastic. Krish and Debi touched the feet of their elders.

Wedding Night and its Romanticism

The bed on the wedding night was decorated with fragrant colourful flowers to create a meadow like effect. A mirror hung on the corner wall of the bedroom. There were dim lights. Mild romantic music was turned on. Rose petals sprinkled from the door to the bed. An essential oil diffuser in the room was set to give a romantic aroma without the flame. This created a cosy, calm and amorous atmosphere. The curtains were dark coloured in order to avoid any outer distraction. On the corner of the room, there was a compact dining table, made of ivory, with two beautifully decorated chairs. On it, oysters, chocolates, and wine, considered aphrodisiacs (a food, drink and other things that stimulated sexual desire) were kept. Upon preparation of the room, Krish and Debi were pushed inside the room by Abhinandan, Rubi and other cousins of Krish. They were asked to latch the door inside lest somebody should hide under the bed when both of them would be lost in a fairy world. Everyone congratulated the couple with cheers and laughter, teasing them saying: 'see you the day after'.

Both of them were wonderstruck to see the marvellous decoration and beauty of the room. The tasteful decoration of the room looked exquisite and was eye-catching. Seeing all this, Krish could not restrain his wish, saying 'I wish every night is my wedding night'. Debi: 'What did you say?' Getting a bit scared but intellectually twisted, saying: 'I wish this day, I mean, our marriage anniversary, is celebrated for many many years'. However, while no sooner had Debi started walking than Krish took her on his lap. He asked her not to walk on the floor lest her feet should get dirty. He walked on the rose petals and dropped her softly on the bed. Getting scared, Debi being deeply intimidated by all the preparations, hugged Krish tightly. It was indeed a blessing in disguise for him. Krish felt that she was as soft as pure silk.

It was 2 am. Krish took out three different sets of attractive lingeries from his cupboard and gifted them to his gorgeous new bride. Handing them to Debi, he informed her that three types of costumes were given to her. There would be three sessions, a break after an hour, and she would change her costume, accordingly. Initially, she was vociferous as all these dresses were ultramodern. Krish reminded her promises. As per that tonight belonged to him only. When Debi appeared before him with a special Bra and Panties, Krish was not able to keep his eyes off of her. He looked at her without batting an eye. Every time he looked at her from top to bottom. He touched her to explore if he were Debi or 'Apsara' descended from Heaven. "You looked like a Barbie doll. Had you been so, I would have showcased you and gazed at you in astonishment day in and day out!" He forgot everything while eulogising her. He emphatically said: "I indeed do not have words to appreciate Him who has made you." After a couple of minutes, both of them were on the bed. Krish came close to her, hugged her and kissed in an affectionate and tender way that conveyed the message: 'We both are made for each other'. Thereafter, they shifted to the dining table. Wine is one of the most enjoyable beverages on the planet. A few brands of imported wines were arranged. They had wine with seafood.

After having a couple of glasses of wine, Debi took her glass of wine and drenched Krish and vice versa. He felt warm and cosy which made him relaxed. Debi felt tipsy, chatty and dizzy after having it. She told him while hugging that she would keep loving him eternally. Krish could understand the effect of the wine. While thanking 'wine', he placed Debi on his lap. He wanted to enquire about her out of fun: 'Are you Rambha, Menaka, Urvashi, Tilottama or Ghitachi?'

Debi retorted: Have you seen any of them?

Certainly, I have seen them, **Krish replied.**

Debi countered: 'When and where?'

Krish: Today at 2.15 am on my lap!

Debi: Haa .. Haa .. Haa .. Brilliant joke.

Krish: I am sure, if you were sent by Indra, in place of Menaka, you could have lured and incited Vishvamitra's lust and passion and broken his meditation much earlier than Menaka.

Debi: Hurled back: Are you taunting or flattering me? If it's flattering, there is no point in doing as you will get what you are yearning for. If you are taunting.......

Krish countered: No way. The wall clock struck 3 am. Krish reminded her that it was time to change her dress.

Debi mildly asked: Are you not enjoying my company in this outfit?

Krish retorted smilingly: For enjoying your company, no need for any ....

Debi: Don't be silly. Action is enough. Need not be translated into words!

Krish : I mean to say in my eyes, "you're the most beautiful one, no matter what you're wearing".

Another damsel appeared after a few minutes. Devi looked glittering, ravishing, sparkling and stunning with her costume.

Krish: I'm grateful to you for having such an incredible time with me. But in this very important hour, I mean one hour only, I wish to share certain serious issues with you which would positively help us when we grow old.

Debi: Are you going to assure me that in this session, there won't be any kind of pushing, touching, kissing, hugging, fondling, loving, caressing, spooning and canoodling?

Krish assured: Your beauty mesmerised me but your jokes sometimes puzzled me a lot. However, there would be nothing like that. For that the last session would suffice.

Krish narrated:

Why Sexagenarians Opt for Sense Gratification!

Krish: There are things that go without saying that both the husband and wife need trust, loyalty, fidelity, and love in order for their marriage to work successfully and happily until death. Many men, even after marriage, go outside for sense gratification. That is what I am going to share with you within this limited one hour. Please listen attentively which will be very useful from our so-called sexagenarian life until demise. It was once narrated by my grandpa. I was very close to my grandpa. Unfortunately, our association was short-lived. My grandpa and grandma had a wonderful chemistry. They were inseparable. They never used to do anything unilaterally. So much so that if one was missing from a place, people would often enquire about his/her absence as they were seldom without each other. People used to say that they are an inseparable duo, much like Bhagwan Ram and Lakshman. As soon as they turned fifty-five, my grandma considered herself old. It became a ritual for her to drag 'age' in almost every discussion. On the contrary, my grandpa used to say: *'Zindagi Zinda Dili Ka Hai Naam, Murda Dil Kya Khak Jiya Karte Hai'*, Quote by Imam Bakhsh Nasikh (Life is meant to be lively i.e. cheerfulness, excitement, happiness, eagerness, liveliness and mirth. Otherwise, it's like the dead hearts if all these are absent in one's life)! If my grandpa ever used to talk of something romantic, my grandma countered: 'We are getting old, it does not suit us'. She reiterated: "Are you infected with *'Bhimroti?*" (It denotes mental infirmity owing to old-age, sometimes shown by foolish infatuations). Earlier Grandpa had a monumental self-confidence. But, thereafter, owing to all these factors, his positivity got drastically affected. He used to say: 'We know what we are, but not know what we may be' ...... By: Shakespeare. It hurt my grandpa to a great extent. The 'love' they had, started vanishing. When grandpa died, I was in London. He left a sealed envelope for me. I was shocked to go through its contents. Presently, I would let you know in brief and the rest I would discuss with you later. My grandpa was initially addicted to tea, cigarettes, tobacco and alcohol. When he learned that all these had adverse effects on his health and many times they proved fatal to many people, he gave those up one by one and became a teetotaler. But he was unable to keep off sex with his better half despite his best endeavour. Unfortunately, he was forced to abandon it as grandma kept him at arm's length. Initially, he found it very difficult to keep off his craving for sense gratification and the happiness of the body. He was infected with sexually transmitted diseases. So, Debi, this mentality and attitude must be done away with as they spoil the cordial relationship and mar the morality of menfolk. My grandpa used to tell me: 'Krish, when you marry, you must balance everything equally irrespective of age factor. Your wife plays an integral part to keep you not only happy but also to maintain your righteousness and morality'.

Debi: 'A lot to know out of grandpa's experience which would positively help us in our married life. Thanks a lot, Krish, for discussing this with me and I assure you that I will positively bear in mind the advice of the wise old man.' But, my dear.....Krish was about to remind. 'Yes, I know, it is time to change,' Debi retorted. It was 1600 hours. Debi came with a sweet nightgown.

Last but not the least, Krish commenced the final session by gifting her a priceless 'diamond ring'. Debi was delighted with the gift but expressed with utmost sincerity that no gift was greater than getting him as her husband. Saying so, she bent herself to touch his feet. Krish was against it. He held her palms and forbade her to do so.

Debi reacted: It is my prerogative, you cannot deprive me of that.

Krish: You would always live in my heart. He also vowed that he would perpetually try to keep her happy, cheerful, gleeful and content. Krish moved to the dining table and gulped a glass of wine. Debi wanted to join. Krish reminded her that she donated her kidney recently. He asked her to hug him while he was enjoying wine. By doing that, she would automatically be under the impression that she was enjoying it too. Krish took out another bottle but kept it back when Debi showed resistance. Both of them went back to their floral bed and deepened their love and affection for each other in a more intimate and sexual way.

Soon after leaving the room, Debi visited the in-house Temple. She prayed to the Supreme, Eternal and Blissful Lord Krishna and conveyed her gratitude: for getting her mother back, an excellent home, parents, in-laws and, last but not the least, a noble-born husband - decent, virtuous and righteous. She cursed herself for casting aspersions on Lord Govinda for His not being helpful to them when they were in trials and tribulations. However, she could well understand that even Lord Krishna is bound by the destiny of human beings. She knelt down and apologised to Madhusudan for her temporary loss of faith in Him. Debi chanted: "You are undoubtedly attractive due to: wealth, power, fame, beauty, wisdom and renunciation. You stayed on this earth for 125 years, 5000 years ago, and played the role of a human being in every respect. Nevertheless you were unattached to all kinds of possessions. That is the reason you are the Supreme Godhead. No one is equal to You and nobody is greater than You!" She kept chanting Govinda's name and glory. Subsequently, she was in a state of Dhyaan and Meditation. When she opened her eyes, she found that all - parents, in-laws, Rubi, Bhai, Krish and Maa - were waiting for her outside the temple for breakfast.

Debi touched her elders' feet and proceeded to the breakfast room. While all were waiting for breakfast, Protima appeared and once again asked her if it was not advisable for her to leave that place. Upon asking the reason, she said that she was anyway working in the capacity of domestic help. Everybody there overheard her. All of them appeared before Protima. Minu and Aroti asked her if there was any problem being with her daughters, son-in-law and the rest of them. She kept quiet. Minu and Aroti told her steadfastly that she was going nowhere. She was not going to stay, but she would live there, and lend her helping hands to them. Protima enquired them if it would be prudent for her to work at her daughter's in-laws. Binoy babu retorted: "You must not throw your education and talent into a waste paper basket by doing minion jobs. Here your education and talent will be potentially tapped. You will maintain my 'bahi khata' (Ledger Account). The salary will be pari passu with your merit'. Protima countered: "Dada, no salary is required. I want to keep myself busy and above that I would happily contribute to my daughter's in-laws who are more than her parents". "Oh, you want to repay your daughter's debts. Didi, I don't know what you realise, but what Debi has done to the Mondal family can never be repaid by any one of us. On the contrary, I fail to understand why we are talking about all this. She is our daughter now. Last but not the least, please note that the salary will be paid to you. You will not be a parasite to anybody. Didi, you should establish your own identity. On the other hand, it will really be a great help to me as my Zamindari is in a dilapidated state for want of an honest, sincere and diligent person to look after the ledger account", snapped back by Binoy. Debi and Rubi were extremely delighted that their mother would not only be living with them but would also be assisting their Baba. All of them enthusiastically had their breakfast.

We should ignite our dormant inner energy and let it guide our lives. Men often become what they believe themselves to be. If I believe I cannot do something, it makes me incapable of doing it. But when I believe I can, then I acquire the ability to do it. Even if I didn't have it in the beginning.

— Mahatma Gandhi

All Indians are not Mir Zafar and Jaichand

One evening, Kedarnath was on the back of his horse to take a round of his estates. Debi and Rubi were adamant to accompany him. Despite his refutation, they kept requesting him. GGF apprised Debi that without the permission of her in-laws, he could not take her with him. In the meantime, Krish appeared on his horse and said smilingly: "How can I be somewhere while my beautiful wife is elsewhere!" Debi forbade him to crack cheap jokes in the presence of Baba. Kedarnath okayed that. Krish took Debi on his horse and all four left to visit their estates. They asked their Baba how the farmers were involved in paddy cultivation in their huge farms. In order to prepare the land, farmers got to work on the fields and finish all the preparations before the rainy season, transplant the paddy seedlings; maintain the field, etc. etc. They got down from the horse and started walking. Kedarnath moved ahead while on the horse. While farmers were transplanting the paddy seedlings, Debi and Rubi observed that a few Englishmen were walking and running on their paddy fields at random, massacring the plantations. They even made fun of the farmers who forbade them to do that. Debi and Rubi intervened and asked them strictly to get away from their farming lands. They got extremely annoyed and started abusing both the sisters badly. A fist-fight broke out.

When one of the Englishmen started pulling Debi's hair, the latter kicked his private part from behind. He fell down in no time yelling in pain. Rubi caught hold of the collar of one of the abusers and threatened to give a smacking punch. When the other came to his rescue, Debi, using Judo, pinned him down. Seeing all this, Abhi ran to their rescue. They got scared, humiliated, embarrassed and it was, in fact, a bolt from the blue to them to come across such strong and athletic Indian girls.

Seeing all this, an Englishman, who was a Zamindar on horseback, got down from his horse and started yelling at them: "How dare you touch your masters? Don't you, bloody Indians, know that all the Englishmen are your masters? You all are our slaves. You are supposed to look at our feet and not into our eyes. You are not going to be spared unless you seek apology".

Krish intervened: You are not our masters. You all are rather beggars, remember it. Your motherland is barren, uncultivable, and that is the reason why you are not able to grow anything in your own country. You should be kind enough to our country and countrymen who are giving you food, shelter and clothing, otherwise, you would have died of hunger.

The Englishman retaliated: "You have not given anything to us voluntarily, we have overpowered you and compelled you to surrender."

Krish: "Then 'jungle' should have been the best place for you to settle down. Because, you know, lions are powerful and they also overpower other animals and that is the reason why they live in the jungle. You Britishers are worse than animals."

He shouted at Krish: "You filthy bastard, damn, rotten Indian, don't know us in spite of the fact that we have been dominating you for more than 150 years. We rape your sistren at our own whims and fancies".

"The same thing is done by stray dogs", shouted Krish at the Zamindar.

Kedarnath noticed the outbreak of a fight, he rushed there without wasting time. When he heard the Englishman hurling all those abusive and derogatory words, he got down off his horse and yelled at him: "You will be living in a fool's paradise if you assume that all Indians are like Mir Zafar and Jaichand. So, keep your bloody mouth shut and get lost from here, otherwise I know how to get you out of here".

Britisher alleged: You bastards.......!

GGF warned: "Don't utter it any more!"

"I'll say a hundred and one times.. bastards..bastards......

Kedarnath moved close to him and slapped him tightly. He was taken aback. He never expected such audacity from an Indian. The rest of the Englishmen turned up to retaliate. Rubi, Debi and Krish were prepared to counter attack them. The Britishers left with the warning: "We shall drag you to the court of law and you will have to face the music."

When they went back home, Krish apprised everyone of the event of the day, eulogising the bravery and temerity of both the sisters. They indeed fought like ferocious lionesses. Debi's kick was indeed a visual treat. Abhi warned Krish to think before squabbling with Debi. Debi smilingly asked: "Come on Bhai, he is my husband, how come I would be so harsh and kick him as hard!" Saying so, she hugged Krish as a gesture of love. In the meantime, GGF appeared with Minu. Both GGF and Minu were quite appreciative of both their daughters. Rubi, in turn, spoke highly of their Baba who were instrumental in their learning of all the warfares. "But, Beta, to learn and to fight gallantly in the battlefield are two different ball games", Kedarnath said in response. All of them engaged in merry-making till late evening.

Court Scene with Brief Interrogation

After a couple of days, Kedarnath received a summons from the court. Debi, Rubi and Binoy accompanied Kedarnath to the court. The District Magistrate (DM) seemed to be an Indian or an Anglo-Indian. Armstrong was the Englishman who filed a suit against

Kedarnath. He alleged to the DM that Mr Kedarnath manhandled his men irrationally and illogically, who were working on the agricultural field. His men, who were youngsters, could have retaliated, but pocketed the insult as Mr Kedarnath was an elderly person. When he, Armstrong, intervened and tried to settle the issue amicably: "My Lord, he badly abused and slapped me. I was humiliated, insulted and made to eat a humble pie in front of my own workers and other bloody Indians. He must first suffer punishment before his complaints could be heard. He should be put behind the bar to prevent him and other Indians from indulging in such humiliating ways to innocent persons". The Magistrate, at the very outset, warned Mr Armstrong for dictating to him the nature of punishment to be given which is absolutely the prerogatives of the Magistrate. He also asked him not to use abusive words and maintain the court's decorum. The Magistrate asked Mr Kedarnath to speak in his defence, if any. Kedarnath pleaded: "My Lord, my daughter, Debi, wants to speak before me with your humble acquiescence as she was physically present and was made a scapegoat by Mr Armstrong and his peasants". Permission granted!

Debi: "My Lord, my sister and I were there with our father on our farms on that day to get to know about rice cultivation on our agricultural fields. Our dad moved ahead soon after telling us alpha and omega of it. We remained there on our farms while the peasants were busy doing their work. We noticed suddenly a few persons were walking and running continuously at random with the purpose of messing with our farmers and ruining our paddy fields. They were making a mockery of the farmers' request as well. They were also abusing them in English. One of them pelted stones at them. While my sister and I forbade them to do so, they started abusing both of us too in their language, English, assuming that we don't understand the language. After some time, one of them said loudly: 'Go away from here, otherwise, I will fuck you'. Saying this, he started pulling my hair. I had no alternative, my Lord, but to kick him hard in an attempt of self-defence. While two others came to his rescue, my sister, Rubi, held one of them and threatened dire consequences if they touched her *Didi* again. In the meantime, Mr Armstrong turned up and was abusive. (Debi told the Magistrate in detail whatever happened thereafter.) The Magistrate was surprised and could not believe what was told. He enquired of Debi: "How both of you, being females, managed to deal with them. My Lord, with your permission, may I ask my sister, Rubi, to come here and stand with me? While the Magistrate was about to answer, all the people present there made a fervent request to the Magistrate: 'We all want to see her.' OK, OK. Upon arriving, Rubi humbly responded: "My Lord, it is all about courage and to do something in self-defence. If our countrymen were blessed with a father like us, who got us trained in Judo, Karate and techniques of warfare, I am hundred per cent sure that we would never have lost our sovereignty". Seeing the Magistrate not much convinced of their bravery, Rubi, being innocent and juvenile, pleaded humbly: "My Lord, with your due permission, we are prepared to give a demo if any Englishmen are ready for that." All those persons who attended the hearing started clapping and shouting in admiration 'bravo, bravo', long live our Debi and Rubi. The Magistrate asked all of them to remain quiet. He ordered Rubi to maintain the court's decorum. Debi apologised to the Magistrate on behalf of Rubi. The written copy of the decision (an order) will be handed over to you, Mr Armstrong, after the hearing. All those persons, who abused barbarically and fought with Debi and Rubi, will be summoned shortly in the Court, retorted the Magistrate. The Magistrate summoned Mr Kedarnath for his statement. Without wasting any time of the Hon'ble Court, the Magistrate informed him that he got to know what had happened from his daughters and how both of them reacted. He asked him whether he would like to add anything over and above what was told by his daughters to this Hon'ble Court. No, My Lord, responded Kedarnath. I was one with my daughters that Mr Armstrong's abusive languages were totally uncalled for. 'But, at the same time, Mr Kedarnath should not have manhandled'. The Magistrate warned and cautioned Mr Armstrong against using derogatory words and hurting the dignity of Mr Kedarnath. But since he committed it for the first time, he had been relieved of all legal consequences.

Mr Kedarnath, it was a war of words. But you were instrumental in aggravating it by manhandling Mr Armstrong. Hence, you were penalised Rs.250, failing which you would be behind the bar for two days. "My Lord, may I know the very reason for penalising me?" It was for slapping Mr Armstrong. "My Lord, if the price of a slap is Rs.250, I am prepared to pay Rs.500 with My Lord's permission to give him another slap on his other cheek." All the people in the Court were stunned and surprised by the exemplary courage and temerity exhibited by Mr Kedarnath; most of the Indians clapped ceaselessly and appreciated him immensely.

Conclusion

What led our countrymen to fall prey to British Suzerainty:

From an Author's Perspective

All I heard about India was '*Satyameva Jayate*'; 'Unity in Diversity'; 'Honesty is the Best Policy' and 'if someone slaps you on one cheek, offer the other one to him'. Most of our people and our so-called leaders hardly thought about the welfare of the country; had the least love for their country and were working at cross purposes. We were fighting among ourselves, hating and envying one another upon race, community, caste, class, education and on many more issues. Unfortunately, these were not new phenomena. All this has been in our society since times immemorial.

The British did not start ruling our country overnight. It happened gradually. If one State of India was struggling with the British, another one was not only happy that the British were destroying their competitors but also tried their best to cause harm to their brethren in the other State by being in collusion with the British to ensure that the State acknowledged British suzerainty. Nevertheless it went on for a long long time. How come roughly 3,000 British soldiers conquered a country of over 150 million people. This is certainly hard to swallow. However, It would not be hard to digest once we know how the country was infested with traitors like Mir Zafar and Jaichand. Mir Zafar was the commander-in-chief of the Nawab of Bengal, Siraj-ud-Daula. The British East India Company led by Robert Clive defeated Siraj-ud-Daula's forces with the help of Mir Jafar during the Battle of Plassey in 1757. There are numerous examples of these types of people even today. There is a Proverb: '*Barbad Gulistan Karne Ko Bas Ek Hi Ullu Kafi Tha. Agar Har Shaakh Pe Ullu Baitha Hai, Anjam-e-gulistan Kya Hoge*' (Quote by Allama Iqbal). It is an old saying which roughly translates: 'An owl is enough to destroy a garden, what will be the fate of the garden, if there is an owl on every branch'. Hence, the answer is self-explanatory.

The British came to India as traders. Their chief motive was to make a fortune. They needed political power to carry on their trade. They imposed heavy taxes on the peasants. The Indian goods lost their demand because the market was flooded with imported English goods. These goods were free of import duties. The British thus ruined the skilled Indians. They had dethroned the Indian rulers by taking advantage of their rivalries. Slowly and steadily they spread their empire all over India.

The country was flooded with betrayer, back-stabbers, turncoat and traitors. They were spread in different parts of India. The British conquered India by following the policy: 'Divide and Rule'. They often addressed India as the 'Jewel of the British Crown' and rightfully so. Many foreign rulers viz. Mughals, Afghans, Iranians, British, Portuguese and French attacked us, plundered us, looted us, lived here for centuries and destroyed our monuments & temples - replacing them with theirs. They disseminated their barbarism, parochialism and rusticity. What our ancestors did! Nothing really! It is said that: If each Indian hurled a stone, the Britishers, who were a handful, would have run away. Many of them (Indians) instead helped the Britishers while the others became silent spectators. The British managed to overpower us because of our internal disputes, dirty politics and unfortunately thanks to our being proponents of 'non-violence (*ahimsa*).

However, there were a few valiant, among them Netaji Subhash Chandra Bose, whose defiance of British authority made him a hero, though an unsung one. Unlike most other freedom fighters, he had a non-compromising attitude on the issue of Independence of India. He firmly believed that Independence had to be fought for and cannot be achieved by means of 'non-violence'. He epitomised exceptional courage and patriotism. "Give me your blood, I will give you freedom." This slogan ignited patriotism in many Indian hearts. Even today, this slogan reminds us of this great personality - Netaji Subhash Chandra Bose. He had the farsightedness long before achieving Independence, that the British would hand over 'divided India'. It was never acceptable to Netaji. That was the reason why he reiterated: '*Aami chai okhondo bharater purno sadhin.*' It can be loosely translated: 'I want complete independence of undivided India.' This slogan was a commitment and not a fake promise made by most of our present leaders sitting at home and bringing about a civil war & bloodshed among the innocent people.

His famous battle cry - Dilli Chalo - was a great pointer to his determination with which the Azad Hind Fauz fought against Britishers. Today's youths must be taught in schools and colleges about one of the great freedom fighters like Netaji who advocated the spirit of 'Nation First'. He was deeply inspired by the Bhagavad Gita in his fight against the British. It is a matter of exuberance for all of us that India is emerging as a superpower under the leadership of the present Prime Minister Shri Narendra Modi as once dreamt by Subhash. Netaji and love for his country are perennial which might end only with the world.

***

SINGAPORE -- A COUNTRY OF DELIGHT

Singapore - A Country of Delight

Introduction

As my daughter and son-in-law have been staying in Singapore for the last more than eight years, I had the opportunity to be in that country and its vicinity a few times. The country is indeed a paragon of cleanliness, regulation, a firm hand, control and self-discipline. The country is truly an example of: 'Cleanliness is Next to Godliness'. Though the country is largely dependent on imports for perishable and non-perishable; consumable and non-consumable items, nevertheless its economy is superlative. It would be very difficult to convince all those about the country who have not personally or physically experienced it. Thomas Fuller rightly said: "A blind man will not thank you for a looking glass."

Purification of the Sea Water

We all are well aware of the dreadful water crisis worldwide. When water is scarce, sewage systems can fail which may lead to the threat of contracting diseases like intestinal, lung, cholera and other infections. It is obvious that climate change disrupts weather patterns, leading to extreme weather events, unpredictable water availability and contamination of water supplies. Many countries depend on an increasingly erratic monsoon for its water requirements since there is no endeavour to conserve rain and flood water. It is often observed that roadside taps keep running even when not in use, leading to huge wastage of scarce water. Climate change also contributes to scarcity of water. If rain and flood water are potentially conserved, it is likely to relieve pressures on water resources. Water is, in fact, the basic necessity for the survival of all life forms that exist on earth. That is the reason why earth is the only planet that supports life. Earth is also known as the blue planet, which is an abundance of water. About 70 per cent of the surface of the earth is covered with water. But a very little part of the whole is actually attainable and useful for us. Humans use it carelessly like it has no value at all. To conclude, scarcity of water has disastrous effects on humans, animals as well as the flora and fauna.

We are conscious of the indispensability of water in keeping our houses neat and tidy, alongside its innumerable other usages. Hence, I enlighten my readers as to how the people of Singapore keep their country as glittering as priceless diamonds. One of the factors which attributes to this is abundant water resources. It is one of the few countries which have successfully attempted to mitigate scarcity of water. Except marine animals, no other form of life can consume or live on saline water. I shall eulogise the Government of Singapore who has not only recognised the value of water but has also made tremendous progress and achievement by converting saline into drinkable water.

They have abundant indigenous water resources of their own. How? The process is called 'desalination' of the sea water. It is being used extensively in Singapore as a result of which it is able to provide people with much needed freshwater. They are quite successful in desalination. Currently, this process is one of the most successful means to obtain fresh water for human consumption and usages for multifarious purposes. In Singapore, desalination is done through a process called reverse osmosis, which separates water from salts and minerals. As desalination is not dependent on rainfall, it makes their water supply more stable regardless of weather conditions. They have indeed done a Herculean task to this effect. In view of this, the houses do not even require water purification devices. The tap water is as good as mineral water. With abundant water supply, they are able to clean their roads and also to maintain a green environment.

Let me narrate an interesting episode from my recent visit. Once while I was in the bus stand, the road was being cleaned with water by that time. I had to miss a few buses in order to watch how much care and interest the road cleaner was taking to clean the road. It is incredible. This has enabled them to get rid of dust and filth. It is indeed a country known for greenery and immaculacy. Having clean water is vital to individual health and for the needs of our environment, it is the foundation of all life and crucial to sanitation. I was indeed amazed to observe that even a heavy storm is dust free. So much so, since the country is free from filth, the trees look gorgeously green, beautifying the country all the more.

I was really surprised when my daughter said that once officials from the water department came to check the reason for consumption of more water for a couple of months. They came to detect if there was any leakage or wastage which led to consumption of an increased amount of water than they generally consumed. Thereafter, they questioned the very reason for it. They were satisfied when they got to know that it was due to a few relatives staying over for a few days. In spite of the fact that they have abundant water resources, they not only discourage its wastage but also ensure that nobody should indulge in any kind of misuse contributing to a potential crisis.

Natural Disaster cannot Jeopardise Traffic System

While I was there, it rained heavily followed by ceaseless thunderstorms for a week or so. I was upset about our inability to move outside owing to possibilities of numerous hazards like blockage of roads, traffic jams, water logging, uprooting of trees, and disrupting transport & communications services. I started cursing nature and my destiny as well for disrupting our tight schedule. But to my surprise and dismay, as soon as I moved out to inspect the status, I was literally bewildered to find that everything was as before. I started rubbing my eyes in utter disbelief. I stepped a few yards away from the apartments and stood on the main road to further explore the real situation. Perhaps the foremost ground of this incredulity is having lived in a country where politicians and bureaucrats are from privileged backgrounds with least interest in understanding the well being of its citizens. 'Privilege' in this context denotes the legal exemption from some duty, burden, attendance or liability to which others are subjected. Water logging, traffic jams, cracks, chuckholes and uprooting of trees are out of question.

Sincerity and Honesty

Integrity and probity of the administration is unparalleled. Once my son-in-law shared with us that he was refunded a few thousands SGD by the Government of Singapore upon working out that the Government received a huge sum in the form of income-tax returns. It is, in fact, incredible, beyond imagination.

No Stray Animals & Beggars are on the Road

Many countries often face the irreparable issue of stray animals. Despite various efforts, this remains a huge challenge to the government bodies across the world. Many countries where there are stray animals like dogs, cows, buffaloes, oxen, pigs, etc. The problem of stray animals has existed for many years but not much has been done by the concerned government department. There is a constant threat of rabies as well as dog bites hanging over the heads of the citizens. Stray cows and buffaloes too often block traffic and create a nuisance. It has also been observed that they frequently cause road accidents and attack the public or traffic abruptly. Nomadic people and gipsies pitch tents on roads, cook, wash clothes and even use the roads for urinals and defecation resulting in an absolute violation of hygiene and roadside beauty and decorum. In such countries, the homeless people too are extremely troublesome. They indulge in various corrupt practices in the form of kidnapping babies using them as a means of their livelihood. Many even take up begging as a profession. It has become an age-old social phenomenon in many countries. Many a time an entire family is involved in this profession. Some of them go as far as posing to be handicapped in order to attract the attention and sympathy of the passersby. It is a blot on Government and society. It is shameful and degrading for the country which must be stopped with an iron hand. In many countries, the system has been politicised to suit the vote bank and hence is being continued. Singapore, however, is totally safe in this respect. There are no stray animals; no beggars in sight to create nuisance. The question of gipsies or nomadic people anywhere in Singapore is tantamount to a fairy tale. It is incredible that every inhabitant parks his/her car in the allotted space, else he/she will have to pay a heavy penalty. They can never escape penalty by bribing a petty sum to officials since officers in Singapore are well paid and far from corruption. Believe me, there is not even .1 per cent exaggeration. I am explaining my own experience of staying in this country.

One fine morning, I set out of the flat to go to the seashore. On the way, I was stunned to watch a man smoking while standing at a corner of the road. Although I was not pleased watching him smoking, yet delighted to observe that each time he was dropping the ash of the cigarette into the nearby garbage pail. It was indeed credulous and unbelievable. While sitting on the sea beach, I wondered if I were in a fairy land! That really not only speaks of the beauty and cleanliness of Singapore but also exhibits how much affinity each citizen has towards his/her motherland. Markets have fixed prices and there is no room for any negotiations which talks a great deal about the authenticity of the pricing. No *feriwalas (hawkers)* are allowed to sell any consumable or non-consumable items. While brooding over all these, I was lost in a reverie for a while.

Culture in Singapore

Singapore's name is derived from the phrase "Singa Pura", which literally means 'Lion City'. The Republic of Singapore is a sovereign island country. Its capital is Singapore, a (city-state) in maritime South-east Asia. Its currency is Singapore dollar (SGD). Presently, January 2023, one SGD dollar is equivalent to INR 62. It well denotes the status of a country's economy. It is immaculately located in South-east Asia. It is a sunny, tropical island. It is a city of not just one island, but 64. It's a city of man-made waterfalls. The city-state is 710 square kilometres and inhabited by five million people from four major communities - Chinese (majority), Malay, Indian and Eurasian. Its official languages are English, Malay, Mandarin and Tamil. The daily temperature range has a minimum usually not falling below 23-25 degree C during the night and maximum not rising above 31-33 degree C during the day. May and June have the highest average monthly temperature 27.8 degree C and December and January are the coolest 26 degree C. It is a diverse country. People of several faiths coexist. There are five major religions: Buddhism, Christianity, Islam, Taoism and Hinduism. A small number of Jews, Jains and Sikhs also live here. The percentage-wise population is: Chinese : 74.5, Malaise : 13.5, Indians : 9 and 3 : Euro-Asian, Arab and tribals.

History of Singapore

In 1819, the British East-India Company bought Singapore. The Britishers used to grow opium in Kolkata, the erstwhile Calcutta, and processed it in Singapore. Britishers used Chinese for this nature of work. Chinese were working in the opium factory which was far away from their home and there were no sources of entertainment for them. They became drug addicts. Thousands of opium addicts were living in Singapore. Because of drug addiction, the percentage of crime went up. People turned to theft. In 1941, it was estimated that there were about 16,500 opium addicts in Singapore. The 1940's was the period of the Second World War.

On 15th February 1942, the Japanese invaded Singapore. Singapore surrendered to the Japanese. During the next three and a half years, the Japanese ruled over Singapore which led to the complete annihilation of culture, tradition, way of life, the ideas, customs, social behaviour and economy of Singapore. Civilians were murdered, enemy soldiers decapitated, prisoners and patients in the hospitals were burnt alive, slaughtered and butchered mercilessly. The savagery and massacre of the local Chinese population was truly shocking. Many prisoners of war were subjected to barbarous punishments. Thousands of people were used as forced labour. Thousands of women were brought from Korea, China, Indonesia and Malaysia to Singapore where they were available to the Japanese soldiers. Women were being used as a commodity. Buildings were heavily destroyed. There was large-scale poverty, high unemployment and the place was crawling with diseases. There were acute food shortages and people were starving to death. All along there was massive crime, violence and Singapore became a slum colony.

Fortunately for Singapore, in 1945, the British defeated the Japanese. The latter lost the war and withdrew from Singapore.

During that time, there were more than 30,000 opium addicts. Thomas Raffles turned Singapore into a free port. In passing ships, they would not have to pay any fees. This led to free trade in Singapore. Most ships in Singapore have refilling stations. People made their both ends meet by means of stealing, robbery and indulging in other corrupt practices. But the British rule of Singapore slowly receded. In 1959, there was a full scale election in Singapore. The young leader, Lee Kuan Yew, Secretary General of People's Action Party (PAP), became the first Prime Minister of Singapore. Thereafter, Singapore merged with the Federation of Malaya to form Malaysia in 1963. Owing to a number of complications viz. Intolerance, racial differences, social bigotry and political prejudices between Singapore's governing People's Action Party (PAP) and Malaysia's Alliance Party resulted in Singapore's expulsion from Malaysia.

An Independent Republic

Soon after becoming an independent republic on 9 August 1965, the country adopted a parliamentary system where the Prime Minister is the head. Initially, the country faced extreme poverty, massive unemployment, overpopulation, illiteracy, drug addiction, civil war, bloodshed and housing crisis. Later, however, it launched a modernisation programme and focussed on developing large public housing estates and investing heavily on education and infrastructure. By the 1990's, it became one of the world's most prosperous nations.

Singaporean culture has transformed greatly over the years. The indigenous culture of Singapore was originally influenced by Austronesian people who arrived here from Taiwan. During the course of many years, Singapore's culture was further influenced and inspired by multiple Chinese dynasties and other Asian countries which have eventually given shape to the Singaporean culture that we see today. Singapore's philosophy is simple: either you take off your shoes or clean my carpet. There is no compromise. While meeting or departing a Singaporean formally or informally, one must ensure to shake hands firmly. A slight bow while shaking hands is a mark of respect. Gender discrimination is a serious offence and sometimes it is construed as a legal infringement. Hence, one must pay respect to every person irrespective of gender and religion. Tipping is not customary in Singapore. It is not only discouraged but also not accepted by the one being tipped. Casual clothes (shorts, t-shirts, flip-flops) are acceptable in most public places. There are many countries where even laws are flouted in this respect despite the fact that there are police forces, courts and fundamental rights. They talk of people looking at the girls and women because of their short or casual clothing hence justifying the misdemeanour. Ironically, they also advise their parents and husbands to clothe them properly perhaps to avoid vulture looks of the men folk at them. Here, however, such misconduct by anyone is considered a serious offence liable to strict legal punishments. As a result, one would seldom find cases of unsolicited staring, let alone eve-teasing. Politics is not a hot topic of discussion in Singapore. That is one of the reasons why there are no differences of opinions, conflicts, disputes among them.

Heaven for Tourists

The country is undoubtedly a paragon of beauty from all perspectives. Its beaches, fun theme parks, shopping malls and world class hotels are picturesque which makes it one of the most popular tourist destinations too. Over and above, Singapore is not only safe to visit but also most enjoyable as well. It is clean, full of energy, greenery and has a pleasant climate. The island does not have definite or precise seasons like summer, spring, autumn and winter. Nevertheless, the average climate is neither hot nor cold. I had also experienced that when it was a bit warm, it was immediately followed by torrential rains. Locals are friendly and welcoming. There is so much to see and explore here and there. For me, It is the safest country on the planet. Women can safely walk on the road without an iota of fear, even at midnight. It is known for its tremendous opulence, gorgeous beaches and fantastic shopping malls. One need not worry much about things like petty theft or any kind of crime.

Public Transport is as good as a Cab

Additionally, the tiny country is the cleanest in Southeast Asia with highly regulated cabs. Undoubtedly, it is an expensive country. However, it is really worth spending money and enjoying life. While taxi fraud and transportation grift are problematic in most of the countries in South-east Asia, you will never come across such issues in Singapore. Public transport is cheap, clean, safe and efficient. Transportation services are the fastest and most convenient method of travelling around the country for tourists and visitors. The taxis will use metres, and they are equally safe even at night. One need not wait for long to get taxi/cab services. Drivers can speak English well with understandable accents and are well-behaved as well as educated. They seldom talk while on duty. Nevertheless they respond politely, gently and nicely. Frequency of buses and public transportation is quite appreciable. Double decker buses are popular. Since many people in Singapore speak English, one should not have a problem. The rides are clean and hassle free. Buses are neat & tidy, well maintained and have air conditioning. Singapore's MRT line will get you anywhere you want to go. It is a fast and efficient way to get around. Commuters are well-behaved. There are no conductors in buses. Sometimes drivers need to serve the impaired commuters. Drivers will happily leave their seats and ensure that these people are seated properly. Actually, the beauty is that nobody has to monitor. People are so responsible and honest that they need not be invigilated. Drivers also notice while sitting on the driving seats if passengers are facing any difficulties while charging their debit cards. There are no seats reserved for senior citizens and women. Generally, seats are available in the buses. But once during peak hours, my wife and I had to stand. I was surprised to find that two local young ladies got up and offered their seats to us. Although it was a petty issue, however, in other countries, passengers would often occupy reserved seats and pretend to either doze off or be extremely busy talking on phones in front of senior citizens which is extremely insensitive.

If someone has to cover long distant areas, they mostly use bicycles. They will cover a few kms on their bicycles; leave their bicycles locked or unlocked at a nearby bus stand and go to their destination by bus. While coming back, they will pick their bicycles and go back on them. Their cycles are safe. What a country and her inhabitants!

Flirtation and Teasing Are Unknown

Eve-teasing or harassment are absolutely out of the question. Solo female travellers too are safe on roads even at midnight. Every minute of the tourists is potentially used as they do not have the fear to encounter political unrest, terrorism, riot, accidents and VIP movements. Tourists are indeed lucky that they rarely combat any such nefarious activities. One should respect the local culture as it is and avoid making a face at those who are in skimpy dresses. You will also not see many people indulge in kissing on the road. Hence, if you are travelling with your partner, keep the PDA (public display of affection) to a minimum. It denotes kissing, loving, touching, embracing or hugging that are given in public.

That might invite stares. This country is literally fairly conservative. There is a law against indecency in public. So, by all means display your affection, but never ever cross the line to becoming indecent and uncomfortable for others. The country has become figuratively a heaven for tourists only because of the fact that it has its own set of rules and regulations. It heavily criminalises many actions which are considered petty crimes or no offence acts in most other countries. That is the reason why the country is devoid of robbery, assault, forgery, smuggling, embezzlement, drug trafficking, lynching, raping, etc. The general offences of Singapore are: possession of chewing gum without a doctor's prescription; walking or crossing the street unlawfully, not using the zebra crossing, or not following the traffic lights, or not using the pedestrian sidewalk; smoking in public places especially where 'No smoking' signs are put up for restriction; urinating or spitting in public; littering on the roads instead of using the dustbin; committing a fight in a public place, such as bar brawls or street commotions. If one happens to travel a long distance in Singapore, there is nothing to worry about restrooms. Every few miles, clean washrooms, dustbins and hand sanitizers are available. It is undoubtedly a sort of great relief to travellers and visitors.

My Experience - Changi Airport & its Surrounding

Changi Airport is indeed a model of beauty. Despite the usual hustle and bustle, visitors are as blithe as a bee. It is one of the world's busiest airports by international passengers and cargo traffic yet rated as the world's best airport by Skytrax several times. It is the first airport in the world to hold the accolade for eight consecutive years. Changi Airport is renowned for its unparalleled global connectivity. We travelled by bus to go to Airport. The bus dropped us close to the entry point of the Airport - Terminal-2. We were really amazed to know that visitors could travel inside the

Airport without buying any tickets. Surprisingly, they can visit up to the counter, issuing boarding passes, take-in luggage, etc. Singapore Airport is a civilian international airport. It is one of the world's busiest and cleanest airports. The airport consists of four terminals. It has a wide range of restaurants, eateries, bars comprising several unique cuisines and drinks from all over the world. One can go shopping, play games, watch a free movie, relax in the breathtaking gardens and sit-down restaurants. Many eateries in each terminal are open 24 hours. Some lounges offer shower facilities and nap rooms at an extra cost. One will find plenty to explore in the hundreds of airport stores. All the greenery, natural light and beautification throughout the airport mesmerise visitors by its unique and unsurpassable beauty. Visitors feel like they are in a fairy land. Travellers regret upon leaving the Airport being deprived of the wonderful privileges anywhere else.

With its iconic architecture, lush indoor gardens, one of a kind of attraction, and unique shopping and dining options, Jewel Changi Airport is a multi-dimensional lifestyle destination for Singapore residents and international travellers to enjoy. A hallmark of Changi Airport's growth and its stunning beauty is unparalleled. It is said that "Beauty is in the eye of the beholder". This saying is used to express the fact that not all people have the same opinions about what is attractive. It differs from person to person. On the contrary, I make an exception when I talk about the stunning beauty of Jewel Changi Airport of Singapore. Its iconic architecture and all round beauty are loveable by all and sundry. The people of other countries, who earlier used to boast of the beauty of their airports, having visualised Jewel Changi Airport, may want to rethink. It would have also changed the travellers' habits and preferences.

The Jewel comprises 135,700 sqm complex, a total of 10 storeys - five above ground and five basement storeys. Jewel connects

Changi Airport's terminals, thus improving the experience for airport users. Bus Terminals are available at the basements of the first, second, and third terminals, providing direct access to Singapore. The glass dome of Jewel is 37.08 m high. It is a domed glass complex with a waterfall cascading through the centre of its roof. The train track ran straight through the centre of the dome. The waterfall running through it collecting the rainwater that falls on the entire building and funnelling it into the structure through the oculus is nothing but fantastic. Since Jewel is part of the Changi Airport, it's open to visitors 24/7. Kids and adults alike will really love this show. The main highlight of Jewel is the HSBC Rain Vortex, a 40-metre high indoor waterfall which is also the world's tallest. There is an enchanting music and light show. Now, this was a rare occasion where I was indeed wishing for more time to spend at the airport! In fact, I must admit that any amount of adjectives is unable to do justice to the stunningness of this place. I am sure and sanguine once you are there physically, you will love gazing at it for hours together. We often hear that people visit the Taj Mahal along with their beloved. But I am sure once you visit the Jewel Changi Airport, you would be infatuated with taking your loved one to Singapore and visit the Jewel Changi Airport (JCA) together. However, if you happen to visit JCA with your beloved, you might miss her company as she will be so mesmerised by the uniqueness and beauty of JCA, she will give least importance to your presence.

Singapore Flyer: Located in Marina Bay, Singapore Flyer is easily accessible. It is Asia's largest observation wheel. It can fit 172 tennis courts or 1,120 parking lots. It is in the form of a Capsule: each capsule is 4 x 7 metres - about the size of a city bus. There are 28 capsules in toto. Each of which can carry up to 28 passengers. The total capacity per revolution is 784 passengers.

Flying Boarding

The Flyer has an overall height of 165 metres (541 ft) and was once the world's tallest Ferris wheel. There are two synchronised doors and two platforms on each side - making it easy for the elderly and those in wheelchairs to get on and off. Each rotation is about 30 minutes. Singapore Flyer is designed and built to rotate smoothly under various wind conditions at high altitudes. On board Singapore Flyer, one can see up to 45 kilometres away. From the flyer, you will be able to see Changi Airport, Sentosa Island and even parts of Malaysia and Indonesia. On Valentine's Day, it provides an additional rotation (30 minutes) and a glass of Champagne each. Enjoy the quiet serenity inside the rainforest. It is a one of a kind experience which no one should miss.

Mesmerising Beauty – Sea of the East-Coast

In Singapore, I stayed with my daughter and son-in-law at Neptune Court, adjacent to East Coast beach. While staying in Singapore, I visited the beach two to three times a day and spent long hours on its coast. Sitting on its shore, I started deliberating about the fact that we need to pay heavily in the form of various taxes for every odd thing in our day-to-day life. But it is the sea which is like a bountiful mother that offers delight, jubilation and exultation and we remain in seventh heaven sitting on its coast, without paying anything in return. It would have been sheer ungratefulness if I had not reciprocated. Thus, its mesmerising beauty inspired me to write on her eternal beauty and its surroundings. Although I do believe that what I have proposed to do is just a drop in the ocean. But the ocean would be less because of that missing (by Mother Teresa). Her panoramic, scenic and picturesque beauty is, in fact, inexplicable in words. They can only be visualised, felt and enjoyed. No words of their glorification are fit enough. There is also a saying: "Loneliness is the distressing feeling of being alone or separated." But East-Coast is such a beach along with a captivating park where I spent hours sitting all alone on its shore, and wondered why I had not felt lonely and isolated. We realise sitting on its shore that there is no greater wealth in this world than peace of mind.

"Life is like a Sea;
We are Moving Endlessly.
Nothing Stays with us.
What remains are just the Memories of Some People
who Touched us as Waves.

.... Anonymous

The sea shore is so pleasant and perhaps it has the magic wand that sitting on its beach inspired me to think, write and forget about life's agony and pain & suffering. But as soon as I resume writing, the sea shore is so gratifying that I become in a state of catnap. After about a few minutes or so, when the sea water wets my legs, and having felt a bit cold, I immediately get up and am full of praise for the sea breeze, the sea waves, the coast, rocky and dramatic or soft and sandy. I am a philogynist. If given a choice between staying a few days on the sea shore or spending some time with a pretty and attractive woman somewhere else, I shall really be at my wit's end to make the right choice. However, as you know the beauty of mortal creatures is not perennial. And especially in the case of a female romantic companion, it is for sure: "Beauty and modesty cannot go together." The change of her temperament is like the weather of Delhi: Where 'Morning shows the day' is generally not applicable. The morning may be sunny with 40 degree C and on the same day, the evening becomes breezy and cool in the wake of a heavy rain and thunderstorm, lowering the temperature to a 15 degree C. which becomes insupportable. On the contrary, on the seashore, the change of climatic conditions is equally pleasant and will not make much difference to our merrymaking.

Maybe that is one of the reasons why Robinson Crusoe could lead a successful, wonderful and popular life all alone on the banks of the seas. He was stranded on an uninhabited island for a few years, enjoyed and survived all alone. Alain Gerbeault rightly said: "I wanted freedom, open air and adventure. I found it on the sea". In fact, the ocean can be described in an endless number of ways. It is refreshing, enchanting, beautiful and humbling. It's gigantic, massive, mysterious and terrifying. Its magnificence has inspired countless poets, authors, lovers - both successful and unsuccessful - novelists, films, documentaries and songs. Its beauty is so enchanting and captivating that it always transforms our sorrow into joy. Hence, if at all there is heaven on this earth, it is nowhere, but on the beach of the East Coast; it is nowhere than the beach of the East Coast. Life is indeed like the ocean. It can be tranquil or harsh, rough or smooth, but in the end, it is always beautiful and full of joy. It has a peculiar quality. Literally speaking, no company is needed to enjoy their mesmerising effects as the ocean stirs the heart, inspires the imagination and brings everlasting joy to the mind and soul. The water of the sea in the East-Coast is blue as it is dust free; when the sun reflects on its water, it becomes multi-coloured. The waves are proud of their strength and beauty. They are in a continual set of motion - every time rising up to touch the sky, splashing amongst themselves, losing their motion and then rising again with full force crashing onto the rocks. Unfortunately, it is noteworthy when the waves strike hard on the shore relentlessly but have to go back wailing for not being able to cross beyond its shore. Nevertheless they never give up their endeavour of crossing beyond its shore.

There are no hawkers, barrow boys, travelling salesmen and vendors to spoil, mar and altogether disfigure the bank or make its water dirty and stained. There it is illegal to feed wild birds. As a result, there are very few common birds like crows, house sparrows, pigeons, *shaliks* - Indian *mynah* - not to talk of owls, eagles, vultures, etc. They believe that they are harbingers of tarnishing the surroundings. They may also cause panic, discomfort, fear and anxiety to all the visitors, especially children and aged ones.

Wild Birds have no Room in Singapore

One late afternoon, sitting on the chair, made of stone, I was engrossed in the beauty of the seashore and its surroundings. It was drizzling with a pleasant breeze shrouded with semi-darkness that made the atmosphere romantic which prompted me to prolong my stay. There were a flock of underfed *shaliks* hopping hither and thither exploring fodder. The fodder was hardly available since insects, ants, flies, fleas, louse, pests, beetles, etc., are invisible in the country. I was indeed surprised when one of them came close to me and started tapping its beaks on my feet. Initially, I ignored assuming that maybe it was by mistake as I was humming the Bollywood song with intense feelings at that time: "*Yeh Raaten, Yeh Mausam, Nadi Ka Kinara, Yeh Chanchal Hawa.......*" I was wonderstruck to know the very reason when it kept on pecking its beaks and staring at me time and again. Slowly and steadily, all others followed and came close to me. I started pondering over whether perhaps its forefathers belonged to India and if it had exactly opened its third eye, which is believed to be linked to perception, awareness and spiritual communication, to get to know that I was a bird lover from India, and hence begging fodder from me. I was really moved but could not help. I found no alternative but to quit. While I was coming back, I started wondering whether it is advisable to maintain the country immaculately at the cost of retaining wild or stray birds ill-fed. I started pondering over if I had fodder with me at that time, what

I would have done. I was indeed in a fix; in a dilemma. My mind was assailed with questions but I was not able to explore any answer. I literally wished to cry to lighten my feelings and sentiments. But, unfortunately, my eyes would not cooperate. I failed to conceive where all the tears had disappeared. Even after one month of coming back to my own country, the tragic scene, characterised by extreme distress and sorrow, has been hovering around my mind intermittently. May Lord Govinda provide them with adequate fodder!

Nevertheless, early in the morning, the entire Singapore reverberates with the continuous melodious voice. On my first morning, I was partially awakened by the golden voice. I was wondering when I kept hearing the musical voice. I started contemplating while in my partial slumber that neither it could be the voice of a nightingale, since people of Singapore do not encourage wild birds, nor could it be the voice of our Lata Mangeshkar as she is no more in this mundane world. I endeavoured hard to sleep. But how can the music lover sleep without sorting out the mystery. I was very pleased to get to know that the lyrical voice was indeed the voice of a nightingale. The voice appeared sweeter as there was no pollution, no contamination, no toxicity and no filth in the air as a result of which the little bird was able to sing without any impediments.

The sea of the East-Coast is further beautified by the flights flying just above the sea after every one and a half minutes. It is moreover packed with ships that appear like glittering stars in mid-night. What a scenic and panoramic beauty! I could visualise it sitting or sleeping right from our flat. Earlier, I used to get irritated when I had to wake up in the dead of night to go to the washroom. But there in Singapore, I didn't mind getting up even two or three times late at night, which disturbed my deep slumber, as I was duly compensated with glittering ships stranded on the sea and the fresh breeze sneaking through the windows. The sea overlooks a huge beautiful park. There are a number of rules and regulations known as "Park Etiquettes" which are followed by all and sundry in letter and spirit. They are:

- Stay on tracks while walking, running and cycling
- Be a responsible pet owner
- Dispose of your trash responsibly
- Observe wildlife from a safe distance
- Do not remove wildlife from their habitats
- Show consideration for others when using the park

I, for one, was delighted to note that the people of Singapore and visitors have the civic sense as they follow the instructions on their own. It is not that they will look all around and spit or discard useless articles here and there when nobody is around. Many are really fond of pets. They always ensure to leash their pets. A few visitors came with their puppies on perambulators. Puppies were as calm and quiet as sleeping babies. Initially, I could not believe my eyes as I was at a distance. I got to know only when I came closer to the perambulator. Dog owners never leave their dogs' waste on the road. They tie the little poo bags or carry rolls of poo bags in their pockets and pick them up and throw them into a poop can. They have even devised a way to solidify the semi-liquid poop in order to discard it easily. So, systematic, exceptionally methodical and well organised! I bent my head as a mark of salutation. There are two restaurants, one being Chinese and another Indian on its bank. Restaurants are open till late night. F&B are broadly defined as the process of preparing, presenting and serving food and beverages to the customers. Different varieties of rental cycles are also available. Interested tourists, visitors and locals come, hire cycles and ride on its track. A large lavatory is there for urinals, latrine, bathing, showering, dressing, etc. There is no dearth of facilities. Surprisingly, there are many BBQ pits (barbeque), arrangements for cooking and provision of pitching tents and staying at nights as well. Generally, people come in groups especially during week-ends and festive occasions. Many celebrate their family functions on the bank of the sea. Once my daughter, son-in-law, I and my wife spent a couple of nights on the seashore. We booked a BBQ pit and the area around it and spent the whole day cooking and merry-making. We also pitched a tent for a night stay. The pit was indeed a larger one enabling us to cook a full-size chicken. We arranged raw crabs and lobsters from the nearby restaurants and got them grilled as well. The cooking, eating, drinking and chatting and enjoyment continued till late at night. What a lovely time! Away from din and tumult, with beer in our left hands, all sorts of delicious non-vegetarian items in our right hands, while enjoying the beauty of the sea in the late evening, it was indeed mesmerising. There were also a number of other people who came with their groups. It was indeed a matter of great pleasure that we all enjoyed ourselves on our own and there were no precedents of any disputes, arguments, quarrels and not even a bit of ding dong. It was really an adventurous night.

A few youngsters used a fish hook to catch fishes. They had a long fishing rod with a hook which they threw into the sea and kept the rod inside their tent. As soon as they felt the big tug of a fish taking the bait on the line, they jerked the rod up and back into the air. The hook will snag the lip of the fish and it will start to fight to get away. They immediately catch hold of the live fish. To catch fish is really enjoyable. I already had a nice talk with those college-going boys while they were smoking in the absence of the knowledge of their parents.

Enjoyed at Sea-Beach to my Heart's content at Night

It was late at night while I was writing my book, one of them asked me jokingly: "Uncle, why are you not enjoying the pleasant night? Is it the right time to study?" I softly countered: "Beta (son), there is no right or wrong time for study. Whenever you feel like studying, that becomes the appropriate time. However, if you allow me to enjoy myself by this time with you, let me cease my study and join you". All of them seated themselves on the nearby table, made of stone, and started singing a Bollywood song:

> *Suhana safar aur Yeh Mausam Hasin*
> *Suhana safar aur Yeh Mausam Hasin*
> *Hamey dar hai, ham kho na jaaye kahin*
> *Suhana safar aur Yeh Mausam Hasin*
> *Ye Kaun Hasta Hai Phoolon Mein Chhup Kar*
> *Bahaar Bechain Hai Kis ki Dhun Par*
> *Kahin gum gum, Kahi Rumjhum*
> *Ke Jaise Naache Zami*
> *Suhana safar aur Yeh Mausam Hasin....*

One of them was singing, the other one was making a beautiful sound with the help of his tongue pari passu with the musical rhythm of the song; the third one was mimicking Dilip Babu's mannerisms. The last one was enjoying the show to his heart's content and at the same time eulogising their performances, sometimes clapping, often chanting loud praises. I clapped and kept looking at them incredulously. I enthusiastically asked them to sit with me and urged them not to go by my age. I assured them that their romantic mood would not be dampened, rather enlivened, by my company. (I recollected my days with my students. When I used to organise trips to different places. The bus and the train journeys were enlivened by singing of filmy songs, chatting, shouting of various slogans, witty remarks, cracking jokes, sher-o-shayaris, and so on. Away from the din and tumult of the city, we experienced a strange repose in the lap of nature. The addition of fair company added to the charm and attraction of the surroundings. Sometimes we broke up into different groups and loitered about, strolling and sauntering aimlessly, but enjoying it nevertheless. We really enjoyed our days with a lot of enthusiasm and fanfare. When I am on the verge of becoming septuagenarian, I long for such kinds of trips to be organised by my ex-students in order to enable me to return to my past life. But I immediately recalled: 'If wishes were horses, beggars would ride on them'. During that time, I was all alone, so I took them inside the tent. I asked about their interest in consuming alcohol. All of them were astonishingly looking at one another with suspicion and utter disbelief. I could well understand that they were a bit hesitant to open up with someone of their father's age. I patted Ashim's shoulder and gestured to him to join me. Seeing him there with me, his other friends followed suit. We all sat together. I opened a bottle of scotch and without seeking their nods, I prepared five glasses and handed over a glass to each of them. I told them what my dad used to tell us: 'When my sandals fit your feet, the relationship between the son and dad turns into friendship'. Hence, I asked them to consider me their friend. They could not imagine perhaps even in their remotest dream that I, who was of their father or grand-father's age, and totally unknown to them, would ask them to join in drinking.

All four delightfully agreed. All of them came close to me. They held the glasses and shouted at the pitch of their voice: 'Cheers'. One of them took a mouthful of it; the other one drank it down with a loud slurp; the third one kept the glass down without taking any sip. The last one put the glass down after having taken a lovely sip. While enjoying alcohol with them, one of them pleaded with me to share my life's experience. I jubilantly informed them that I would share my knowledge and experience initially on drinking alcohol.

At the very outset, they were told that soon upon saying 'cheers', the glass must not be put down without taking a sip. I eulogised the way Ashim had taken the sip. It should always be taken like that. It should be sipped like taking 'tea'. All of them were surprised and wanted to know how I came to know his name. They were taken in when I told all of them their names. They shouted: 'How come! How come!' Actually, when I was writing and you all four were roaming leisurely, smoking and talking loosely about girls, I thought to write about you. Hence, I watched your activities meticulously, with my third eye, escaping your notice and attention, while pretending to be busy in writing. I got your names when you were calling one another. All of them shouted together: 'Very dangerous'! I enlightened them about what Kabiguru Rabindranath Tagore once told:

"WHERE RAVI (SUN) CANNOT APPROACH OR PENETRATE;

KABI (AUTHOR) CAN HAVE AN EASY ACCESS".

I made it clear to them that the sun does not have accessibility everywhere – in the deep jungle, in slums, bustee and jhuggi areas. On the contrary, the accessibility of the author is everywhere. 'The imagination is a very very powerful tool. It enables authors to reach everywhere without the least hindrances. It allows him to be creative, to see with new eyes or the third eye and endless possibilities'. Many of us do not know the spiritual energy: 'At the speed of the mind, we can go many thousands of miles within a fraction of a second. But even more powerful than the mind is intelligence, and even more powerful than the intelligence is spiritual energy. For a person with spiritual energy, nothing is impossible.' "Aarey, Sir, uncle, *dada*, *jethu* (big uncle), you are a reservoir of knowledge", one said. The other one cheered while clapping: "very nice, very nice. It really adds to my knowledge".

In the meantime, I made all of them know that the quantity of the first peg was generally uniform. Thereafter, you might drink as per your capacity for which no permission needs to be sought. Mind it! The alcohol must be diluted with an adequate quantity of plain water. Never mix it with cold drinks, soda or anything other than plain cold water. I would also apprise you that smoking cigarettes is much more dangerous than taking alcohol. Further, it is a slow poisoning or fatal to smoke while drinking. Once I was a chain smoker. Leave it! I must not dampen your enthusiasm. You are here to enjoy yourselves. All of them enthusiastically urged me to continue. I obliged and continued. At that time while drinking alcohol, smoking cigarettes used to be mandatory. I could not think of drinking without smoking. My smoking while drinking was as mandatory as for the bridegroom to take his 'bride' on a 'honeymoon' after marriage. As was certain, I was infected with heart disease, lung disease and chronic bronchitis. It was at the prime age of 40 years onwards. I had to pay a heavy price and as a result of which I had to suffer a lot. I had to make Herculean attempts to quit smoking in order to lead a trouble-free life. There was a long history of my ceaseless suffering and how I successfully got rid of smoking. Even at 70 years of age, I am bearing the brunt of my mischievous and reckless acts. Earlier, I was slim and well built. But given my old leisures, I had to take medicines for years which has made me overweight and caused a protruding belly. It is far from genetics. My parents, four brothers and a sister are all thin and lean. Hence, for a few hours of enjoyment, it is nothing but stupidity to suffer life long. If you are interested to know all about that I would tell you later if you keep in touch with me. Today, we are here to make it a memorable night". My only intention was to highlight injurious and harmful effects of smoking and drinking by mixing with them as a friend.

Background of Clinking Glasses

At the very outset, why do we clink glasses and say "Cheers?" Most of you will say it is almost second nature to clink glasses with others before a drink. It is a custom that has been practised for centuries. Drinking is also for coming close or mingling with fellow drinkers. So, by physically touching glasses, it is all about sharing joyous events and drinkers become part of a celebration. But the origin of the phrase 'cheers' is somewhat different. It is said that there were some theories that it was a way of being poisoned. Back in the days, there used to be disastrous wars among kings from dawn to dusk. Soon after the sunset, they all assembled together to celebrate and forget what had happened during the day and what was going to happen in the coming days. But poisoning foes' drink was the most convenient way to get rid of those who could not be defeated in the war. It was believed that if glasses were filled to the brim and then clinked hard, a few drops from each glass would pour into the other. Mixing drinks and then taking a sip was a gesture that the drinks were unharmed. But one of them countered: "Uncle, how can it be? If the glasses are clinked hard, how do they not break!" I answered swiftly, the reason being there used to be wooden glasses. All of them retorted: 'Uncle, you are great!' Three cheers for this!" With this sensational and fabulous knowledge, I would like to drink one more peg, certainly, with adequate water. I asked them to go ahead and advised them to have snacks at the same time, to neutralise the effect of alcohol. I further added, generally drinkers follow certain moral principles or ethics, that govern a person's behaviour or the conduct of an activity. When we raised the glass with cheers, the glass should not be kept down without taking a sip. The next one is also equally important: We should not drink on an empty stomach and should also not be taken while taking certain types of antibiotics. Wonderful! Excellent! Knowledgeable! We would share it with our friends.

Last but not the least, my dad used to say: "When one is young, he acquires good or bad habits. One starts doing a certain act for the sake of pleasure, enjoyment and fun. He does not know when he starts feeling the necessity of doing it again. It gradually takes the form of a habit and eventually an addiction. Every chain smoker, habitual drunkard, gambler and trickster never starts all these as a habit. One simply begins with such an act for the sake of the company of friends, for the curiosity of taste, or for fun. People enjoy doing all these but when the habit of smoking and drinking becomes essential; so rightly said, 'habit is a good servant but a bad master'. That is the reason, it is said that 'Habit is second nature.' Hence, keep them as your servants and enjoy their company, the secret of enjoying life to the fullest extent". But you should not allow the habits to control you, dictate you and conquer you.

"Sir, lovely and unparalleled. We study, watch TV and read many gospels of religious books. But we never get the opportunity to learn all these virtues sitting with an elderly, knowledgeable and experienced person. The fantasy is that you are drinking with us while cursing and condemning drinking. You are very intelligently discouraging us to form the habit of it, and, if possible, to abstain from these bad habits. Finding us smoking or drinking, our teachers, elders, and parents as well, would have taken us to task. But here the man is encouraging us to enjoy these, nevertheless keeps reminding us of how injurious, harmful and dreadful they are". They came very close to me and sincerely assured me that they would positively take care of and never allow the habits to control and harm them. Two of them were in the habit of smoking. They promised to quit sooner than later. As regards drinking alcohol, they assured that they would try their best to have it with plenty of plain water occasionally or once in a blue moon. They then exchanged their contact numbers with me. They further promised to keep in touch with me. Further they invited me to their tent as per my convenience. I assured them that I would surely be with them for some time. They left my tent one by one, seeking my blessings. Seeing them leaving, I was not able to control my tears. It was good that the darkness of night made their tears invisible to me.

Education System

Once while sitting with my daughter in Singapore, I was wondering whether the incomes of doctors were limited as there are hardly any diseases since the level of air pollution in Singapore is almost nil. Hence, there is hardly any risk of respiratory illness, cardiovascular problems and of cancer.

The number of patients is literally very few. The climatic condition is also conducive. Its education system is among the top-performing globally. Singapore aims to bring out the best in every child. It is probably the best organised education system in the world. Its teachers are well-trained. Over 50 years, Singapore has moved from low literacy levels to become one of the highest performers globally. The percentage of teacher-students ratios:

In 1994: 1:23.79; in 1995: 1:25.27; in 1996: 1:25.40; in 2007: 1:21.14;

In 2008: 1:20.18; in 2009: 1:18.22; in 2016: 1:15.06; in 2017: 1:14.69

The aforesaid percentage of teacher-student ratios makes it crystal clear why literacy rate in Singapore is one of the best globally. Students do not indulge in any dirty political activities. The true aim of education is to give students adequate knowledge, to equip them intellectually and morally for the struggle of life, and to develop their personalities. Education aims at character building. Accordingly, the gaining of knowledge and the development of personality are the prime focus and concern of students. They have nothing to do with the rough and tumble of politics. In the field of politics, shifting loyalties, changing alliances, and mere lip-services, diplomacy or cunningness are frequently employed. In fact, politics is not dirty. People are dirty. It's dirty because basically the people who are into it are mostly illiterate, goons, thugs, greedy and work only for their personal and vested interests. The tactics or politics are often mean. Students should, for this very reason, always keep away from politics.

Good quality of education has the power to inculcate necessary skills and bring about necessary changes in the community. It has the power to impact individuals, communities and future generations. The lawyers, judges and policemen there are having free days as there is hardly any lawlessness. Hence, they are able to channelise their competence and potential on the development of their country. Since the people of Singapore are well educated, there is hardly any poverty. People there are not over-drunk as a result of which the country does not have negative effects of alcohol. Hence, hospitals have very few patients hardly infected with manifold diseases and ailments. In view of these, Government expenditures on patients are minimal. The Government need not employ an excessive number of doctors for treatment of patients. Since there are a few patients, they can afford to have the best treatments as doctors can concentrate more and more on the patients.

Peace of Mind Gives Passions to Life

'The fragrance of flowers spreads only in the direction of the wind. But the goodness of a person spreads in all directions'.

.... By: Chanakya

Since there are no stresses, threats, menace, bullying, terrorism, agitation, strikes, lawlessness, kidnapping, rapes, murder and hooliganism, all these might mean helping the countrymen to pursue their passion or motivating them to reach their fitness goals without much difficulties. All these lead to peace of mind which is also described as inner calm and an internal state of tranquillity. When you have mental peace, you might feel at ease within yourself, a sense of self-compassion, undisturbed by day to day worries. Peace of mind is a great way to reduce the stresses of day to day life and can help you become a calmer, more relaxed person overall. This can lead to a happier existence. Peace of mind over all the turbulences and misfortunes of life enables one to accomplish one's cherished aspiration with ease and comfort. Happiness that lasts can lead to a blissful state of mind that would be akin to peace. Peace is a way of living together so that all members of society can accomplish their human rights. It is an essential element to the realisation of all human rights. Peace of mind is a great way to reduce the stresses and strains and drudgery of day to day life. Peace simply means being in a place where no hatred exists and every corner is filled with love, care and respect; where conflicts are handled peacefully. Peace of mind teaches us not to be in a hurry and do everything quietly and in a calm spirit. Their dictum is:

"We are here to heal, not harm. We are here to love, not hate. We are here to create, not destroy".

By: Anthony D. Williams

And

"A person's most useful asset is not a head full of knowledge, but a heart full of love, an ear ready to listen and a hand willing to help others!"

.... Daily Inspirational Quotes

Singapore was in a Topsy-Turvy state

In 1959, there was a full scale election in Singapore. The young leader, Lee Kuan Yew, became the Prime Minister. He believed that Singapore would not be able to survive as an independent country and they must unite with Malaysia. He got Singapore merged with Malaysia in 1963. The Malaysian Government was not thrilled to have Singapore be a part of their country. The principal reason was that in 1964, there would be an election in Malaysia. Even the people of Singapore were not happy with that merger because of the agreement that 40% of Singapore's revenue was to be paid to Malaysia's Central Government. Even though the population of Singapore was only 17% of the combined population. The Chinese and non-Malays did not like this discrimination too. They observed how Malaysia was turning into Malays' Malaysia, while minorities were not given the same rights and equality. Owing to these differences in 1964, there was a communal tension and racial riots were also seen. Because of these riots, in 1965, Singapore was separated from Malaysia and became an independent country - the Republic of Singapore. By this point of time, there was some remnant of British control over Singapore. In 1967, the British announced that they would withdraw their troops and leave the country once and for all by the mid-70s.

PM Yew a Superhero

"Do or Die" is outdated. "Do it before you Die" is the updated one.

Had there been some other Prime Minister, he would have been positively delighted to get an opportunity to rule over the country as it happened in many countries. It was for the hunger of power of the leadership that led to the partition of several countries in the world. But the Prime Minister, Lee Kuan Yew, was honest & diligent and had a tremendous amount of farsightedness. He was also passionate about the development of his country and solution of its multifarious problems. He was sure and certain that the sudden pull out of the British forces would present serious and grievous problems to the defence and economic security of Singapore. This might sound good news for the people in general. But, in fact, for the Government, it was a complex, complicated and knotty problem. The British contribution was significant in running Singapore as an independent nation. British forces provided a large part of jobs to the Singaporeans. On the top of it, Singapore did not have their own army and no defence forces. Had the British left, they would have been defenceless. That was the reason why Yew requested the British to postpone their departure and give them proper time to transition. He was the Prime Minister whose only passion was to develop the country. The British agreed to the request. The deadline for the British to leave the country was set for 1971. Hence, Yew had only four years to get a hold of his country.

From here the miraculous story started. A story where the Prime Minister, Lee Kuan Yew, became the hero before Singaporeans. He jumped into work at once. First of all, he made peace and solved political tangles and other issues with the neighbouring countries. In 1967, he collaborated with few other countries viz. Indonesia, Malaysia, the Philippines and Thailand.

Cooperation in the Socio-economic Fields

That did not mean the country was not in need of any army. For the defence of the nation, Lee introduced national services. When the boys in the country attained sixteen and a half years of age, he made it mandatory to register them for national services. Later, it was necessary for every boy of 18 to compulsorily join army, national forces and defence services. Lee laid prime emphasis on the need for education of the countrymen. High quality public education was made compulsory and provided almost free of cost.

The Prime Minister promised that Singapore would be a multi-racial country and that they would be an example for the world. He reiterated that "We are not a Malay nation; we are not a Chinese State and we are not an Indian State; our country is not based on any particular religion; our country is not based on any particular language and any particular culture. We are a secular nation where every citizen is equal. No group would be allowed to oppress others. We would work all together harmoniously. The PM was fully aware that to write 'secular' in the Constitution, the country would not automatically be secular. The population of Malay was 43%, Chinese 41%, Indians 10% and others 6%. People became sceptical since many people with different religions were living together. People doubted one another. Communal tension was also very high. This ideal co-existence was not as easy as Lee had expected.

In order to solve this knotty problem, Lee took a proactive approach for assimilation. He reiterated that equality would never come by writing that people were equal in the eyes of law. When people from different religions and ethnicities lived in a country with high communal tensions, people doubted one another. They did not want to socialise with others. He introduced Ethnic Integration Policy. According to this policy, he scrupulously made a fixed ratio for the people living there based on ethnicity for the Government housing. For example, in a building, he made it mandatory that there have to be 22% Malays, 42% Chinese, 10% Indians and 6% minority groups and so on. The percentage of ethnicity should be reflected in each building. This would enable Chinese, Malays and Indians to co-exist. This was an outstanding move. Because in reality, if people are allowed to live with their own will, the communally brainwashed people will not live with others. They would create their own *ghettos*. This area is for Hindu because Hindus live there and this area is for Muslims because Muslims live there and so on. So, there would be a demarcation in the city. In order to break this self-segregation, he ensured the different ethnicities would live in all buildings so that they could interact with one another and would live harmoniously. What a great idea and its implementation!

Additionally Singapore introduced a Racial Harmony Day as well. Every year on 21 July, school kids in Singapore dress up in the traditional costumes of other religions. For example, a Hindu may dress up in a muslim traditional costume and vice versa. Right from the school level, children are taught that the principles of secularism, diversity and unity need to be upheld in the country.

Cleanliness is the Hallmark of Civilization

In the opinion of O'Rourke: "Cleanliness becomes more important when godliness is unlikely." So, he launched a campaign to keep Singapore the cleanest and greenest city in South Asia. And this campaign was in effect every 2-3 years between 1958 and 1988. This was not a superficial event where politicians stood in front of cameras and moved a few leaves here and there and their sycophants would clap and eulogise. The PM made a concrete campaign with multiple steps. A large number of public toilets were created. He also ensured to keep toilets neat and clean and well maintained. There were no compromises in the name of cleanliness. Heavy fines were imposed on spitting, littering and smoking. The next problem was the slums. Singapore was full of slums. What could they do about it? More than 26,000 families were relocated from slums to high rising buildings. So, public housing was developed. Meanwhile, free water supply, gas and electricity were provided in the free public housing.

The school students read: 'Declaration of Harmony'. In the year 2021, 80% people were living in public housing. The houses were provided by the Government. As a result of which, the homelessness was almost eradicated. More than 4,900 hawkers were relocated to food centres. New wholesale markets were developed for vegetable sellers. Rivers were cleaned. 2,800 industries were relocated. Public and private health care were made very cheap. Under the Ministry of Health, thousands of beds were made available in the hospitals.

In a country as small as Singapore with such a high density of population, if every citizen owned a car, it would not leave space for residential areas and it is a sheer wastage of a lot of precious and scarce land; it would have made roads congested and the city would automatically shrink. So, in order to discourage easy purchase of vehicles, heavy taxes are imposed on buying cars. But in order to neutralise the effect of transportation, the current Prime Minister of Singapore promoted better transport. That is the reason why even today Singapore is the most expensive city if anyone wants to buy a car. This country encourages a limited number of cars on the roads. If any one wants to add a new car, first of all, some other vehicle needs to be moved out of the road. The status quo of the existing number of cars on roads is maintained. On the other hand, public transportation like buses and metros are one of the least expensive forms of public transport in the world. It is affordable as well as one of the cleanest, safest and most comfortable modes of transportation.

The question may arise in the minds of the people: how does the Government manage funds for providing all such facilities as housing, hospitals, schools and transportation to its citizens? Does the Government charge high taxes from its people as in the case of several European countries? In countries like Sweden, Finland, Denmark and Austria, income-tax rates cross even 50%. But in the case of Singapore, it is quite low. So, how does the Government manage funds? It can be elucidated with an example. The Government of Singapore owns many companies in the transport, power and media sectors. Public sectors, very sorry to say that, are not mismanaged as in the case of many countries that the Government finds no alternative but to privatise them. In Singapore, all these public sectors are managed scrupulously and systematically. There is another source of revenue i.e. wealth-tax, property tax and GST. There is a huge fiscal surplus as they earn much more than they spend. On top of all these, people deposit a large chunk of their salary into the Central Provident Fund Scheme. That is why Singapore has one of the highest savings rates in the world. The Government is managing their funds quite prudently and efficiently as there is the least corruption involved. Another question struck in my mind while I was in Singapore. It does not have any natural resources where the Government and the people can invest and earn money. So, the curiosity is valid as to how people are earning in a country like Singapore. At the time of independence, they had barren lands. In such cases, the economy needs to be kick-started. They did it in two ways. First, the Government invested on a large scale. They also fired the lazy and corrupt workers from the agencies. Second, the Government encouraged foreign companies to invest in the country by opening up the economy. PM Yew practised both. He invested the government funds in big infrastructure purchases such as building a world class port. These purchases provided a large number of employment to the people and that became the backbone of the economy. Since the country did not have any natural resources, it meant that the location of the country was its only advantage. Generally, a small island can never be self-reliant and also made a hub for creating flights; and to facilitate international trading. To attract the foreign investment, Singapore had to be a stable country where it is easy to carry on a business. So, they reduced taxes; ended red-tapism; bureaucracy and useless paperwork and attracted business magnets from other countries. As a result, today in terms of ease of doing business, Singapore is the fourth least corrupt country in the world. It is the only Asian country to rank in the top 10 in the list.

Yew's Magic Wand to Remove Corruption

What was Kuan Yew's magic stick to put an end to corruption? He raised the salaries of the government employees as well as salaries of politicians and ministers. They are paid unbelievably high remunerations. The Prime Minister of Singapore is the highest paid Prime Minister in the world. The salary of the present PM, Lee Hsien Loong who is the son of the erstwhile PM, whose salary is $16,10,000; Joe Biden's salary is $400,000; much more than the US President. It is with the purpose that there will be no corruption. The salaries of the Government employees are also performance based. Third, if a minister is so greedy as to engage in corruption despite a high salary, they are given heavy punishment; with a heavy fine and imprisonment up to five years. In 1960, the Prevention of Corruption Act was introduced. There is an Investigation Bureau, an independent agency, that investigates corruption without any kind of interference. This autonomy is very important since if any politicians engage in corruption, this agency can take any action against it. It allows this agency to remain independent to explore corruption, even the PM cannot interfere in their working.

In terms of the environment, in 1972, the Singapore government launched an initiative of 'Tree Plantation Day.' A specific day on which all residents come together to plant trees. This initiative was so successful that within ten years, the number of trees planted was more than the number of people living in Singapore. The indoor gardens in Singapore are the best in the world. Singapore's greenery has become a tourist attraction now. They clean their river every ten years.

But Lee Kuan Yew did not want his country to become a low cost factory for the rest of the world. He ensured that the people of Singapore learn skills in technical schools and internships. By the 90's, Singapore became the global chain for sophisticated technologies, such as biotech engineering, aerospace, integrated circuits, pharmaceuticals, petroleum chemicals and semiconductors. They provided good quality training to their citizens and taught them useful skills to enable them to work in industries that did not require natural resources.

Deadly against Personality Cult

After doing so much, Lee Kuan Yew knew that under all circumstances, he could not allow a personality cult to develop around him. Today, if you visit Singapore, you will find no temples and monuments to worship him. Literally, he took the country to its present pinnacle of glory from rags. He could have very easily turned his people into his followers, sycophants, yes-men, flatterers or even devotees or an avatar. He instead focussed on his work to develop the country rather than developing his own image. In contrast, people in other countries often deify the so-called celebrities. If any cricketer hits six over-boundaries in one over or hits a few centuries and a couple of double centuries in matches, he will be like god to their supporters. The temple and monuments would be erected in his honour in the country. On the contrary, Lee Kuan Yew was an educated person; he was pragmatic and was not a believer of any kind of ideology. It is said that his ears were always listening. He paid attention to all suggestions. These qualities are rarely found in most politicians. He openly said: "I have spent a whole lifetime to build my nation. As long as I am incharge, I will not allow anybody to even harm the hair of its head". If we loosely translate it into Hindi: *Mai kisiko iska baal bhi baaka karne nehi dunga.*" What magnanimous leadership!

Was Lee a Dictator

Today many people categorise him as a dictator. But if at all he is a dictator, he is certainly a benevolent dictator. Because to some extent, he was against free speech and freedom of the press. The people of Singapore are vociferous that he was a dictator. In order to check and for accountability of the leaders, free press and media cannot be done away with. But the case of Singapore was exceptional because here the leader knew how to be accountable to the people of Singapore. He listened to others. If we want to take any lesson from this story, they should be the exact policies implemented by him which took the country to its great height. Had there been a free press, I am sure and sanguine, the country would not have risen to the peak as there is a proverb: 'Too many cooks spoil the broth.' If too many people are involved in a task or activity or in a leading role, the task will not be done well. There is a good chance that it will not have good results. There will be severe criticisms of somebody or something, castigations and allegations against one another. Finally, there would be wastage of time, energy and money. The result of the development of the country would be big 'zero'. Hence, nobody should pay heed to unnecessary gossip against him.

Establishment of Ram Rajya

In literal sense, Singapore is a country where people are free from all these and they are as happy as the people used to be in the kingdom of Purushottam Rama. During the rule of Lord Rama, there used to be 'Ramrajya'. 'Ram Rajya' is the 'Sovereignty of the people, for the people and by the people'. It also symbolises the ideal society without any crime and war; and there was no sorrow, suffering, poverty, greed, grief or inequality in the country where He ruled. Every sin was met with retribution. Truth and non-violence reigned supreme.

However, it was also observed even in Lord Rama's Ramrajya, people did not spare Mata Sita and there was a lot of gossip about Her. Some of them went to the extent of doubting Her chastity and integrity. Mata Sita is the silent figure of strength in the Hindu epic, the Ramayana. She is the epitome of devotion as a wife, daughter, and a mother. Unfortunately, even after giving Agni Pareeksha, Mata Sita was not let off by the countrymen. Lord Rama was omnipotent, omnipresent and omniscient. Though He was fully aware of all these yet in order to appease his subjects and fearing ill repute of the country, ordered an unwilling Lakshmana to take the pregnant Janaki Devi, Sita, whom He loved more than His own life, into the forest on the pretext of showing her the hermitage of the pious sage Valmiki and left Her there. Nevertheless Rama's decision was made with the aim of regaining trust of His subjects at the cost of His own personal life. In order to uphold Lord Rama's righteousness, Mata Sita welcomed the decision of Lord Rama with open arms. Nevertheless, both Lord Rama and Mata Sita had to suffer a lot and went through trials and tribulations in their endeavour to keep their kingdom free from crimes and wars and to bring about peace, prosperity, justice, equality and tranquillity amongst His subjects. Lord Rama was referred to as *Marayada Purushottama*. It is to be noted that maryada means 'limit' and Purushottama means 'the greater than the greatest man'. Purusha means 'man of honour'.

PM, Yew, Mastermind of Today's Singapore

Prime Minister, Lee Kuan Yew, was instrumental for today's Singapore. He received barren, poverty stricken; drug addiction, crimes, criminals, forced labour, prisoners of war, murders, theft, full-fledged prostitutes; rapes, goondaism, communal tensions and disharmony in *Viraasat*. He was quite unmindful and not at all vociferous of what he had received. He virtually rebuilt his country by virtue of his sheer will, determination, patience & perseverance and above all giving earnest, prolonged, honest and industrious efforts from rags to smiling heaven. He removed all the problems one by one. As far as I understand, while going through PM Yew's life history, he must have kept himself busy day in and day out. He was passionate about the development of his country and prosperity of his countrymen. He must have paid a heavy price for that in the form of sacrificing his own comforts, spending sleepless nights, devoid of relations and family life, scrapping vacations with the members of his family and relations, no time to take care of his health, no family functions and bearing stresses and strains owing to overwork and curtailing hours of rest.

Singapore remains one of the world's strongest economies. Its success is only attributed to the pragmatic leadership of the late Lee Kuan Yew. Today Singaporeans enjoy the benefits of housing, additional universities, hospitals and a good transportation system, stable Government, good justice and securities. All these have attracted foreign investments. Disputes are settled in a fast and efficient manner. Corrupt practising is absolutely out of the question. Police senior Officers or Civil Servants were punished for corruption as per the rule of the law in Singapore. Singapore police and justice system serves all on an equal footing. Religious intolerance amongst Singaporeans is tantamount to nil.

Nevertheless, today many people categorise him as a dictator. He was known for practising political pragmatism in his governance of Singapore, but has been criticised for using authoritarian and heavy-handed policies. Very few said that his actions were necessary for the country's early development. If at all he was a dictator, for sure, he was a benevolent dictator. That is natural. How can Lee be spared when people dared to be critical of *Maryada purushottam*, Lord Rama, as well as Mata Sita, who is the quintessence of incarnation of Goddess?

Conclusion

Many people focus on amassing their own empires and estates. They disregard the purpose for which God gave them the human body. True human beings live for others and are unmindful and are not vociferous of allegations and castigations against them. Those who live for the world always lose their personal, intimate life. They welcome it as they are always under the impression that God created human beings that would serve others. There are numerous ways we can be of service to others. Life is filled with several opportunities. We can help others by doing physical, intellectual and spiritual service or service of the soul. Physical service encompasses all those activities performed to help others in order to meet their primary needs in life which are food, clothing, shelter, safety and peace & tranquillity in life. There are many people who fulfil the intellectual needs of society - teachers, professors, writers and journalists. Service of the soul is helping seekers satisfy their spiritual quest. To truly perform selfless service, one must act without any desire for a reward or recognition, motivated by an innate desire to help another. It is up to everyone to work out his own salvation or damnation (Zarathushtra).

In this context, I wish to highlight the magnanimous act of Mr P. Kalyanasundaram, retired librarian from Tamil Nadu, India.

- He has been donating his earnings for the last 30 years.
- He even donated his pension amount of about Rs.10 lakhs to the needy.
- Mr Kalyanasundaram donated all his life-long savings as well.
- He worked as a server in a hotel to meet his day-to-day needs.
- He is the first person perhaps in the world to donate his entire earnings to a social cause.

- In recognition of his service, the American Government honoured him with the "Man of the Millennium" award.
- He received a sum of Rs.30 crores as part of this award which he distributed entirely to the needy.

It is very easy to force or direct others to obey you. It is also easy to use brutal force to subjugate others. You may be a winner, but if you are asked to change your life and to give up any kind of lust, you will find it impossible to do so. For any man relinquishing the empire is not possible. But Gautam Buddha did it. Though Nadir Shah defeated a number of kings with a brute force, he cannot be equated with Gautam Buddha. Samrat Ashok became great only when he renounced the throne, but not on defeating the Kalinga war. It is rightly said that the man who could conquer himself is indeed great, magnanimous, benevolent, generous and ultimately human. But who conquers others is simply powerful or strong.

The Greek philosopher, Plato, once said:

- People are often unreasonable and self-centred. Forgive them anyway.
- If you are kind, people may accuse you of ulterior motives. Be kind anyway.
- If you are honest, people may cheat you. Be honest anyway.
- If you find happiness, people may be jealous. Be happy anyway.
- The good you do today, may be forgotten tomorrow. Do good anyway.
- Give the world the best you have and it may never be enough. Give your best anyway.
- For you see, in the end, it is between you and God. It was never between you and them anyway.

***

www.ingramcontent.com/pod-product-compliance
Lightning Source LLC
LaVergne TN
LVHW041920070526
838199LV00051BA/2681